PROTECTING YOU

LENA HENDRIX

ABOUT THIS BOOK

One moment of hesitation and I lost Maggie forever.

Since then, we've spent the last fifteen years in this small town, circling each other and pretending neither remembers **how right it felt** when we were best friends.

Now she's a single mom and she doesn't need a "broody, grumpy cop" like me complicating her life. No matter how many times her heated gaze scorches my skin, I can never have her in the way I want.

Completely.

So I push her away—but it's for her own good.

Because if she knew the truth of what I did, she wouldn't just have hurt feelings—she would truly hate me.

She has a guarded heart, and it's all my fault.

But I don't have a heart at all. **I gave it to Maggie O'Brien a long time ago**.

ONE

MAGGIE

Now

Fuck the bake sale.

Blowing the hairs that had escaped from my sagging ponytail out of my eyes, I quickly looked both ways before crossing Main Street and barreling out of my flower shop toward Biscuits & Honey. The local bakery had been open about a year and was owned by Honey McCoy. In the short time she'd lived here, she became one of my best friends. She had swiftly become a leader among the busiest shops in town. She and the bar owner, Colin, had gotten married and shared the offices that joined their two spaces. Honey was an outsider who had successfully integrated herself into life in Chikalu Falls, Montana.

As I hustled across the street, I pulled my chunky sweater tighter across my chest. I'd left my heavy coat in the car after leaving my flower shop, and that was a mistake. Autumn had settled into our little town, and as the cold evening wind slapped at my skin, I blew out a quick breath.

Outside the glass door of the shop, I glanced back down

at the text that had come from my daughter just as I was
wrapping up a long day at the shop.

Lottie: I need something for the bake sale tomorrow.

Me: Well, did you bake something?

Lottie: Seriously? Mom.

Irritation rolled through me as I nodded and gave a tight
smile to the couple walking into The Dirty Pigeon, the bar
and dance hall next to the bakery. I swallowed down the
wave of humiliation at having to ask for help—something I
was sure the other mothers didn't have to do. Thank god for
Honey, because there was no way I could muster the energy
to bake something tonight for Lottie's Halloween school
fundraiser. I figured it was typical for a fourteen-year-old
not to tell her mom *in advance* that she needed something as
time-consuming as a baked good.

With all the pity glances I got from the other mothers at
school, I couldn't flake on the fundraiser. Most of the other
moms were older, stylishly coiffed, and ready to judge. I was
seventeen when I had Lottie and, save for *one night* of reck-
lessness, I had always been the most responsible teen I knew.
A pie from Biscuits & Honey would still receive judgment
from the other mothers, since it wasn't technically homemade,
but at least it would be the most delicious item on the table.

Maybe I'll buy two, just in case . . .

The dusky fall sky was losing its last streaks of pinks
and oranges, but inside the airy and bright shop, patrons sat
along the wall, chatting and sipping coffee while enjoying
pastries and pumpkin-spiced dessert. Cinnamon and brown
sugar aromas wafted from the kitchen, and pride for my
friend's success swelled in my chest. I offered smiles and
nods to friends and neighbors dotting the small interior.

As I took one step toward the counter, I saw *him*.

Cole Decker was three customers ahead of me in line, and I lowered my head a bit, hoping he wouldn't notice me. That man was fucking infuriating—always finding ways to make my life a little more miserable. Sometimes I didn't know if he did it on purpose or if he was just wired to make my body hum and inconvenience me in as many ways as possible.

He still looks delicious, though.

I steeled against my traitorous thoughts. It may have been almost fifteen years since Cole and I had been best friends but my physical attraction had never died. In fact, as he aged annoyingly well with his gravelly voice, broad shoulders, and tiny smattering of gray in the dark brown at his temples, I only struggled to keep my hormones in check around him more.

I peeked around the person in front of me to watch the way his dark police uniform hugged the curves of his ass and clung to his muscular thighs. Despite his bulletproof vest, you couldn't mistake the expanse of his chest and taper of his waist. My body clenched with desire, and I felt hot in my cozy sweater.

Who the hell still has a six-pack at thirty-three?

Cole Decker, that was who.

The veins on the back of his hand entranced me as he pointed out pastries for the gal behind the counter to stuff into a white box. She plucked cinnamon buns, Italian wedding cookies, peanut butter and butterscotch scotcheroos—a wide assortment of treats that caused the box to bend under the weight.

"Leave some for the rest of us."

The words tumbled from my mouth, and before I realized my inside thought had become my outside thought, Cole turned his head to glare at me over his shoulder.

Damn it.

My spine stiffened, and I lifted my chin a notch. The icy stares he shot my way would not intimidate me. I knew that big, strong asshole had cried at the ending of *The Notebook*.

He muttered something under his breath and reached for his wallet. I sighed and looked at the sparse display case. A handful of cookies and a lonely cherry pie.

Sorry, Lottie, looks like we're only getting one pie. At least it's my favorite.

I tapped my foot, impatience buzzing down my leg. It was dark now, and I still had a lot to do for the weekend's upcoming wedding. Cole shot another look over his shoulder and paused with the cash in his hand.

"You know . . . ," he said. His voice was deep and commanding and definitely did *not* make my stomach flip-flop. "I'll take the cherry pie too."

"Wha—no!" I shouted before I could help myself.

Heads turned and heat rose from my chest to my cheeks.

A smirk danced across his face, but he paid for his order, gathered the boxes, and stepped out of line. It moved forward while he took one imposing step toward me.

"Is there a problem, Ms. O'Brien?" The dull, slightly bored tone of his voice only spurred my aggravation.

I clenched my jaw and swallowed past the pebble lodged in my throat. "Actually, yes. I was going to buy that pie."

He set the box of pastries on the empty high-top table next to us. "This pie?" he asked, gesturing to the package still in his grasp.

"Yeah. It's the last one." I planted my hands on my hips in an effort not to choke a police officer. Cole and I hardly ever spoke, and energy zapped under my skin. "You have enough treats, don't you think?"

"Guys at the station get hungry on the midnight shift." His eyes flicked down my body, and I felt my nipples pebble beneath the thin camisole I wore under my sweater.

"I need that pie. It's an emergency." I crossed my arms in an X over my chest to hide the splotchy red patches I could feel blooming under my collarbone.

Cole flipped open the box with one hand and grabbed a fork with the other. "A pie emergency?" he asked, pointing to the golden pastry with the fork.

I rolled my eyes at him. I did not have time for his shit tonight. "Yes," I hissed. "Just let me buy it from you."

He pressed his lips together in a *hmm* as if he were really considering helping me out. "Well"—his voice dipped low, and he leaned toward me slightly, the plastic tines plunging into the flaky crust as he pulled up a huge, gooey bite of tart cherry goodness—"this pie is mine."

The way his voice deepened on the word *mine* had my body screaming. I stared at the fullness of his lips as they closed around the warm pie, and I licked my own, imagining what his kiss would taste like—sweet and tangy and masculine.

I shook my head to clear the fog of desire.

He's cocky and an asshole, I reminded myself. *And he just stole your fucking pie.*

I pulled a blank expression over my face, allowing fire to seep into my eyes. "Real nice," I scoffed. I pushed past him and sailed toward the exit door without looking back.

"Wear a coat before you freeze to death."

Ignoring him completely, I kept moving. I didn't need

him to tell me what to do, no matter how logical it was. I hustled down the sidewalk and across the street to my car. Cole Decker was infuriating and, as usual, I let him get under my skin. Quite literally the only man who could make me angry and horny at the same time.

The frigid wind was biting, and my numb fingers fumbled with my car keys as I replayed the scene in my head. I could never seem to keep my cool when Cole was around, and as much as I tried to avoid running into our hot-as-sin local detective, he was popping up in my life more and more. To add inconvenience to irritation, now I had to figure out what the hell I was going to do about Lottie's bake sale tomorrow.

I typed out a frenzied text to Honey. I needed to call in a favor, because with my frazzled nerves, there was no way I could pull off something edible for the bake sale.

~

"You're a lifesaver." I sighed in relief as Honey slid a white box toward me.

"I got you, girlie." She winked and perched herself opposite me at the high-top table.

After I'd frantically texted her from my parking space, she had assured me she would take care of it and had told me to meet her at The Pidge, what everyone called The Dirty Pigeon.

"I seriously can't thank you enough. I came in to buy a pie, and he stole it out from under me!" I seemed irrationally pissed and childish, but I didn't give a fuck. He could have let me purchase it, and instead, he *ate it in front of me.* What a prick.

"I saw," she said with a smirk. "I was cleaning up in the back."

Embarrassment colored my cheeks. Honey needled me about Cole often enough, but I always brushed it off and claimed she was crazy to think there was ever anything between us.

"Someone liiiiiiikes you," she teased.

I rolled my eyes. "Please. We aren't seven."

Honey laughed a little to herself as a waitress placed our usual drinks in front of us. There were definite perks to being close friends with the bar's owner.

"I don't care what you say, that man is stupid for you."

"Well, he's certainly stupid." I sipped my drink and tamped down the guilty feelings of name-calling Cole. He was many things, but stupid wasn't one of them, and even I realized I was the one being childish.

"Look, buying the last pie if he knew you were going to was a dick move. He may be Colin's best friend, but I can take care of it." A slow smile spread across her face, and mischief danced in her eyes. "His next order can have him shitting his pants for a week and not knowing why."

Honey was ruthless and the most loyal friend I'd ever had.

Feeling lighter than I had in weeks, I laughed. "No, don't do that. Who will keep this town safe if Captain America is out of commission?"

"That's true." Crestfallen, Honey swirled her drink. "It's too bad he's actually a decent human." Honey winked at me. "Mostly."

I simply rolled my eyes. It was common knowledge that Cole was the local golden boy, but for some reason he had a serious bone to pick with me. Rumors had spread far and wide through town as to why and ranged from a land dispute to high school drama to unrequited love—*ha*.

Honey pointed to the pie box and bumped my shoulder with hers. "So what's the deal?"

"Lottie informed me, *tonight*, she signed up for baked goods for the school fundraiser tomorrow."

Honey nodded as she sipped and swayed to the beat of the house band. "That sounds fun." She laughed.

"She's killing me. One minute she's the spawn of Satan, and the next she's begging to cuddle on the couch. I can't keep up."

"You're a great mom." Her hand covered mine. "She's lucky to have you."

I smiled at my friend. Being a single mother was never easy, and times like these, when your friends showed up for you with no questions asked, flooded my system with guilty feelings. It only served to remind me that I couldn't manage to do it on my own.

Our attention turned to the stage as Honey's husband, Colin, crooned into the microphone. A friend of his since high school, I felt nothing but platonic feelings for him, but it was undeniable that the man was handsome and could sing his heart out. Bluesy and warm, his voice was pure velvet.

Honey's blonde head swayed to the music, and her eyes filled with lust as she watched her man. A ping of jealousy shot me in the chest.

The soulful song faded, and I rubbed my hand against my thigh, willing the ache in my chest to release. "I should get going," I said to Honey. "I can't thank you enough for saving my ass tonight."

Her eyes softened. "I've always got your back. See you at the fundraiser?"

I lifted the pie box. "You know it." I kissed her on the cheek and left the bar, but not before letting my eyes flick past my favorite photo hanging on the wall. It was of Cole, Colin, and the third of their trio, Lincoln, dressed in football gear after a win, their youthful faces radiating charm and excitement. I had snapped the photo, and it always took me back to a time when life seemed full of promise, simpler.

The naive dreams of a young girl had been incinerated the moment I found out I had gotten pregnant on prom night by a boy who'd used me just for sex.

David had known how to charm me that night, and while he'd made a half-assed attempt at dating me after, he was never serious about a relationship with a shy girl who preferred books and country drives to field parties. A few weeks later, when my period was late, I drove twenty miles to a town where no one knew me and got a pregnancy test over the counter. I emptied my soul as I cried, alone in the smelly stall, and stared at the twin pink lines in the public bathroom.

When I tried to tell David, his response of "Is it even mine?" was a bullet to my chest. David was old money, and I was trailer trash who put out on prom night.

What a fucking cliché.

Mama wrapped me in a hug, and we talked about options. David's family offered me money to not have the baby, but I refused and steeled myself against the judgment that inevitably came my way.

After David's death, a large part of growing up had been letting the dreams of a younger me float away on the breeze. The chance at being Cole's girl had been one of those dreams.

The crisp air blew my hair back, and I gripped the box tightly. The whole town would turn out for the school fundraiser, and with Honey's help, I wouldn't show up empty-handed. Balancing the box in one hand, I fumbled for my keys.

A flash of yellow on my windshield caught my eye. "You have got to be kidding me."

I placed the pie on the front seat and reached to pull the paper from under the wiper. Stamped in dark ink was a parking ticket: multi-space, illegal parking. I glanced down at the white line beneath the wheel of my car. Sure, I was not *between* the lines, but illegal parking? No way.

I scanned the ticket and found exactly what I suspected —Cole Decker's signature scrawled across the bottom.

That fucking guy.

I sucked in a steadying breath to keep from coming completely unhinged. Deep down, I knew with a pretty bouquet arrangement and a sweet smile, I might get Arlene Johnson, the elderly secretary at the police station, to dismiss the ticket. Add it to the ever-growing list of things I needed to get done in the morning.

I looked over my shoulder in time to see Cole pass in a squad car. Not giving him the satisfaction of seeing how much he got to me, I ground my teeth together and slipped into my Honda. I pulled out of the parking space and wound up the dark mountain highway without allowing myself one last look at the infuriating boy who once held my heart.

TWO

MAGGIE

Ten Years Ago

"Thank you for dinner." I smiled at my date as I pushed through the door at Francesca's, the only nice "date night restaurant" in Chikalu.

"It was my pleasure, Margaret."

I tried not to sigh at the use of my full name—especially since I had already told him I preferred Maggie. I gritted my teeth through my plastic smile. One date. I had promised my mother I would give her coworker Michael one date while she watched Lottie for the night.

As far as dates go, he was perfectly fine. Polite, attentive, respectful.

Boring as fuck.

I sighed at myself a little at how harsh I was being toward Michael. He was a nice guy, but there was nothing about him that was exciting. Maybe I was being too judgmental. Heaven knows no one else was trying to break down the door for a date with a single mother to a four-year-old.

"Michael, I've had a nice time. Would you like to have a glass of wine at my place?"

A spark of hope bloomed across his face, and I immediately regretted asking him. I simply wanted to give him, and myself, a little more time to get to know each other before I gave up on him completely.

"Yes, Margaret. That would be lovely."

I gave him a small smile, and as Michael pushed the door closed, I noticed Cole Decker slowly creeping past in his squad car. I lifted an eyebrow, then purposely looked straight ahead.

Ignore it. Ignore the flutter. Don't let him ruin the first date you've had in a year. You don't mean anything to him.

By the time Michael rounded the hood of his car, I had regained my composure, and my pulse returned to normal. I adjusted the hem of my dress, pulling it closer to my knees.

One drink. Give him one more drink, and if you still don't feel a spark, then you know.

Michael drove up the winding road toward my home. Just as we reached the edge of town, I heard a familiar *whoop whoop*, and red and blue lights filled the dark interior of the car. My eyes shot to the side mirror, and Michael eased the car to the side of the road.

"This is unexpected," he muttered. "I was well under the posted limit." Michael was visibly nervous, wringing his hands and running them down his thighs.

I was about to reassure him when Cole stepped his large, very muscular body out of the squad car. His face was set in a hard grimace. The words of comfort withered on my tongue, my mouth suddenly bone dry. That man could wear the hell out of a police uniform, and I rubbed my thighs together to stop the buzz that seeing him in uniform created —the friction only intensified it.

Fuuuuuck.

Michael adjusted his glasses and fumbled with the car buttons until his window squeaked down. "Uh, good evening, Officer. I assure you—"

"License and registration." Cole's deep voice was cold and hard.

"Yes, sir, but I—"

"License and registration."

Why was he being such a prick?

I gently placed my hand on Michael's forearm as he fumbled through the glove box for the paperwork. I put on the sweetest smile I could manage and leaned forward. As I looked up at him, Cole's jaw ticked once, his eyes flicking down to my chest. I tried to ignore the tingle that shot through my belly at his chiseled jawline.

"Hi, Cole," I said sweetly. "Michael and I were just finishing up dinner. Is there a problem?" My voice was strong and never gave away the lifetime of adolescent secrets shared between the two of us. Any outsider would think we were simply acquaintances who lived in the same small town. I had perfected that voice over the last few years.

"It's Officer Decker." His thick arms were hanging at his sides, and when he stood tall, I had an unobstructed view of his trim waistline and the noticeable bulge in his work pants. "Your *friend* rolled through that stop sign back there."

Michael's head swiveled back as if he were trying to locate the stop sign. His voice rose and wavered nervously. "Oh, stop sign? No. Certainly not. I came to a complete stop."

"And besides"—I smiled through my teeth—"is not coming to a *complete* stop really that big of a deal?"

"It's breaking the law, ma'am."

Ma'am? Okay, Captain America. This man is fucking infuriating.

Michael handed Cole his driver's license and car registration, and without another word, he walked back to his squad car. Michael blew out a shaking breath.

"You know him?"

My eyes flicked back to the mirror. I could just barely see him typing on the computer in the car. I pushed away the memories of Cole and me laughing and spending hours together after school when we were kids.

"Everyone knows everyone in this town." My heart hurt to think about how hopeful I had been then. At the time, I thought surely Cole and I were going to end up together—half the town assumed the same. Instead, we'd stayed friends until he left for college. I was pregnant, and despite promises of visits and letters, we set out on living very different lives.

By the time Christmas rolled around and he was home for winter break, we were practically strangers, and I didn't have the time or the energy to heal my broken heart.

"Well, hopefully your connection helps me get out of this with just a warning." Michael smiled weakly at me.

"Failure to fully halt at a stop sign."

Michael blanched as Cole handed him the yellow ticket.

"Seriously?" I shouted at him and then immediately bit my lip at my outburst.

Cole leaned over and pinned me with a look that could make a grown man piss his pants. "Also," he continued slowly, "you were in a school zone, which will now require you to appear in court."

What. A. Dick.

I rolled my eyes and didn't miss the satisfied smirk that

lifted the corner of his disgustingly handsome face. Anger bubbled up and I shouted, "This is a gross miscarriage of justice! An abuse of power!"

He turned his back on us and threw over his shoulder, "Then file a complaint."

Without another word, he whipped his squad car in a wide U-turn and headed back toward town.

Fuming, I crossed my arms and ground my teeth together. Michael stared at the ticket in his hands.

"This is unbelievable," he said. "I've never gotten a ticket before." When I didn't respond, he continued: "You're sure you don't know him? That just seemed . . . I don't know. Personal, maybe?"

"Ha!" A barking laugh escaped me. "No. There is nothing personal between Cole Decker and me. I am no one to him. He's just an asshole on a power trip."

As Michael eased the car back toward the road, I pressed the heels of my hands to my eyes, suddenly weary and ready to curl up on my couch with a good book and a glass of wine.

Alone.

As we pulled into my driveway, Michael turned off the engine and went to remove his seat belt. I placed my hand on his to stop him.

"Michael," I started, "thank you for dinner tonight. I appreciate it, but I am going to have to call it a night."

"Oh." He paused. "It's just at dinner we'd discussed having a glass of wine at your place."

"I know. But it's getting late, and I have to get Lottie early tomorrow morning."

"Hmm. I understand. Can I call you tomorrow?"

I hated that part. The part where I had to be very direct to a perfectly nice guy because I was the broken one.

Because I didn't know how to date anyone without there being that invisible, unmistakable pull toward them—a feeling that I hadn't had since *him*.

"Thank you again for dinner, Michael." I forced myself to give him the dignity he deserved by looking him in the eyes. "I had a nice time, but I have to be honest. I am not sure I see a relationship between us beyond friendship."

Michael looked down and nodded once. "Thank you."

I looked at him quizzically.

He continued: "I appreciate you being up-front and honest with me about your feelings. I had hoped that this had the potential to develop into something more, but I appreciate you not leading me on."

"I'm sorry," I offered.

"No need," he said. "Good night, Margaret."

After unlocking the door, I pushed it closed and leaned against it. My small farmhouse was bathed in moonlight, the quiet more eerie than peaceful. There were countless nights when I was raising Lottie alone that I wished for some help, a break, *one night* that I could forget all my responsibilities and just be left alone. Now I hated it. Part of me wanted to call up my mother and let her know that I was on my way to pick up Lottie, but it was late. They would be sleeping, and then I would have to explain to her that her matchmaking had missed the mark.

After slipping off my shoes, I made the familiar rounds of checking the doors and locks in the house. A single woman raising a daughter alone, I tended to be a little paranoid. As I pulled the curtains of the living room closed, I saw a car slowly drive past my house.

Is that a squad car?

It was too dark to see, but the hairs on the back of my neck stood up, and the familiar burn in my chest was back. I had worked hard to grow into a strong, independent woman, and I needed to let my foolish heart break for Cole Decker once and for all.

I pulled the curtains closed tightly, and instead of enjoying that glass of wine, I wrapped myself into a cocoon on my bed and tried to sleep. My dreams were filled with the past and present colliding, as they always did when I was faced with interacting with Cole.

Sadness.

Hurt.

Desire.

Frustration.

Longing.

Emptiness.

The emotions rolled through my dreams, and as I awoke and stared at my ceiling, I couldn't help but blame myself for where we went wrong. I knew the answer when I was seventeen, and it was as clear today as it was then.

I missed my chance at happiness when I slept with David and wound up pregnant.

THREE

DECK

Now

Sucking in a deep breath, I paused before pulling open the doors to the school gymnasium. As Chikalu Falls's detective sergeant, attending things like school fundraisers was a part of the job. My father had been an officer, and his dad before him. It was in our blood.

Friendly smiles and waves, always being welcome at businesses, never paying for a cup of coffee—perks of small-town law enforcement. I enjoyed my job, and I was damn good at it. From early on, I understood that it was more than ensuring the citizens were abiding by the law. It was taking care of people. I earned those cups of coffee by understanding the nuances of small-town life. Listening to people. Understanding that while Mitzy's husband was a drunk, he was a happy drunk who never drove, and it best served everyone if we just offered him a ride home when he needed it.

It was also dealing with small-time, petty criminal shit. Which is another reason I made sure to make an appearance at the school fundraiser. For well over a year, someone had been tagging buildings—cartoon dicks with top hats, of all things. Whoever had done it even got one on the water tower last year. Shaking my head, I knew it was a matter of time before I caught the punks who evaded me at every turn. After a few months of silence, another one popped up on the window of Maggie's flower shop.

Now it's personal.

The warm furnace air in the gym was stifling. Sweat and stale coffee clung to the air as the whole town turned out for the fundraiser. Long tables were set up on the perimeter for the silent auction. Businesses donated gift certificates, tools from the hardware store, and merchandise. The county vet offered a free visit, and the largest table was for piles and piles of baked goods.

A hot ball formed under my sternum as I stared at the table. Buying the last pie when Maggie was eyeing it was a dick move, and I knew it. I wasn't an asshole to everyone in my life, far from it, but Maggie pushed my buttons like no one else could. My brain was wired to pick at her and push her away, and even I knew that was completely fucked-up. Everyone loved Maggie, and she was nothing but joyous and kind and warm.

I had my small circle of friends, and with her and Honey striking up a friendship last year, she'd been nudging her way into that circle more and more. I couldn't stand it. Just being around her brought deep, gnawing feelings clawing to the surface, and I didn't need that shit in my life.

Control.

That was what I needed. Small-town law enforcement could border on mundane, but there was a lot more to it than shaking hands and kissing babies. Dealing with the darker shit—alcoholism, drug abuse, kids growing up with nothing to do but get into trouble. Fuck, we'd even had to work with the county sheriff on suspected mob activity last month. That was hard enough, and I didn't need Maggie getting under my skin.

My eyes scanned the room for her, as they always did, without even meaning to. I spotted her auburn hair, curled and in waves tumbling down her back, and my body instantly felt warm. Fifteen years and I hadn't managed to stop the involuntary reaction of sharing the same air as Maggie O'Brien.

Mostly, I tortured myself. I knew the parking ticket would piss her off enough to send her sailing into the station, where I could get a glimpse of the fire in her eyes. I had intentionally left key information off the ticket, essentially rendering it a worthless piece of paper, but she didn't know that.

I have lost my goddamn mind.

I continued to scan the crowd and saw Maggie's daughter, Lottie, talking with her friends. The dark eyeliner around her eyes was smudged, and her mouth tipped down in a scowl. She was another one who got under my skin. She looked like David more and more each year, and the knife in my skull only twisted when I thought of him.

His life was over, and only I knew the truth behind it.

The reality that little Lottie was fatherless and that it was my fault was a catalyst for pushing Maggie so far away. It physically *hurt* to be near them, knowing what I'd done.

"Well, you look psychotic." Colin's firm grip pressed on my shoulder and snapped me back to reality.

Had I been staring?

I blew out a breath and steadied my heartbeat. "Just taking it all in."

"Ha!" Colin's lopsided grin spread across his face. "No luck yet with the Dick Bandits, I take it?"

I shook my head in frustration. "No, they've been quiet for a while. But it's going to happen again. I can feel it."

"C'mon, man. Let it go. It's just stupid kid shit."

He was right, but I couldn't let it go. This was my town. I also knew what happened when kids were left with too much money and too little time. Kids who didn't have accountability. Kids like David who took a wrong turn and never managed to get themselves back on track. My thoughts drifted to Lottie, and I'd be damned if she ended up like her father.

I shrugged and did my best to stay calm and focused. "My girl's over at the bake sale table with Maggie." He raised his hand to Honey, and my eyes immediately went to the gorgeous woman next to her. I turned my head to stare out above the crowd, and my jaw tightened. "Come say hi."

"Nah," I said. "I have a few things I need to take care of."

I hated lying to my best friend, but I couldn't muster the energy to pretend like any kind of proximity to Maggie didn't make my heart pound and my ears ring. Plus, I'd already acted like a complete asshole, and I didn't want to give her yet another excuse to hate me.

She has enough of those already.

I watched Colin's back as he sauntered away toward his wife. I hated to think that there was a little part of me that was envious of my best friend. He had it all—a successful business, a beautiful wife, a town that loved him—and I fell short. On the outside I was living a fulfilled life, but only I knew how bone-deep *lonely* it felt sometimes.

I slanted my eyes to the floor and pushed down the unrequited feelings that Maggie dragged to the surface. Tiny patent leather pumps came into view, and I pulled my eyes up to see Ms. Birdie, Lincoln's mama, smiling up at me.

She was arm in arm with Ms. Jean, Colin's mother, and one look was all it took to see they were up to no good.

"Ma'am." I nodded to the pair of them.

"Deck, honey, I'm afraid the Women's Club is in a bit of a pickle." Ms. Birdie peeked out from under her lashes as she feigned worry. It didn't take a detective to know that the Chikalu Women's Club was known for their meddling nearly as much as their philanthropy.

"Is that so?" I asked. "How can I help?"

"Well," Ms. Jean began, "you see, Matthew Bailey *may* have found out that he was signed up for the date auction . . ."

"Is that so?" I couldn't help but laugh. Old man Bailey was still the town hard-ass, and the thought of him being auctioned off on a *date* was ludicrous. I probably would have paid actual money to see that.

Ms. Birdie sneaked a sly smile to her friend and continued: "But it is a fundraiser, and we need someone to fill his spot."

"It's for the children," Ms. Jean pressed. She glanced down at the clipboard she held with the auction date names. Three rows from the bottom, my eyes stilled on *Maggie O'Brien*.

Without thinking, I grabbed the clipboard and scrawled my name on the bottom of the page. There was nothing stopping Maggie from going on a date, and there was zero reason I couldn't do the same.

Besides, it was for the children.

∾

"IN A DELIGHTFUL AND UNEXPECTED TWIST, our first date up for auction is our very own Detective Sergeant Cole

Decker!" Ms. Birdie gave an exaggerated wink to the crowd and fanned herself with her clipboard.

"Come on over, Officer," she urged.

I gave a tight-lipped smile and nodded to the crowd, but I stayed rooted in my spot. Being auctioned up like a prize heifer was degrading as fuck, and the thought that Maggie had to suffer through the same fate caused my pulse to skyrocket.

Through Ms. Birdie's embellishments of my *amazing qualities* and the bare-bones list of interests I gave her, I drowned out the crowd. Using my peripheral vision, I had a keen awareness of Maggie standing between Honey and Honey's sister, Jo.

Did Jo just nudge her? What the fuck was that about?

My heartbeat hammered and pounded in my ears. My face stilled, and I used my police training to look completely unfazed by the snickers and whispers that simmered through the crowd. After an agonizing few moments, Ms. Birdie told the crowd, "And remember, it's a secret, hidden auction so make sure that you submit your best and final offer for each date!"

The crowd milled around the gymnasium, and my mind went briefly to my savings account. Surely I could bid enough for a date with her. I smirked.

Wouldn't that just chap her ass.

I was a chickenshit, and instead of draining every last penny for a real date with Maggie, I stood like a ponderosa pine and let the silent auction unfold around me. It nagged me for two weeks after the auction ended.

So close and you couldn't man up.

Again.

Instead, I was sitting across the table from my auction date. The cloyingly sweet stench of Stacy's perfume overpowered the lemon and garlic of Francesca's best menu items and dragged me out of my own head. Despite the fact that Stacy didn't even live in Chikalu, she'd weaseled her way into the auction and come away with the highest bid for my date. We were off-again, and I had no intention of riding that crazy train once more.

It's for the kids.

It's for the kids.

It's for the fucking kids.

"You could at least try to have a good time." Stacy's voice cut through the noise in my brain, and I looked at her. At one time, I thought her sexy demeanor was confidence, but it'd rapidly become clear that she loved attention. Any attention. When I realized she had a thing for men in uniform and I wasn't the only person keeping her bed warm, I'd walked away for the final time.

"Sorry." A shrug was all I could muster.

"Maybe you're actually made of stone. There's just no getting through to you." She rolled her eyes, and I knew her comment was meant to get a rise out of me, but I stared blankly at her. I felt . . . nothing. I hated that a big part of her was right. I hated that I had become an angry, closed-off version of myself.

I sighed, trying to be better. "I *am* sorry. Work's just been a lot lately. Tell me what you've been up to. How's your brother?"

Stacy took the opening and ran with it. For the next forty minutes she droned on and on about how mundane small-town life was, that she was definitely moving again, and something else I didn't give a shit about.

The air sucked out of my lungs when Maggie breezed through the restaurant door. Her heady, floral scent hit me before I even realized it was her, and adrenaline coursed through my body. She was in jeans that clung to her curves, the swell of her hips and perfect ass directly in my line of sight. She was on her auction date with Shawn Evans, a fucking firefighter. I could tell she'd done something different with her hair and makeup. She'd made an effort for this date. My fist clenched around my fork as I pushed the pasta around my plate and pretended to not notice them sitting across the restaurant from us.

Maggie caught me staring and tipped an eyebrow at me just as she sat down, but I quickly looked away and tried, half-heartedly, to focus on Stacy again. I forced myself to take a deep breath and shove down the sudden urge to stand up and run, or flip the table, or ram my fist into Shawn Evans's chiseled fucking jaw. A surge of real, honest jealousy rode me hard, and I had to kick it down.

Maggie deserved a man like Shawn. From what I knew of him, he was good looking, had a great job, and was a pretty stand-up guy.

Fuck that guy.

The disastrous date with Stacy finally ended. I turned to drop a generous tip to our waitress and punished myself with one last glance at Maggie.

My world tilted and spun out of control.

She was leaned back, her eyes toward the ceiling, delicate hands clutching her throat.

She's fucking choking.

Instinct took over, and I toppled chairs as I cleared a path to her. Her body was feather light, and I pulled her back to me, her toes lifting off the ground as I spun her out of her chair. I wrapped my arms around her, centering my fist just below the swell of her breasts and closed my other hand around it.

As I was about to pull and save the life of the woman I'd obsessed over since high school, her hands clawed at my forearms. Shawn pushed toward me, and it finally registered that Maggie's voice was yelling at me, clear as day.

"Cole! Cole, stop! What the *fuck*?!"

I set her down and turned her by the shoulders to face me. Confusion clouded my brain. The entire restaurant was dead silent, all eyes on the three of us.

"I . . . I thought . . . I thought you were choking."

"I was *laughing*, you psycho. Jesus!"

I stepped back, and when I realized I was still clutching her shoulders, my hands dropped to my sides. She'd been laughing at something Shawn had said, and when I thought she was dying, I'd spent a minute dry humping her while attempting the Heimlich. Heat rose in my cheeks, and my mind went blank.

Laughing? Who the hell laughs like that?

Irrational anger boiled through me, and I couldn't even acknowledge the horrified expression Stacy gave me. Without looking any of them in the eye, I stormed out of the restaurant.

Add that to the list of exchanges with Maggie that ended in fucking disaster.

FOUR

DECK

Two Years Ago

"The usual?" Colin asked me as he wiped down the makeshift bar table. It was Saturday night, and he was working the taps at the beer tent at Chikalu's annual Fall Sagebrush Festival.

"Yeah," I said and threw down two beer tickets on the table.

Colin nodded toward the tickets and scoffed. "Get outta here with that. You're actually not working Sagebrush for once. Your drinks are on me tonight."

"Appreciate that, man." I grabbed the cold beer and slugged down two hearty gulps. "You working all night?"

"Nah," he said. "I'll be helping here for a while, but then the band's got a set in about an hour. Meet up after?"

"'Course. Linc around?" I scanned the crowd for our friend but didn't see him.

Colin shook his head. "Nope. Finn was going to try to get him to come, but you know him. It's a lot of people here."

I nodded. Lincoln had been our friend since grade

school, but he'd served in the Marines and come back a changed man. He carried his demons, and things like a crowd and people and actually *talking* to someone was a hard no for him.

"Plus, he's still torn up about Jo," Colin added.

I shook my head. "Yeah, he fucked that one up good. Think they'll work it out?"

"Hell if I know. He's a dumbass if he doesn't run after her, but he doesn't listen to anyone. Jo's great."

"Just like her sister, right?"

"Fuck off." He laughed at my ribbing—Colin had hooked up with Jo's sister and was still hung up on the girl. "We had a good time."

Avoiding the subject, he nodded over my shoulder. "Speaking of a good time . . ."

I turned to see Stacy, a waitress from Canton Springs, walking toward us. We had an on-again, off-again relationship that mostly meant she called me when she broke up with someone, and I warmed her bed.

"Ah, fuck." I sighed and drank a deep pull from my beer. Colin slid a fresh one in front of me, and I grabbed it before heading toward Stacy. "I'll see you later."

"Funny running into you here, handsome!" Stacy grinned at me and leaned in for a hug. It was awkward, and my hands were full, so I mostly stood there while she wrapped her arms around my midsection and pressed her impressively large breasts against me.

"Hey, Stace."

She jutted her lower lip out in a pout. "No uniform tonight?" My being a cop was a definite highlight for her, but I was used to that.

"Not tonight. Sorry to disappoint," I mused.

"Well, you can make it up to me with a dance."

I glanced up at the crowded dance floor. It was a makeshift plywood floor set up in front of the main stage, and the bands that Colin had booked for the Sagebrush Festival were incredible—everything from old country classics to new stuff, band originals, and classic rock. Chikalu loved a good line dance, and men and women of all ages were dancing in unison to the song.

My traitorous eyes immediately landed on Maggie. She was an incredible dancer—knew every step to every dance and was confident enough to add little twirls and ass shakes that made my blood simmer. She had always loved dancing, and I made it a point to avoid seeing her in her element like that.

I knew the steps and I was a decent dancer, but I wasn't nearly drunk enough to line dance. As if the universe were conspiring against me, the band transitioned to a slower song, and most people paired off to two-step. Stacy dragged me by the wrist into the edge of the crowd.

I was reluctant, preferring to babysit my beer and people watch. That was, until I saw Maggie accept the offer to dance with some schmuck. He twirled her around and bumbled the steps a few times. Each time, she laughed it off and her eyes smiled up at him.

Fuck that guy.

I emptied my beer, tossed the empty cups into a trash bin, and pulled Stacy onto the dance floor with a twirl. Her dress hugged her curves and stopped profanely short on her ass, leaving her long legs bare until they met the tops of her cowboy boots. We moved and swayed to the music, falling in rhythm with the other dancers, but I intentionally maneuvered us closer to Maggie and her partner.

His hands were dangerously low, nearly cupping

Maggie's ass, and if I hated him before, I wanted nothing more than to break his hands for touching her.

You have no claim on her. She doesn't want you.

Circling around each other, my glare caught Maggie's green-and-gold-flecked eyes. On a normal day, I would force myself to look away and not get lost in those beautiful pools, but tonight, with the sun sagging in the sky over the mountain and the twinkle lights blinking on, I couldn't help myself. Years of longing and regret churned just below the surface. She felt something too. I knew in the way she refused to look away.

As we danced, I ran my hands down Stacy's sides, my eyes never leaving Maggie's. To an outsider, it could seem like I was showing off, just a little, but in reality, all I could think about was how much I wished it was Maggie in my arms. I hated that instead of feeling Maggie's body move with mine, it was someone else. Heat roiled in my stomach.

That anger fueled my fire to push thoughts of Maggie away. I dipped Stacy low, her legs straddling my thigh, and pulled her body flush against mine, just to be a dick.

Finally breaking our eye contact, Maggie stepped away from her partner and grabbed the arm of her friend Chalene, midsong. "Come on, this song sucks. Let's do the wine tasting."

Fresh irritation rolled through me—the women working the wine tasting were notoriously heavy-handed and Maggie was already on the wrong side of tipsy. As they moved through the crowd past Stacy and me, they bumped into us, and I instinctively steadied her arm. Maggie looked down at my hand, and her eyebrow tipped up in challenge, but I was rooted to the ground, not releasing my grasp. My palm tingled, and her skin felt like silk under my rough hands.

Stacy cleared her throat, breaking the spell I was under. "Let's get another round."

With my attention on Stacy, Maggie melted into the crowd, disappearing.

~

"You've GOT to be fucking kidding me." I pressed the pads of my fingers into my eyelids and tried to unsee what I just saw. Driving past the intersection of Main Street and Elm, down the old dirt road leading out of town, I saw a very intoxicated Maggie singing and swaying with an equally drunk Gertie Mills. Trouble was, Gertie was eighty-one years old and topless.

I pulled to the side of the road and typed out a quick text to Stacy.

Me: Change of plans. I got called into work.

I felt a tinge of guilt at the small lie. Technically I was *always* a cop, and protecting my community meant I was never off duty. I needed to be sure these women got home safely, and walking down a dark road, half naked, was something I couldn't just let go.

Stacy: Want me naked and waiting for you when you're done?

While I appreciated Stacy's enthusiasm, it wasn't happening tonight. There'd be hell to pay tomorrow, in the form of pouting and snide messages, but I didn't give a fuck. My overwhelming need to protect Maggie would always outweigh a mediocre fuck. I ignored the text and spun my truck around to double back toward the women. Just as I approached, a rookie cop pulled up behind them, lights on.

I parked and ambled toward them. I was dead in my tracks when I realized that not only was Ms. Gertie completely topless, but so was Maggie. The women were giggling and singing off-key country songs and completely oblivious to what was unfolding around them. My heart hammered, and I cursed myself for immediately getting hard at the sight of Maggie's perfect round tits. How many nights had I imagined what they looked like? How many times had I gotten myself off on the fantasy of having my mouth and hands all over her tight little body? Seeing it, actually seeing it in real life, was a thousand times more tempting than any fantasy I could create.

I stormed past the rookie cop toward the women. "Put your shirt on, Maggie." My voice was harsh and demanding.

"Aww, the good-time assassin is back!" she teased. With a deep voice she continued: "I'm Officer Stick-in-the-Mud. Gruff. Gruff. Gruff." Ms. Gertie giggled and brushed back her white curls.

I pointed at the rookie. "You. Take Ms. Gertie home." I rattled off her address from memory, and he nodded, following his superior's orders. After he guided her toward the squad car and tucked her into the back seat, he made his way toward the driver's side. I squared up with him, feet planted wide.

"This never happened." I pointed a finger at him. "You came across Gertie Mills, drunk and topless, but she was alone. You never saw anyone else with her. Ms. Gertie is known for a good time, and everyone will laugh this off, but Maggie doesn't need people talking shit about her."

"Yes, sir." He was a good, loyal cop and understood how much weight small-town gossip held.

I narrowed my eyes at him. "You'll also forget all about seeing her topless." I leaned my head toward Maggie as she continued to fumble with her inside-out T-shirt.

"Of course, sir. I didn't see a thing."

I nodded at him once before turning my back and stalking toward Maggie.

"Jesus, put that fucking thing back on!" I raised my voice at her, and she stopped, partway into getting her shirt on, so her head was still covered and her tits bounced.

I reached out and pulled her shirt down, her head popping through the neck hole. I glanced down, and I don't know what was worse—seeing her naked breasts out on full display or seeing how the tight fabric stretched over her chest. I could see her nipples popping through the thin fabric, and I immediately grew hard again. I wanted to take those perfect nipples into my mouth and taste her.

Tease her.

Pissed off at my own physical reaction to her, I put my hand on the small of her back and walked her toward the cab of my truck. She wrestled away from me.

"Don't you tell me what to do! I'm not doing anything!"

"The fuck you are. You're walking down a dark road half naked in the *opposite* direction of your house. Get in the fucking truck!" I rounded my hood and yanked open the passenger door. I was irrationally angry. I hated the fact that someone could have seen her naked, hated that someone could have taken advantage of her, hated that I couldn't think of much else besides seeing *all of her* naked and writhing beneath me.

"Make me." Maggie's mossy eyes glowed in defiance. Without a second thought, I reached into the glove box and grabbed my handcuffs.

I held them in one hand, the cold steel pressing into my palm. On an empty threat, I called to her, "Don't make me arrest you, Maggie."

The fire in her eyes burned brighter. "You wouldn't dare—"

Before she could even finish her sentence, I had her pressed against the side of my truck. Her ass pushed against me, and I knew she could feel the hard length of my cock. I held her arms behind her, gently. Every soft curve of her body was pressed against the hard lines of mine, and I wanted to devour every part of her.

My voice was thick with lust and anger. I had taken it too far. I would never, *ever* abuse my power as a cop, but Maggie had a way of picking at me like a scab. I took a deep, steadying breath.

"Please don't make me arrest you," I repeated.

The tip of my nose grazed the shell of her ear as my words danced over her skin. A low hum in her throat nearly broke me—nearly made me take her right there against the side of my truck in the dark shadows of the road.

"Cole . . ." Maggie's voice was breathy and needy as she pushed her ass firmly against me. She turned, and I kept my hands at her sides, caging her between my truck and me.

"Yes, Magpie." I shifted my hips as she pressed into me and hitched one leg over my thigh. I inhaled her perfume—something floral and musky and completely devastating. Years and years of wanting this woman came rushing to the surface. I wanted to take her face in my hands and tell her all the secrets I had been keeping from her. Tell her that she was the first and only girl I'd ever loved and that I didn't think I was built to love anyone else.

"Why do you hate me?"

"I could never hate you." My voice was husky and low, my eyes never leaving hers.

I watched her chest rise and fall with her breaths, her breasts swelling and straining against the fabric of her T-shirt.

"Then what is this?" Her voice was barely above a whisper.

"I'm trying to keep my fucking hands off you." It was a losing battle, my hands clenched into fists.

"Cole, I—"

She puked. Over and over she emptied herself at the side of my truck. Instinct took over, and when she was through, I lifted her into my arms, held her close to me, and gently placed her in the truck. The anger I felt before had fizzled, and I wanted to do whatever I could to take care of her.

"Where's Lottie? Do I need to get her?" I asked, my voice still thick with unfulfilled lust.

"Pshhh," she slurred with heavy eyelids as she snuggled into my shoulder. "Lottie is *way* too cool to be seen at Sagebrush with her *mom*. She's having a sleepover at Molly Ann's house."

I wrapped my arm around her and relief flooded my system. At least I had to take care of only one of the O'Brien women tonight.

When we arrived at her farmhouse, she was barely awake and drunk as fuck. It helped that she no longer resisted my help, and together we got the front door open, and I tucked her into bed. I quickly got a glass of water and placed it beside her. Maggie looked up at me, her hair splayed across the pillow, and I allowed myself one touch. I ran my fingers through the long, silky strands as I looked down on her beautiful face.

Mmm, she hummed. "Cole."

I leaned closer to her, taking a hit of her scent as I tucked the blankets around her. "Why don't you call me Deck?"

"Because everyone else does."

I harrumphed.

Always stubborn as fuck.

Then she added, "Cole makes you mine." My chest squeezed as she rolled over.

"Cole?" she asked, her eyelids sagging and drunken slumber seconds away from taking her.

"Yes, doll."

"Am I your girl?"

I brushed a sticky piece of hair away from her face. My chest pinched at her words, but in the darkness, I couldn't give her anything other than honesty. "You'll always be my girl."

I leaned down, kissed her hair, and closed her bedroom door behind me. I sighed, leaning against the back of her bedroom door and feeling the weight of the evening hang on my shoulders. In every story, there's a villain. I knew this. But it tore at my soul to know that I had become the villain in hers.

After checking the rest of the house locks, I pulled her front door closed with a snap and walked away.

FIVE

MAGGIE

Now

"Hear me out, Mama." Hope rose in Lottie's voice as she perched her school laptop on her knees. "I have a whole presentation!"

Turning from her, I couldn't help but laugh. She may be hormonal and irrational and a nightmare teenager, but my girl had spunk. I frowned down at the skillet—my Denver omelet was quickly becoming a Denver scramble because I never could get an omelet quite right.

"Okay." I sighed. "Let's hear it." I plated up our breakfast as a grin split Lottie's face wide open.

That's why you do it. When's the last time she smiled at you like that?

"I know my birthday is not for a little while," she started.

"Three months."

"Right, but still . . ." Lottie turned her laptop toward me. She did, in fact, have a presentation.

"Oh, Lottie, no." I shook my head at the title—*Unusual Pets That Make Amazing Companions.*

A well-practiced, disgusted scoff erupted from her throat. "You didn't even listen!"

I took a deep breath. "You're right, I'm sorry. Please. Go on."

The smallest of smiles teased her full lips, and she began clicking through her presentation.

"Potbellied pig," she started. "Not only are they intelligent, but—"

"They make delicious breakfast?" I teased. My hilarious joke only earned me an eye roll. Figures.

"No. Mom, be serious. We aren't eating our pet."

"Well, I haven't agreed to a pet. Besides, we have chickens! We don't need another animal around here."

She cleared her throat and angled her head toward the laptop. I raised my hands in surrender. "You're right. Please continue."

"Potbellied pig," she began again. "Not only are they intelligent, but they eat food scraps and can protect the family. Next option would be a capybara. For a rodent, they are surprisingly doglike."

My eyebrows inched up my forehead. Lottie had clearly done her research. The pudge ball was kind of cute, but a giant hairy rodent? Hard pass.

Unfazed, Lottie continued. Sugar glider, wallaroo, tarantula.

Fuck. No.

I had a sinking feeling I was going to have to disappoint my daughter, yet again. Somehow this ridiculous venture would be my fault, and I would *ruin her entire life* because I wouldn't let a tarantula run loose in my house. A knot of tension formed at the base of my neck. These days it seemed as though we connected less and less, and there was always something I was screwing up.

"Finally, we come to the pygmy goat." Lottie beamed at me. I had a sneaking suspicion she'd saved the least disgusting pet for last.

Why couldn't she just ask for a cat? I can totally lean into the crazy-cat-lady phase of my life.

"The pygmy goat would assimilate to farm life seamlessly. It's cute, small, and would save time and money by eating the grass so we don't have to mow it!"

I had to admit, the goat did have the whole "I don't have to mow" thing going for it. "Lottie, where would we keep it?"

"That's the best part! They're little, less than thirty-five pounds. They only need a small outdoor space. Isn't goat cheese your favorite anyway?" My girl sure was laying it on thick.

I knew I had to tread lightly where Lottie was concerned. Unfortunately for her, she may have inherited my fire, but she got her daddy's impatience laced in there too.

"I'm not saying no. But," I continued, "we'd need to get the logistics worked out. Besides, it's a big commitment, and it's already coming into cold months. Maybe this is better for spring, baby."

"So it is a no." Lottie's face fell. She'd perfected the crestfallen pout, and even though I knew she was being a brat, it still tore my heart out every time. It wasn't easy being both mom and dad to Lottie. There was no good cop / bad cop when you were the only person making the tough decisions.

"Where in the world do you even get a pygmy goat?"

Lottie saw the cracks in my armor and in an excited squeal wrapped her long arms around my waist. I reveled in her affection, pulling her arms tighter to me. Lottie had also gotten her dad's lithe frame, and it was only a matter of time until she was taller than me. "The vet on Route Seven knows of a farmer who is looking to sell some of the new babies. It's how I came up with the whole idea!"

Leave it to Lottie to already have a perfect plan in place. I was just trying, and floundering, to keep up here.

"Fine. First things first. I will talk with the veterinarian and make sure this information is correct. If we can get the logistics worked out, we can *consider* getting your weird little goat."

My sweet Charlotte's rich laughter filled our kitchen, and my heart swelled. Nowadays it was rare that I could find genuine ways to make her happy. If that meant that I had to bust my ass to build a pen and care for a little goat, then so be it. I could look at it as another adventure for the two of us to have together.

It wouldn't be until later, when I lay in the darkness of my empty bed, that I let myself think about how different my life could have been. On a day-to-day basis, I never allowed those thoughts to creep in. I loved Lottie fiercely, and I would never change the circumstances that brought us together. She was my world. But sometimes there were moments when I wondered what it felt like to not have to carry her world *and mine* on my shoulders. To have someone to lean on and laugh with. Just knowing that even though you had a shit day, you had someone to share it with.

Inevitably my thoughts would drift to Cole. At seventeen, I'd cried all my tears over him until the bone-dry ache took root in my chest. After I told him that I was pregnant, the immature and selfish part of me wished he would have stayed home from school, scooped me in his arms, and rescued me. Instead, David and I did the only thing that two wildly unprepared teenagers could do—we tried to pretend that we had anything in common until our relationship fizzled out before my belly even started to show.

Despite the fact that I had written and crumpled letter after letter to Cole, I couldn't tell him what had always been in my heart. It was selfish to take away his future because I had made a mistake and he was my only comfort. I knew that even then. So when our unshakable friendship began to fade, I let him go.

I couldn't face him in town. The daily rumors about David and me became incessant, so I went to live with my widowed aunt Gwen on her ranch a few towns over. There, I learned how to farm and be self-sufficient. She was rough and a little scary and never once let me feel sorry for myself.

I grew up fast, and part of that growing up meant never allowing myself to stand in the way of Cole becoming the man he was meant to be. David was unconcerned with me or our baby, so I stayed away even after my aunt's cancer took her far too quickly. Then, just after Lottie's second birthday, my mother called me to tell me that David had died in a car accident. He had fallen back on drugs, and it had been months since he had called to ask about Lottie— even longer since he'd seen her.

I was truly alone.

My mom convinced me it was time to move home, and by the time Lottie and I settled back in Chikalu, Cole was a stranger. Worse, he'd grown prickly and dismissive. For the past decade, it seemed as though my presence angered him more and more. Gone was the shy boy with kind eyes who'd sneaked me lemonade candies in class and given me ridiculous nicknames. In his place was a delicious, broody man whose scowl lit me on fire every time he drove past my flower shop.

SIX

DECK

Now

"So, is that . . . pubic hair?" Ms. Trina stood outside her shop, the Blush Boutique, with her hands planted on the wide expanse of her hips. Her stark cobalt eyeliner slitted as she tipped her head to the side.

"Yes, ma'am." I blew out a breath. "I believe that is a somewhat anatomically correct penis."

This fucking job, man.

Beside me, Ms. Trina's shoulders began to shake. On the painted white brick of her boutique, someone had spray-painted another giant dick—top hat askew, arms akimbo, its wide cartoon grin taunting me.

She should be furious. Hell, I was furious for her. But instead, she wiped tears of laughter from her face, smearing the blue eyeliner as she giggled and sighed. "Ah, Deck. This is really something!" A fresh fit of the giggles erupted from her chest.

Ms. Trina was a bit of a wild card in town. She owned and operated the ladies' clothing boutique, and rumor was she had a not-so-hidden talent of selecting the perfect set of lingerie to make any man fall to his knees. A rogue thought of Maggie popped into my head. I wondered if Ms. Trina had ever helped her find the perfect set of lingerie for a hot date. For some lucky asshole who wasn't me.

An irrational flare of anger balled in my chest, burning a path down to my gut. "It's vandalism." My voice came out harsher than I intended, cutting through her laughter.

You're such an asshole.

I cleared my throat to soften my voice, to remember that I was here to serve and protect my community. "I can have someone out here later this afternoon to take care of this," I said.

"Oh, there's no rush." A hint of laughter still danced at the edge of her voice. "People around here need to loosen up a little, and this might just be the thing to do it!"

Ms. Trina patted my shoulder, wiped another tear from the corner of her eye, and giggled her way back into her shop. I knew she meant the comment about people in a small town in general, but it still felt pointedly direct. I hated that I came across as stiff and uptight.

I took a few pictures for evidence and called in to the station. The new rookie on the afternoon shift could come up here with a can of paint to help cover the smiling cock.

As I finished, the door to the Blush Boutique opened, tinkling the small bell that hung from it. My eyes barely registered Casey Mae, and I started back toward my vehicle.

"Oh, hi, Deck," she called over my shoulder.

I turned to face her. "Hello, Casey Mae." I nodded in her direction. She was a few years younger than me in school and worked as an accountant, if I recalled correctly. Duty kept my feet planted when she made no attempt to move away.

"Are you just starting your shift or just ending it?" She

twirled her hair around her finger, and my police training registered a slight nervous flit of her eyes.

I shifted in my uniform. I may have the title of detective sergeant, but Chikalu was still small enough that I worked the streets and wore all the same equipment as the street guys. Despite the title, I couldn't imagine being a desk jockey for the rest of my career.

"Putting in a few more hours."

"Well," she continued, "it's Saturday. Some girls and I are meeting up later at The Pidge. Sure would be nice to take a lap around the dance floor." Casey Mae took a slight step forward, and instinct made me mirror her movement backward.

I gave a noncommittal nod, but my heart hammered beneath my vest. I knew Casey Mae was friends with Maggie, and I couldn't help but wonder if she'd also be at the bar tonight. I had fully planned on a workout, a beer, and turning in early, but I felt a buzz of energy just below my skin. I knew I'd never grow the balls to dance with Maggie, but the chance to sneak a few glances at the way she rolled her hips or how her tits bounced when she hopped during a line dance made my blood run warmer.

I started walking toward my squad car, effectively ending the conversation. Casey Mae called at my back, "Well, if I want to call you later, should I get your number?"

I turned to see Casey Mae's tongue flick out to drag across the corner of her mouth before I opened the driver door. Goddamn, she was irritatingly persistent.

I smiled my best Officer-of-the-Year smile and said, "If you need me, you call 9-1-1."

～

"This is fucking dumb." Lincoln glared into his amber drink as I leaned my back against the bar.

"Yeah, pretty much," I said and took a deep pull of my beer. It was a Saturday night, and The Pidge was crawling with kids from the local community college. Somewhere along the way, the girls at the community college had stopped being hot and started being really, really young.

Nah. You just got fucking old.

"We can go," I said. My mood had soured when I realized that Maggie wasn't at The Pidge. She was a hard-working single mother—she was probably at home being responsible and taking care of Lottie.

Lincoln exhaled a sigh beside me. "I can't," he said. "Jo's out on a fishing guide, and I promised her I wouldn't hole up in the house all week."

Jo had been a godsend for Lincoln. She'd pushed him outside his comfort zone in ways we'd tried for years and somehow had gotten him to go along with every demand she made, no matter how much he hated it. That man had it bad for his woman, and I was man enough to admit that, deep down, I envied their relationship. Neither asked the other to change, but rather they loved each other just as they were.

I was about to leave. About to tell Lincoln that we could head out to the cabin and leave the noise of the bar behind when the heavy door pushed open.

I sensed her before I even saw her.

Maggie sailed into the bar, completely oblivious to the heads that turned in her direction or the appreciative stares of the men she passed. I wanted to rip their fucking heads off just for looking at her.

"All right," I said. "We can stay." I felt shitty letting Linc believe that the only reason I wanted to stay was because Jo wanted him to socialize, but I had no choice. I'd buried my magnetic pull toward Maggie for so long that it felt more natural to push her away than to give in to the twitch of my fingers that begged to touch her.

I turned toward the bar to order another round and used the opportunity to track Maggie as she joined a table of women on the edge of the dance floor.

She wore a white eyelet blouse with long, billowing sleeves, but it left her neck and shoulders completely bare. It was completely inappropriate for the chilly autumn weather. Never mind the fact that I couldn't stop thinking about licking the delicate shadow underneath her collarbone.

When Lincoln's gaze followed my own, I signaled to the raven-haired bartender, Isabel.

"Another round?"

"Please. And a shot of whiskey."

Both arms sleeved in intricate tattoos, she paused, tipping up an eyebrow. "You got it." Shaking her head, she poured two shots of rotgut whiskey and pushed them forward. I slid one toward Linc.

"Fuck you, man. I'm not drinking that shit."

I swiped the glass before he could even finish his sentence, slugging the burning liquid down my parched throat. Lincoln's stony expression never wavered, but I could feel his eyes assess every move I made.

"Tying one on tonight or what?" he asked.

I angled my chin toward Maggie. "Or what."

Lincoln shook his head, laughing to himself as he sipped his beer. In an instant, Maggie's hazel eyes skimmed the crowd before stopping on mine. I stared ahead, feeling her gaze pause on my skin. My practiced look of cool indifference cracked, only slightly, when my eyes darted in her direction and got tripped up in the way her eyes held mine.

My heart stopped in my chest, my breath burning in my lungs.

When her friend bumped her, she looked down, breaking the spell.

An hour later, Lincoln and I were swapping stories and laughing. His demons weren't so demanding tonight, and sharing a few beers with someone who had known you your whole life felt natural. I'd never let Maggie out of my periphery and knew the schmuck she was dancing with had to be at least ten years our junior. He must have lived at the gym, and I hated the way his hands dipped low on her waist as they two-stepped to the bluesy country music.

When she inched away, he crowded her space again, and I stiffened. The overwhelming need to protect her caused a demanding rhythm to pulse in my jaw.

"Hang tight," I said to Lincoln.

"Just say the word." He'd seen it too.

I kept the scowl fixed on my face as I slowly worked the perimeter, moving toward her in a lazy arc. The next song was flirty and fun, but the tension wound around her delicate neck and bunched in her shoulders. She was uncomfortable, and this chump was getting too close, not reading or caring about her signals.

"Casey Mae." I nodded in her direction as I walked up to their table, never taking my eyes off Maggie on the dance floor.

I glanced in Casey Mae's direction in time to catch her cheeks flush. I felt like a prick leading her on, but I needed a solid reason to get out on that dance floor. "How about that dance?"

A muffled squeal behind her tugged a small smile to my lips, and I led Casey Mae toward Maggie. I rarely danced, though I knew how and had been told I was decent at it. I knew how to move and twirl my partner to show her off and make her feel like the center of the universe. Casey Mae was a bit clunky and tried to lead a time or two, but my wide palms would stretch across her upper back, leading her around the floor with confidence.

As we inched closer toward Maggie, I could see her partner was getting bolder, pressing his hips into her ass as they swayed. She pulled away, turning to push her palm against his chest. A low rumble vibrated within me at seeing him completely oblivious to her discomfort. The song faded, and I thanked Casey Mae for the dance, effectively dismissing her and ignoring the pout she clicked into place.

Two steps forward and I was pressed against Maggie's back, my hand wrapping possessively around her trim waist. "You okay, doll?" My voice rumbled low against the shell of her ear.

"There you are!" Her eyes were wild as she turned and threw herself around my neck. Instinct took over, and I wrapped her in my arms. For a moment, I pulled her close to me, drowning in the warmth of her body, the delicate scent of floral perfume and her skin. My cock thickened at the closeness of Maggie's body pressed against mine.

I've waited fifteen years for this.

Maggie still clung to me as I shot her dance partner prick a murderous glare. He took one step back, both palms in the air. Shaking his head, he backed away and wound himself around the next girl who smiled in his direction.

I should stop touching her. Let her go.

I couldn't. Maggie hadn't released her arms from around my neck, and I couldn't force myself to peel my arms off her. Instead, I took a deep inhale of her sexy, floral scent and filed it away in my memory for later. Around us, the mood shifted. The lights slanted, and the low bass of a slow country song reverberated through the speakers.

Instead of releasing my shoulders, Maggie's plush hips began to sway. "I think he's still watching," she whispered against my skin.

"Definitely," I said. That douche had all but forgotten about us, but if that was what she thought, I was going with it.

One hand ran up her back, settling between her shoulder blades, and I pulled her chest against mine. I knew it was a mistake. My carefully crafted detachment was the only way I knew how to protect her from all my bullshit. Her heart hammered through the delicate fabric of her top, and I could feel the diamond tips of her nipples press against me.

I swallowed a groan as we swayed and moved to the music. Slow, practiced breathing was the only thing that kept me from completely unraveling in her arms. Up close, Maggie was even more beautiful than I could stand.

She was everything I needed but had no right to want. Not after what I had done. I shoved my demons down and focused on the fact that Maggie O'Brien was swaying in my arms, humming along with the band.

"You smell nice," she said quietly. Her voice was barely audible above the noise in the bar.

"Mmm," I harrumphed, unable to form a coherent thought, let alone actual words. A thousand thoughts tumbled through my head, but I couldn't seem to find a way to give voice to a single one.

You smell nice too.

I miss you.

This feels too good.

The song faded, melted into a new one, and my ability

to form a singular thought returned. My back stiffened as I pulled to my full height, causing her fingers to untangle from my hairline. The cold left behind by the absence of her hands prickled down my spine.

What the fuck are you doing? You've done nothing but ruin her entire life.

Dread pooled in my stomach as I thought back to all the choices that brought us here, all the things that I had done. I thought of David. I had no right to enjoy the feel of Maggie's soft breath tangling with mine.

Steadying her on her feet, I held her at arm's length and leveled my breathing. Her long fingers curled around my wrists, pushing against my pulse points as they hammered against her fingertips.

I'd let it go too far. How had I let her creep past my defenses and seep into my bones? The swirling greens and amber of her eyes burned into me. Everyone around us melted away.

I could do it. I could pull her into me and crush that full mouth against mine and finally claim her.

"Cole . . ." Maggie took the tiniest step toward me.

I swallowed past the gravel in my throat.

"You need to be more responsible." I pushed past the undulating crowd, fleeing before I could do something epically stupid, like finally caving to my deepest desires. Bitter self-loathing washed over me as I caught the disgusted look that marred Maggie's gorgeous face. I'd hurt her with the very words I knew would cut deep. But I had to protect her, and her heart.

Even if it cost me everything.

SEVEN

MAGGIE

Fifteen Years Ago

Cole: There in 5.

Excitement skittered through me. I checked my makeup, fluffed my hair, and closed the door to the double-wide trailer that Mama and I lived in. It was cramped and run down, but it was clean and it was ours. Cole was one of the few people who never made me feel bad for living in Chikalu Heights, the trailer park on the outskirts of town.

One day, I mused. One day I was going to leave this trailer behind me. Maybe I'd be a teacher or an actress or an artist. It didn't matter that I didn't particularly know what I wanted to do or have the skill set for any of those careers. Once I realized that a scholarship was the only way I was going to have a shot at going away to school, I was relentless in my studies. I'd earned every penny of my scholarship, and leaving couldn't come soon enough. Senior year was coming to a close. I was leaving for Montana State University and had a world of options ahead of me.

Sure, I would miss Mama, but she had big dreams for me too.

"You coming or what, Mayhem?"

Lost in daydreams of my future, I hadn't seen Cole pull up in his truck. I rolled my eyes at the newest, stupidest nickname. Secretly, I loved that he came up with ridiculous things to call me. Because of it, I made it a point to call him only Cole and not Deck like everyone else.

My Cole.

"It's late. Where are we going?" Mama was working a night shift at the café, and she'd be pissed if she found out I was sneaking out. But it was Cole. Plus, she'd never have to know.

"Just figured we could go for a drive." Cole gripped the steering wheel, and the muscles in his arms bunched and flexed. A familiar tingle started in my belly and worked its way down.

Why does he have to be so freaking hot?

He glanced over and totally caught me staring, but instead of calling me out, he continued, "You should have come out tonight."

Someone had thrown a barn party tonight, and Cole had invited me. Instead of having a good time, I chose to stay home to study for finals. Senior year may be practically over, but I couldn't screw this up.

"I can't revoke my nerd status before school is over," I teased.

"You're not a nerd," he countered as he pulled down the dusty roads that led out of Chikalu Falls.

"Psh. Sure I am. But it's okay." I shrugged. "I'm only a nerd to people here. When I leave, I get to be whoever I want to be."

I closed my eyes and leaned my head back on the seat. His truck bumped down the rocky country road, and I felt the warm breeze from the open window cool my face.

I could feel his eyes on me.

He cleared his throat and turned the volume up on the country song that flowed from the old radio. That was one of my favorite things. Cole was as comfortable with silence as I was, and we'd collected hundreds of miles on these winding dirt roads. We laughed and sang and talked about whether aliens existed or whether the alternate timelines were really a thing.

I got to see a part of him that he kept hidden. With me, in the cab of his truck, we got to be ourselves. He could shed the expectations of his family and his jock status, while I got to be more than trailer trash.

Such a shame they live there—she's so smart. I'd once overheard some old women in town gossiping. More like talking shit, but they would never see it that way. They spoke as if living in a trailer meant that I couldn't possibly be intelligent. I was so over that town and their gossip.

"Can I take you somewhere?" Cole's voice was deep and thick, and I felt its low tones rumble through my chest.

I quirked an eyebrow when he flashed a wicked grin. "You're up to no good."

Cole feigned shock but kept driving. He knew I trusted him, and it couldn't be more true. He eased his truck down a familiar road and came up behind old man Bailey's property.

"What are you doing?" My voice was hushed in the darkness. "You know he's crazy." Mr. Bailey may be a distant relative of mine on my daddy's side, but my dad left before I was born, and we didn't have a true familial connection. Old man Bailey was crabby and gristly and rarely left his house.

"Trust me." Cole flashed a grin and my legs felt melty and my face got warm. He flipped off the headlights and slowly crept his truck past the large, looming house. It was dark in the house except for a small light in what I assumed was the living room. My heart was pounding so hard I clamped one hand across my chest for fear he could hear it and we'd be found out.

Cole reached across and grabbed my free hand. He squeezed it a few times but let go, and I could still feel the tingle where his large hand covered mine. I desperately wanted him to hold it again.

After winding his truck across the property and behind old cottages near the river, we came to a stop behind a crumbling barn. I slipped out of the cab, and Cole reached into the bed of his truck, holding one of his faded sweatshirts with his name and jersey number on the back and a quilt his great-grandmother had made.

"Over here." He tipped his head toward a copse of trees. After stepping through, there was a clearing, and Cole fanned open the blanket and plopped his large, muscular body down. He stretched, pulling his arms behind his head. My breath hitched as his T-shirt rode up, revealing tight, muscular abs and a hint of hair dipping below the waistband of his jeans.

My mouth went dry when he patted the spot next to him. "C'mon, Magpie. Take a load off."

Snatching up the hoodie, I pulled it over my head and hid the fact that I indulged in a deep pull of his scent. I carefully sat next to him, drawing my knees to my chest and tucking my hands into the shirtsleeves. Butterflies swooped low in my belly, and I suddenly couldn't find any words.

Is this it? Are things finally changing between us?

Hope bloomed in my chest, and I adjusted. After a deep breath, I carefully laid my body down next to him. Cole smelled warm and spicy and masculine. I could feel the fraction of space between his body and mine and wanted nothing more than for him to lean in so our bodies touched.

I pulled a breath to the bottom of my lungs and looked up. A riot of stars covered the ebony sky. Beautiful, starlit skies were common in Big Sky Country, but the sheer number of stars tonight took my breath away.

Cole stared up at the sky and kept his voice low. "You said last week that you'd never seen a shooting star. We're changing that. There's supposed to be a meteor shower tonight."

I could hear the excitement in his voice, and a slow-spreading smile stretched across my face. No one had ever done anything so romantic for *me*.

My voice felt airy when I said, "I don't see anything yet."

"Sometimes you have to be patient."

I looked at him, and he had a strange expression. Like maybe we weren't talking about stars anymore, and my nerves were going haywire.

I cleared my throat and focused on the expanse of the sky and not the way my skin felt on fire. "Okay, what-if number three hundred twenty-five." I glanced at him and smiled. The what-if game was something we'd started years ago. "What if you become the chief of police in Chikalu? All the single women in town speed, just hoping it's you who pulls them over. Your parents are retired and travel around the country, sending you postcards, but you're happy in Chikalu. Your wife is obsessed with you." At that, he laughed. "It's gross, actually," I teased. "Everyone in town loves her too. She worries about you when you're at work but knows that you're careful and makes you dinner every night when you come home."

Cole stayed silent for a beat but then said, "Tell me more about her."

"She's funny. Maybe a teacher or an artist. You have a group of friends that always get together and get rowdy, and they're more like family than friends. You can be yourself around her, and she lets you in to see the weird side of her too. When you met her, you knew she'd be yours forever, and she knew it too. You have a big house—something old and on a huge piece of property. Together, you have a family—mostly boys as wild as you, but secretly your daughter is your favorite. She holds a special piece of your heart. You protect them fiercely. Your favorite place is at home with them, and you couldn't be happier than when you dance with your wife in the kitchen."

"I do have some pretty sweet moves." He tried to make light of it, but the hitch in his voice gave him away. "Hmm. Okay, my turn."

I pinned my eyes to the stars, willing myself to breathe. We'd played the what-if game many times before, and it was always fun and silly. What if I had purple hair and worked in a coffee shop? What if he was gay and madly in love with his husband? What if everyone had scales or blue skin? What if our butts were in the front? The more ridiculous we could make it, the better, and the harder we laughed. But in that moment on the blanket, something shifted.

"What if all of your dreams come true?" I closed my eyes and imagined an older, more mature version of myself as Cole's deep voice flowed over me. I felt him shift his body, and the heat from his arm warmed my skin. "You do something creative like make jewelry or write poetry. You live in the nicest house in town and have a big garden with chickens and flowers, and it's your favorite place in the whole world."

"Am I married?" My voice sounded brave, but I was trembling.

"Of course. You knew him all your life, but one day something changed, and you finally saw him in a new way. He knows he doesn't deserve you, but he tries every day. He's strong and handsome and protects you with every fiber of his being. He dances with you whenever you want, and you don't care that he doesn't know all the steps."

My whole body warmed at his version of my future. I opened my eyes and stared up at the millions of twinkling stars.

What if that really came true? What if you ask me to prom and everything falls into place, just like we imagined?

I wasn't brave enough to speak the words clawing in my brain. Just as I was about to open my mouth to say something—*anything*—a tiny bright blaze of fire shot across the sky.

"Oh!" I shouted and pointed straight up at the trail the shooting star had left. Another, then another and another until the sky was streaked with movement. Some blinking and dim, others leaving long tails of brilliant light. Giggles erupted from the purest parts of my heart, and it was so beautiful I wanted to cry.

I felt Cole lean toward me, his breath on the outside of my ear. "Make a wish."

I swallowed hard and pinched my eyes closed. I squeezed them as tightly as I could. I had never wanted anything more than for my wish to come true. After sending my wish up to the universe, I peeked through my lashes to see Cole. His handsome face pointed up at the sky, eyes closed just as tightly as mine were.

I want your wishes to come true too.

Love, pure and bursting, filled my chest. I had to tell

him, but I was scared. It felt like we were on the same page, more than ever before, but what if I was wrong? Maybe Cole just saw me as a friend, and I would mess up what we had by falling for him. His eyes met mine, and his mouth opened to speak. My breath caught in my throat.

Blinding light flashed into my eyes. A booming voice echoed through the field. "Hey! Who's out there?"

My eyes went wide as the outraged voice cut through the darkness.

"Shit!" Cole yelled and bolted upright. He pulled me up with him and against his hard frame. I moved as he bent to scoop up the blanket. "Go!" He pointed to the truck, and I took off like a shot.

Jumping into the cab, Cole tossed the blanket at me and slammed his door shut and cranked the engine. He hit the accelerator, and his truck fishtailed as it struggled to get a grip on the gravel. He blew out a strong breath, and I looked in the side mirror to see Mr. Bailey's flashlight illuminate his angry face. He shouted something at the back of the truck, but I dipped low in my seat, praying he didn't recognize us.

Cole drove quickly as his eyes flicked to the rearview to make sure Mr. Bailey hadn't decided to come after the truck that had trespassed on his property. Nervous laughter fizzed up and out of my chest, and it lightened the tension that clung to Cole's jaw. His eyes glanced at me, and he started to laugh too.

Whatever heady moment we'd shared on the blanket under the stars was gone, and we were back on familiar, friendly ground. His truck pulled onto the road that led to my house, and I tamped down my disappointment that Cole hadn't asked me to prom or told me he felt what I was feeling. When the truck came to a stop, I hopped down and started toward the trailer.

Before I reached the door, Cole's hand grabbed my forearm, and I turned to see his midnight eyes darken in the dim light. His mouth moved as if he were about to say something, but then he paused. A heavy beat passed until his head moved a fraction, his lips set in a thin line.

"Good night, Maggie."

I stared hopelessly at the expanse of his back as he walked to his truck and left.

What if he never feels the same way I do?

EIGHT

MAGGIE

Now

My breath puffed out in large white plumes. The icy air burned in my lungs as I pushed up one last ridge. Years ago, I discovered that running was better than therapy—it cleared my head, flooded my overactive brain with endorphins, and helped keep my obsession with jalapeño kettle chips in check.

You keep running from your life, and all you're gonna have is tired feet.

Aunt Gwen's words hung in the corners of my mind, but I just pushed harder.

"Are we lost?" Honey's breath was as ragged as mine.

"Just down this path. It'll wind around to the right, and we'll come out on the south side of the backyard." My feet screamed in protest.

"I feel like you said that twenty miles ago." She stopped midstride, crumpling in half and sucking in deep breaths. "Fuck, it's cold today."

I stretched and jogged in place to keep the sweat on my body from icing my muscles. I didn't always run outdoors when the November weather turned frigid, but I had been carrying pent-up energy that could be burned only by a grueling run.

It had been three weeks since Cole rescued me from the handsy douche at the bar. Since he'd held me close like his life depended on it and then flipped a switch and pushed me away.

Again.

"Hey, what's that building over there?" As light snowflakes fluttered around us, Honey's voice cut through the crisp air, and she pointed down a narrow path just off the main trail. A small, derelict cabin was secluded, nearly hidden from anyone who would run along the path that bordered my property line.

I rolled my eyes. "That's Cole Decker's murder shack."

"Deck owns a cabin? Huh. Isn't it awfully close to your property?"

"It butts right up to it," I said, giving up on trying to keep warm and wrapping my arms around my chest. As we walked down the path, I pulled my knit hat low over my ears and willed myself to not look toward the dilapidated shack. "Forever ago it was all part of the same property. Somewhere along the line, it was parceled off and sold. The cabin has been in his family for generations."

Honey nodded and blew hot air inside her hands. "It's quaint."

A small, disgusted laugh escaped through my nose. "It's not. It's practically falling apart. I'm sure that's where he brings the badge chasers after the bar. It's disgusting."

"No shit?" Honey fluffed her full blonde ponytail. "Deck's got himself a stabbin' cabin?" Her laughter floated on the thin air as she hip checked me.

I pulled a lip up in a snarl.

"Oh, come on!" she teased. "Don't tell me you never thought about what it would be like if he used his handcuffs on you."

Heat flushed my cheeks, and I was grateful I could blame the cold for the pink that was surely spreading across my neck.

I had. *A lot.*

Over the years I'd tried to ignore the obvious pull I had toward him, but that took considerable effort. Sometimes, in my weakest moments, I would lie in bed and imagine exactly what it might be like to be Cole Decker's woman. I always knew he would be attentive, but as his shyness gave way to the brooding, stoic man he'd turned into, I'd bet my ass that he was assertive in bed. Demanding even.

A deep, low flutter had my thighs quaking. I squeezed them together—the pressure agonizing as I walked.

That fantasy paled in comparison to standing on the dance floor, his thick biceps holding me tightly to his chest. I had been milliseconds from pulling his full mouth to mine and devouring him right there in front of everyone. Everything about Cole was brawny and steady and warm. Everything except for the cold, dismissive way he shut me out.

"He's a prick." I was reminding myself more than telling Honey.

"Then have yourself some good ol' fashioned hate sex. Trust me. It is *so choice.*" A scandalous grin, the kind she often sneaked her husband, Colin, spread across her face.

I laughed. Honey had a knack for always seeing the bright—and usually kinky—side of life. I tossed my arm around her shoulder and pulled her close to whisper, "No."

We held on to each other, our heads dipped low, stealing warmth from wherever we could. "You say that now," she hushed, "but when it happens, I better be the first to know how it was with those handcuffs."

THE WORN SPRINGS in the bench seat of my truck bounced against my ass as we bumped along Route 7 toward the local veterinarian. It was a 1983 Chevy C20, white with a red stripe and a four-speed manual transmission. The truck had spent years sitting in old man Bailey's barn, and when I'd needed something sturdy for jobs around my property, he'd given me a fair price. I rarely drove Peppermint, except for odd jobs on the farm, but I was not about to use my car to transport a baby goat.

Beside me, Lottie's face was pure sunshine. Excitement sparkled in her dark eyes, and her cheeks were pinched in a wide smile. When taking care of the goat inevitably fell to me, I would think back to how happy she looked in that moment.

I buried the guilt that burned in my gut. Just yesterday we'd gotten into a knockdown, drag-out screamfest over the jeans she was wearing. Trying to surprise her with something nice, I'd spent a ridiculous amount of money on a new pair of jeans at Ms. Trina's clothing store, the Blush Boutique.

When I walked into her room to find her taking a pair of scissors to the denim, I'd lost my mind. I told her she was ungrateful. Irresponsible. A child. She yelled right back and said that I was overbearing. Out of touch. Old.

Lottie had only the faintest idea of how much Mama and I had struggled. New jeans happened only once or twice a year, and I wouldn't have *dared* to take a pair of scissors to them. Hell, I still had a pair from high school tucked into my drawer. They may have been soft and worn-in and threadbare, but I still cherished them every time I put them on to work in the gardens.

"You ready for this, Lottie-tot?" I sneaked a peek at her, hoping we were back on solid footing. I also reminded myself that time was moving way too quickly, and sometimes she hated when I used silly nicknames.

"I can't even believe you said yes!"

My chest pinched. Too often, I had to say no to Lottie's outlandish demands, and it was harder and harder to find moments of actual joy. Like her friends, she was often sullen and hesitant to share herself with an adult.

"It's a big responsibility," I said. "I'll need your help in taking care of it."

Lottie rolled her eyes—*there she was*—and faced the window. "I know, Mom. You've said it a thousand times."

I quieted the sigh that threatened to escape and smoothed my hand against my purse. In it was a plain white envelope that had arrived in the mailbox last week. It was one of many that had arrived since David's death. I'd searched and searched for the source, but with the envelope unmarked, save for "Maggie & Lottie" typed on the front, I found it nearly impossible. Any of the leads I tried to chase down ended up being dead ends.

For the most part, I assumed it was from David's parents. They'd shared early on that they had no interest in having a relationship with me or their granddaughter, even after David's death. I assumed it was their wealth and maybe a small sense of duty to help take care of their son's daughter. Whatever the reason, when the envelopes of cash started showing up, I saved every penny for Lottie. Early on, the money saved us from total destitution—paying the bills, buying new school clothes, allowing for more than one present under the tree at Christmas.

Today it was buying a goat.

Once we'd gotten into the vet's office, we were bombarded with paperwork. For a farm animal, the pygmy goat was a diva.

"Just remember"—the vet looked between Lottie and me—"this is still an animal, cute though she may be. If the gate on the pen isn't latched, she'll run. And boy is she fast." He had a warm, hearty chuckle, his eyes crinkling at the sides. The mischievous grin told me this plucky little goat likely had given him and his staff a run for their money.

Lottie tucked Sassafras—heaven only knows where she came up with that name—under her arm and nuzzled her nose against its soft fur and headed for the truck.

NINE

DECK

Now

My shoes pounded and crunched through the snow along the path as I huffed out icy breaths. I was freezing my balls off and needed to get warm before my run started to have any sort of rhythm to it.

I could have used the gym at the station, as I usually did when it was shitty out, but curiosity had gotten the best of me. Yesterday I watched Maggie pull out of the hardware store with her old truck, Peppermint, loaded down with two-by-fours. My run through the path that separated our property allowed me a perfect view of her backyard. A path I was ashamed to admit I took anytime I felt like I hadn't seen Maggie in a while. It helped calm my nerves to know that, though her house was tucked into an outcrop of forest at the base of the mountain, she wasn't totally alone.

Lottie's friends were always hanging around the expanse of the back deck, which looked out into the forest. Over time, Maggie had redone the backyard, and it was built for entertaining. Though my cabin had been in my family for generations, and I had originally planned to buy back this house, once I got wind that it was Maggie putting in a bid, I didn't interfere. A small part of me liked knowing that she was thriving on what used to be my family's land.

As I wound around the curve of the trail that allowed a perfect view through the trees into her backyard, my steps faltered, and I stopped. Hopping through the snow was a tiny goat, and little Lottie was patting her knees to call the animal to her. It had been a long while since I'd seen Lottie look like the adorable, happy kid I'd always known her to be. In fact, she wasn't little at all anymore, and the thought of how fast time was passing ached in my chest. Lately around town she wore a scowl more often than not. I always nodded to her, and instead of the cheeky grin that made my chest feel tight, nowadays she just kept walking.

My eyes scanned the yard and stalled on the perfect heart-shaped swell of Maggie's ass as she bent over to screw a board into place on what looked to be some kind of makeshift animal pen. My mind immediately went to all the intimate, dirty things I could do with her if she were my woman. In public, I would worship her, taking care of her every want and need. People would talk about how Maggie had tamed the incorrigible Deck, and in the bedroom? In the bedroom, she'd be all mine. I would take care of her wants and needs there, too, but also show her new ones she didn't even realize she had.

I could feel my resolve slipping. I knew it was the worst idea to let her wiggle under my skin, but it never ceased to amaze me how one strong-willed, hazel-eyed woman could absolutely wreck me. It was downright frigid, and she was out there busting her ass to build some kind of structure for what I assumed was their new pet. Only Maggie would okay a goat for a pet.

The winter air was heavy, making everything eerily

quiet. My breaths were the only sound I could hear as I watched them through the thicket.

Keep running. Stop staring. Fucking creeper.

I knew damn well I should pick up my pace and continue on home, but my feet were rooted to the ground. Maggie was almost done with the pen but struggling to level and secure the last few boards. Over the frosty air, I could barely make out their conversation.

". . . just for a minute," Maggie called to Lottie. "Help me on this side . . ."

I glanced at Lottie, who'd clearly heard her mother and promptly ignored her. I was about to leave when I heard Maggie yell in pain. My shoes gripped the icy path, and I pushed past the brambles and trees into her backyard.

"Let me help you."

Maggie's eyes shot to my face, and her head whipped around. "Where did you come from? What are you doing here?"

Being a creep.

"I was on a run, and I heard you yell out." It was a struggle to keep my rabbiting heartbeat under control with her so close. I gripped her hand, examining why she held it close to her body.

"Ow," she said, yanking her hand out of mine. "It's just a splinter."

I should have been gentler.

Her smell alone caused a deep pull in my belly. That pull moved lower, settling between my thighs. I fixed my face into an impassive stare, crossed my arms, and gave the pen a once-over.

"Deck!" Lottie called out to me, holding the baby goat like a prize Simba. "It's a goat!" Her cheeks and nose were pink, and her deep-brown eyes radiated joy.

"It sure is." Her happiness was infectious, and I caught myself shaking my head and chuckling quietly as she danced in snowy circles with the goat cradled in her arms. I could see Maggie's mouth drop open slightly as she stared at the side of my face. I held my gaze steady, unwilling to look over at her. I didn't trust myself to look at her and not crush my mouth against hers. Heat balled in my stomach just thinking about feeling my arms around her again. I'd gone fifteen years without it, and one embrace at the bar had me aching like a fiend.

"I don't need help." Maggie's voice was defiant.

I cleared my throat and bent to grip the board, holding it steady. I looked at the drill and raised an eyebrow. I could have grabbed the drill and finished securing it myself, but I knew Maggie. Doing things on her own had become a part of who she was, her independence and pride intertwined. She didn't need my help—and likely didn't want it—but that didn't mean I couldn't lighten the load a little.

We worked swiftly and silently as my fingers numbed in the bitter air. By the time we finished, the sun was sagging low in the horizon, and after the last few boards were tightened, we both stepped back. I moved past her to set a scrap of wood down, and as she stepped back, the tips of my fingers dragged along the delicate skin in the gap between her jeans and cropped parka. The heat from her skin danced up my arm and spread through my chest.

The warm, complex pools of her irises drew me in. My body moved toward her as her chin tipped up.

"Warm up inside with a drink?" Maggie's sultry voice wound around the base of my neck, massaging the aches and kinks that lived there.

A man could get used to hearing that voice every day. My heart screamed to say yes—to go inside and attempt to rekindle the friendship I had valued so deeply in high school. To feel that friendship melt and change into something unshakable. To discover the softness of Maggie's skin as I traced lazy circles over her naked body. To whisper my secrets in the darkness to her and feel her arms wrap around me in comfort.

But I knew that could never happen. Once Maggie discovered those secrets were the reason she was forced to live her life as a single mother, she would hate me. I would lose the very precious thing I couldn't stand to lose. It was easier to lie to myself and hide the fact that she had any effect on me at all.

So I let the coldness of the air seep into my eyes and stiffen my posture. "No, thanks," I rasped. My voice was more bitter and harsher than I'd intended, but it was for the better.

I forced my legs to carry me out of the backyard and back onto the path. Though my legs were lead and my will to work out had run dry, I convinced myself that hearing her mutter "asshole" as I stalked away was a good thing.

I would never be the man who deserved a place in Maggie's home.

TEN

DECK

EIGHT YEARS Ago

Career Day for Chikalu Falls was an event in itself. On the last day of school, Career Day centered on the locals and their trades. Ranchers rode their horses to the school, tractors and combines took up most of the spaces in the parking lot, and rodeo cowboys came in their best leathers. In the staff parking lot, there were cop cars, an ambulance for the kids to ransack, and a fire truck with a hose out for misting the kids. Most of the women in Chikalu wandered over to see the volunteer firefighters doing various challenges—pull-ups, racing to put their gear on, hauling hoses around cones—fucking show-offs.

I adjusted my vest and tugged at the polyester of my collar. It was goddamn hot with all my gear on, and I was melting in the June heat. I walked into the school building, and the cool air blasted my face. I scanned the crowd to find something cold to drink.

"You're hot."

I swiveled at the sultry voice behind me. Marissa Randall, a waitress at a bar in town, eyed me up and down while pressing a bottle of water to the side of her neck. The water bottle was sweating in the heat, and droplets of water rolled down her neck, disappearing between her cleavage.

"Uh . . . ," I managed.

She laughed and said, "Oh, I'm teasing you. Here's some water, handsome." She reached out to give me the water. A small laugh escaped her as I twisted off the top and emptied the bottle.

"Thanks."

Marissa took one step toward me. I instinctively stepped back, looking out over her head. I had no interest in flirting with Marissa, and getting felt up inside the school was not the impression I wanted to give the gossips in town. My eyes landed on a little girl, huddled against some lockers, her raven-black hair spiked out in little pigtails.

"You'll have to excuse me," I said, barely noticing Marissa's continued advance toward me as I put my hands on her shoulders to move past her.

"Well, but . . . ," she called at my back.

Stepping up to the lockers, I lowered my voice and took a knee. "Hey there, Miss Charlotte. What's up?"

She turned her small, six-year-old frame toward me and threw herself into my arms. As she openly sobbed, I wrapped my arms around her in a gentle hug. With my radio and gear strapped to my vest, it couldn't have been comfortable, but she didn't seem to notice.

"Is your mama here?" The words choked out of me as the image of Maggie's perfect face flipped through my mind. I patted Lottie's shoulder. She smelled like peanut butter and dirt, and my pulse hammered against my skull.

"Mama's workin' the flower booth outside."

"Do you need me to get her for you? Are you lost?"

"No. She said I could come inside. I just don't have a

daddy for Daddies and Donuts." Fresh sobs racked her tiny body as my heart sank into my boots.

What right? What right do you have to be here when he isn't?

"Oh. Well, um."

Fuck.

I was out of my depth and not sure what to do, so I continued to awkwardly pat her shoulders as she wiped snot on my sleeve.

She looked at the streak she'd left behind, and her sweet face twisted. "Gross."

Her watery laugh made me smile as she tried to wipe the boogers off my sleeve, smearing them around.

"I got you." I smiled and leaned to pull a napkin from the table nearby to wipe my shirtsleeve and her hand.

"Can you be my daddy?"

I stared into the dark pools of her hopeful eyes as my heart tripped in my chest.

"For the donuts," she continued. "I *really* like donuts, and you can't get one unless you have a daddy—it says so on the sign."

"It says so on the sign?" I asked, and she nodded solemnly. My fist clenched at my side.

Fuck those insensitive assholes.

"Well, that seems silly. But I do love a good donut." I used my best silly thinking face to eke out a little giggle. "Lottie, I would love to be—to get a donut with you."

I stumbled on my words. *I would love to be your daddy* had been dangerously close to flying out of my stupid face before I caught myself. I cleared my throat and took her small hand in mine. The warmth from her sticky palm spread through my hand and up my arm. Lottie's face transformed and beamed up at me as she led me through the hallway. Curious glances flew our way as I nodded at my friends and neighbors. At the end of the hall, set up in one of the classrooms, was a large banner that read "Daddies and Donuts." The sign didn't *specifically* say that you had to have a dad, but you couldn't tell that to a six-year-old. Given the misunderstanding, I lightened up my attitude and tried to ease the hard line of my mouth.

"Come on, Deck!" Lottie pulled my hand toward the door. Her eyes grew wide as she danced up to the table filled with donuts. They looked crusty and day-old, but to a six-year-old, it was donut heaven. Desks were arranged in twosomes with slips of paper and crayons piled in the center and falling onto the floor. I recognized most of the people in the room. Men with the children hunkered down in chairs, their knees at their ears as they smiled with their kids over stale donuts. My heart squeezed in my chest for little Lottie.

As she stood in line, she bounced on her tiptoes, bubbling with excitement. When it was our turn to step up to the table, Lottie smiled at Mrs. Coulson, who both owned the café and waited tables there. Lottie said, "I'm here with my daddy, and we want a donut, please!"

Lottie tried to wink up at me, and I scrubbed my hand over my mouth to hide my grin. This kid was something else. Despite being older than dirt and about two feet shorter than me, Mrs. Coulson still managed to look down her slim nose at me.

"Uh, stand-in." I shrugged. Tension wound up my back, and I absently adjusted my utility belt.

I didn't miss the hint of pity that flitted across her face as Mrs. Coulson looked at the little girl. Her features softened when she smiled at Lottie, and she handed us each a donut. I followed Lottie, who found an empty space at the desks. I adjusted my belt and did my best to fit on the small chair. She immediately started devouring her donut, all traces of her earlier meltdown somehow forgotten.

Between bites, Lottie drew a rainbow on a scrap of paper and rambled on about how great life as a first grader would be. I took that moment to look at her. Her dark eyes were so brown they almost appeared black, but when she looked right at you, you could see flecks of gold around the edges. Her hair was inky and smooth. She bore such a close resemblance to David it hurt to even look at her too long.

Familiar anger rose like a raging tide. David had everything, and he never saw it. No amount of pills or liquor could have ever been better than having Maggie and Lottie in his life. Anger was replaced with the sickening twist of guilt—David wasn't sitting here because of me, and that was my weight to carry. Branded a hero, I felt sick at the thought.

Lottie is a great kid, and, damn it, she deserves to have a daddy for Daddies and Donuts, even if he was a fuckup.

"You gonna eat that?" Lottie's tiny voice broke through my troubled thoughts. She pointed a purple crayon toward my half-eaten donut, eyebrows up.

"All yours, Char-lottie." I slid the napkin toward her, and she giggled at the silly nickname.

"Mama calls me funny names too."

I swallowed past the hard lump that burned in the back of my throat. "Does she now?" I asked.

Lottie smiled around a huge bite of donut. Mouth still full, she said, "Yeah, she said her very best friend in the world used to call her all kinds of silly things, and she does it now too."

My heartbeat ticked faster. "Well, maybe I should just call you Sassafras then."

She popped the last bite of donut into her mouth, and her cheeks puffed out in a goofy grin. She stood, dusting the crumbs from her jean shorts onto the floor.

"I should go." Sadness laced her voice. "Mama gets worried if I wander off for too long."

I unfolded myself from the chair and scooped the rest of her napkins and crumbs into my hands. "I'll walk with you and make sure you get back okay."

Lottie nodded and slipped her tiny hand into mine. We walked slowly out of the classroom and down the hall toward the back parking lot. Lottie rambled on and on about everything and nothing.

"What's it mean to protect and serve?" she asked, pointing to the slogan on my uniform.

I eyed her as her gaze roamed over the patches I wore. "That's pretty good reading, kid. Well"—I cleared my throat —"it means that it's my job. It's my job to protect you and to serve my community."

"That's a big job." She spoke quietly and seemed to think over what that meant.

"It is, but my dad and *his dad* were also police officers. So it's like a family job."

"I don't know what my daddy did—my real one, I mean." She sneaked a peek at me through her dark lashes, as if she were spilling a secret. I gently squeezed her hand. "He went to heaven when I was really, really little."

My jaw ticked, and a riot of emotions raged through me. "I know, sweetheart."

Lottie's eyes fell back to the floor, and I was desperate to have the happiness return to her voice.

"You don't know this, but I knew your dad in high school. He was a funny kid."

Her eyes met mine, and she smiled. "You knew him?"

"I sure did. He was funny and smart, and I remember he really liked to draw."

"I *love* to draw!" Her smile was so wide her face looked as though it was about to crack open. My chest ached. I knew a lot about David. We'd shared a lot of classes together, and before he drowned himself in drugs and alcohol, he was a pretty cool kid.

We reached the large metal doors leading to the outside parking lot. I pushed them open and blinked into the afternoon sun. I looked around and spotted Maggie. Over the years, I'd learned to hide my reactions to her well. She was radiant behind the small plastic table—laughing and taking money for bundles of flowers that she had arranged in metal buckets all around her.

"Mama!" Lottie yelled across the parking lot and waved as Maggie's eyes lifted. She briefly glanced down at our joined hands and pinned me with a glare.

Ignoring her and the staccato rhythm of my heart, I crouched down. "See ya later, Lot-a-mus."

She smiled a cheesy grin and hugged my neck before flouncing off to meet her mom. I stood, purposely not looking in Maggie's direction again, and turned toward my squad car. I pounded the pavement with my boots, and when I sat in the car, I exhaled the breath I didn't realize I was holding.

I thought about Maggie and how different I wish it could be between us. I thought about Lottie and pulled a scrap of paper from my pocket—Lottie's rainbow. I had taken it when we finished the donuts and had slipped it into my pocket.

Easing from the curb, I headed toward the station so I could change clothes and hop on my motorcycle. I could head out of town and throw the hammer down on the accelerator and forget all about Maggie and her ridiculously charming daughter. I didn't need to think about unrequited feelings or funny little kids or donuts, because none of that mattered now. And it definitely didn't matter that it was the best fucking donut I'd ever had in my entire life.

ELEVEN

MAGGIE

Now

Biscuits & Honey was closed for the night, but I sat nestled inside, away from the whipping wind and plummeting temperatures. The meteorologist was calling for more snow and ice, and I was taking advantage of a quiet girls' night in with Honey and her sister, Joanna.

"Is there anything better than cinnamon crunch coffee cake?" I hummed as I licked the last crumbs from my fork.

"Sex." Honey giggled into her coffee mug as she bumped shoulders with Jo.

"Definitely sex," Jo agreed. The three of us were perched on the row of stools that ran along the main window counter of the bakery.

"I wouldn't know. I haven't had sex in . . ." I thought for a few moments. "Shit, I can't even remember the last time. And I'm pretty sure it wasn't even that great. Definitely not better than your crumb cake. How pathetic is that?" I frowned at the empty white plate.

"John was a nice guy," Jo offered.

"Eh," I sighed. "He was nice enough, but there wasn't

any magic. No spark, ya know?" I huffed out a breath. "Maybe that's my problem. Maybe I'm just too picky."

"No such thing," Honey chimed in. "You deserve to feel that fire."

"Well, what about Deck?" Jo asked as she collected our plates and turned toward the kitchen.

"Real smooth, Jo." I laughed. "Definitely not. He's a pain in the ass."

"You can't tell me that there's no fire there," Honey added. "I call bullshit."

I toyed with the inside of my lip. I had buried my yearning for Cole so long ago, but after he helped me at the bar and then again with the goat pen, those feelings hit me like a freight train. Giving voice to them would make them grow only stronger—I was sure of it.

But these women were my closest friends. It made it exponentially more complicated that their husbands were also best friends with Cole, but we'd managed to coexist in this small town for fifteen years. Surely we could go on ignoring each other.

"Lincoln mentioned that someone was getting a little handsy at the bar. He said Deck put the guy in his place?" She asked it like a question, but I had no doubt that Linc had told her everything that had happened that night in the bar, including how I'd stood like an idiot clutching on to Cole even after the music had changed.

"Oh, yeah." I tried to play it off like it hadn't been running in an incessant loop in my head since it happened. "Some guy wasn't getting the hint that I wasn't interested, and Cole pretended to be my date so the guy would back off."

A sly smile spread across Honey's face. "Huh."

"What?" I lifted a shoulder and tried to busy my hands by wiping down the counter to avoid looking at them.

"You know what," Honey continued. "You're not the only one with a bullshit detector around here. I'm calling it. Bullshit."

I sighed when Jo gently placed a hand at the center of my back.

"It's just…complicated. Things with us got so off track that I don't really see any way we can ever go back to being friends." Sadness had crept into my voice without me even realizing. I hadn't ever truly mourned the loss of my friendship with Cole. "He's different now. I don't even recognize him anymore."

"I think that friend might still be in there somewhere," Jo said.

"He really is a great guy," Honey added.

I shook my head. "Cole may be a good friend to you and the guys, but to me, he's not. I can't tell you how many times he's gone out of his way to make my life miserable. I try to see the best in everyone, but he makes it so damn difficult."

I could feel the anger bubbling up inside me, pushing out any sadness that had crept in. Cole had always been a bit of a cocky asshole, but I was slowly realizing that I might not have been so hot for him if he wasn't. But he had also once been funny and kind and a safe haven for me to be myself. Being annoyed and angry at Cole was far easier than feeling the aching sadness of missing my friend.

I pulled my arms through my parka and tightly wrapped it around my body. We hugged and said our good-byes before facing the slapping cold of a Montana winter.

It wasn't until I was alone in the darkness of my bedroom, wrapped in a nest of blankets, that I allowed myself to think about the what-ifs.

What if Cole really was a good guy?

What if we were friends again?

What if I allowed myself to admit that a part of me might always love him?

~

THE HARSH WINTER dragged as the darkness came earlier and earlier. This time of year, flowers were trucked in, but orders were far fewer. On the farm, the bulbs were planted and resting until spring, giving me plenty of downtime to just *be*.

I hated it.

Lottie had convinced Jo to take her ice fishing for a few days over the long Thanksgiving weekend, and the quiet calm that settled into the house after the holiday was unnerving. Every creak of the old farmhouse made my heart leap into my throat.

Stirring cream into my steaming coffee, I stared out the kitchen window into the darkness of the forest. The inky blackness seemed infinite, and the glow from the back porch light did little to illuminate the expanse of the backyard. I loved my home and the space that allowed us to carve out our lives. My eyes scanned the chicken coop, and though I didn't want to, I knew I should check on the girls one last time before turning in for the night.

I pulled on my boots and parka and tossed a knit cap on my head. When I pushed the large wooden door open, the yard was still and quiet, but the bitter cold pinched my cheeks. It was downright frigid, and I needed to be sure the chicken waterer hadn't frozen.

I tramped through the inches of snow, head down. In the coop, the chickens were cozied up in the rafters and on the branches I had secured for them. Their low clucks were a comfort. Thankfully, the electric platform for the waterer was working just fine. The hens were safe and cozy.

As I secured the door to the coop, I thought about Sassafras. Her house was heated, but she was so tiny I felt a tug of worry. Digging my hands deeper into my coat pockets, I made my way toward her pen. I would take Sass inside with me to watch TV for a little while. She was a lot like a cat and loved to cuddle.

Dread pooled in my stomach as I got closer. Before she left, Lottie had gone out to the pen to say goodbye. The door to the pen was open, just barely, and little goat footprints tracked around in playful circles before disappearing into the darkness of the tree line.

Shit.

Shit.

Shit.

I tore off into a run into the forest. "Sassafras! Come here, girl!" I shouted into the darkness and stalled, listening for a rustling, a bleat, any sign of her.

Nothing.

"Sassafras!" I trudged deeper into the dark forest, calling and calling for that stupid goat. I couldn't have Lottie come back from her trip just to break her heart by telling her that Sassafras was lost or eaten by a coyote or worse.

Adrenaline coursed through my veins as it got darker and darker around me. I turned my head, keeping the light of my house at my back so I didn't lose my sense of direction in the dark forest.

I stilled, calming my breathing, and heard a rustle to my left. My heartbeat ticked up as I saw the flick of Sassafras's fluffy tail. I tore out in a run, trying to catch her as she trotted away. Brushing past low limbs and stepping over fallen logs, I pushed forward. I barely felt the wind whip at my cheeks as I kept my eyes pinned to the goat's back. I ran, fast as I could, into the blackness. I stumbled once and surged forward so I wouldn't lose her.

One leap over a fallen log and the ground gave way beneath me. I sank, deeper and deeper, as icy water filled in around me. I clawed at the surface, trying to understand what was happening. I hadn't seen the stream in my run toward Sassafras and winter runoff from the last thaw must have deepened the water even more. Panic clutched my throat as the weight of my boots and jacket pulled me lower. My arms heavy, the bone-deep cold threatened to consume me.

No. Lottie. Please, no.

My mind screamed as I bobbed to the surface and gasped for air, but I plunged back beneath the pitch-dark water. I was going to drown. I would die alone in the freezing waters of the stream. No one would find me. Lottie would be alone. My lungs burned and my muscles seized as I clawed toward the surface of the water.

Above me, I stared at the stars, blurred by the water above my head, and wept.

TWELVE

DECK

Now

I had never been more terrified in all my life.

Years as a cop had hardened me. Violence, guns, dead bodies of people I'd known and grown up with—none of that fazed me anymore. But seeing Maggie running toward me, then disappearing below the surface of the stream, was my undoing.

Nursing a scotch in my cabin, my ears pricked when I faintly heard shouting in the distance. Pulling on my boots and coat, I eased onto the front porch and listened to the darkness. Sure enough, I could hear Maggie's panicked voice through the trees. I took off in her direction, worried that something had happened at the house.

As I got closer to her shouts, I saw her running through the trees. Just as she leaped over a log, I shouted, "No!"

It was below freezing, but the running waters of the stream meant that any ice that formed was thin. The weight of her cracked through the ice, and she disappeared below the surface. I took off like a shot, and the sight of her attempts to surface tore through me. As I moved through the woods, I started stripping. My coat and boots were all I had time to remove, but I knew their collective heaviness would only weigh me down as I reached the edge of the stream.

Breaking through the thin top layer of ice, I pushed through the frigid water. My breath was stolen from my lungs. My body rioted against the cold, but I pushed forward, reaching down into the water until my fingers brushed the slick arm of Maggie's coat.

I hauled her toward me, her gasp the only thing holding me together. Maggie clung to me. She sputtered and coughed and was so cold that her teeth rattled through her blueing lips.

I hoisted her into my arms, the weight of her clothes making my biceps burn as I pushed toward the bank. Her ragged breaths were my only comfort. Her body shook violently, and I knew I had to get her warm.

I raced through the forest toward my cabin. The damp and cold soaked straight to my bones. I barely registered the sting of the forest floor beneath my socks. Pushing through the door, I settled her on her wobbly feet in front of the small wood-burning stove.

"We need to get you warm," I ground out.

Panic still licked at the base of my skull, and I tore her coat from her shoulders. Her body was racked with uncontrolled shivering.

"Th—the—the goat . . ." Her teeth clacked and rattled around the words, her throat tight.

"It's fine. I'll find the goat."

Who cares about a fucking goat? I could have lost you.

Our clothes suctioned to our bodies in soggy, limp clumps. Maggie's breath was coming out in short gasps, an involuntary response to the shock of the cold water. If her breathing didn't calm, she would hyperventilate. I ran my hands down her arms, her skin a sickly temperature.

I peeled off my shirt and pulled her toward me, offering any trace of warmth I could. Her shoulders trembled, and the clacking of her teeth cut through the silence in the cabin.

It wasn't enough.

I pushed her from me. Her eyes were glazed, and panic thrummed in my ears. When I lifted the hem of her shirt, her eyes met mine.

"We have to get warm so you don't go into shock. I'm going to undress you and hold you until you can stop shaking."

My voice was harsher than I meant it to be, and I took a breath to calm my jittery nerves. Maggie's eyes went wide, her pupils dilating as she shivered. Her lips pressed into a thin line, and she nodded.

It was all the permission I needed.

I unceremoniously peeled the soaked clothes from her body and tossed them in a soggy pile on the floor. I let my jeans sag to my ankles and kicked them away. For a heart-beat, we stood, staring at each other in our underwear.

After grabbing a blanket off the couch, I wrapped her in my arms. I couldn't just stare at the perfect curves of her body without doing something completely irrational, like slamming my mouth against hers and owning her body in ways only I knew I craved.

Her muscles continued to quake as I settled us on the rug in front of the fire. My pulse was whumping in my ears, and I molded my body around hers. I pressed as close to her as I could manage, hiking my knees up behind hers. Together we shivered, but heat coursed through my body.

"You're all right, doll," I whispered in her ear.

Her shakes dulled and gave way to sobs. Maggie cried and cried until she was wrung out. I held on to her tightly, not saying a word, until her breathing slowed and deepened, and I knew she was asleep. My mind couldn't rest. The overwhelming need to make sure she was safe had my intrusive thoughts lingering in the darkest corners of my soul.

She could have drowned. I could have lost her forever. Flashes of nameless bodies suddenly had her face, and my stomach rioted. I closed my eyes and willed myself back to reality. Compartmentalizing the awful was a large part of being a cop, and I had to separate my anxiety from reality.

Maggie is here.

She is safe.

The firelight danced across her skin. I dropped my forehead to her shoulder and barely swept my lips across the smooth curve of her shoulder. It was subtle and intimate, and the heat pumping out of the stove was nothing compared to the fire in my veins.

Stop that shit. You don't get to kiss her.

Time had crawled by when, finally, heat from the fire finally thawed my toes. I propped myself up on an elbow to take Maggie in. Now that she was safe from the elements and warmth from the fire was flushing her cheeks, I could relax. From her straight nose to the long swoop of her eyelashes, Maggie was perfection. Even her low, quiet snore was cute as hell.

The air in the cabin was thick as I let my gaze drift lower. The soft skin of Maggie's back was pressed against me, and the swell of her hips gave way to long, lean legs. Maggie worked hard at her shop and on the farm, and it showed in the delicate but strong muscles in her body. Just the sight of her creamy skin against the black of her bra and panties was enough.

Desire had my cock growing thick, and I had to remind myself that waking up with a hard-on pressed to her back was the exact opposite of what Maggie needed right now.

I should have moved. I should have given her space, now that I knew she was safe and warm. Instead, I wrapped my arms around her again, breathed in the freshness of her skin, and held her close.

Five minutes.

I allowed myself five minutes of pure, blissed-out torture before loosening my arms and shifting away from her.

I padded across the cabin to my bedroom and dug out a pair of gray sweatpants and a white T-shirt. After I dressed, I grabbed another shirt, sweatshirt, socks, and a pair of sweatpants for Maggie in case she woke up and wanted to change.

When I walked back to the living room, my heart tumbled in my chest. Curled in a ball in front of the crackling fire, Maggie looked so fragile. The old wooden floor was uneven and rough, so I carefully bundled her up in my arms. She shifted, her long lashes opening only slightly as she peeked at me before nuzzling back into my arm. I carried her to my bedroom, lay her on the bed, and bundled the blankets all around her. I wouldn't be sleeping anytime soon, especially knowing that Maggie was here in my most personal haven.

The cabin was mine.

A place where I could go and simply exist. I didn't have to be an officer or a friendly neighbor or an untethered bachelor who needed marrying off. I could disappear with a good scotch, some books, and a television for watching all the shitty kung fu movies I wanted. The fact that the cabin was nestled in the forest and butted up to Maggie's home was merely an added bonus.

Digging through my cupboards, I found a can of chicken.

Do goats even eat meat?

It would be risky to leave it out on the porch and likely attract a host of unwanted houseguests in the form of raccoons, vermin, even bears. No, I had to go on foot in search of Lottie's tiny goat. I returned the can to the cupboard and found some oatmeal. Tossing a few shakes into a plastic container, I headed out. Hopefully the sound and smell of the oats would tempt it enough to come to me.

If it hadn't gotten eaten already.

Fuck.

I had ditched my coat and boots before I hurled myself into the stream after Maggie, so I pulled on an old coat and muck boots from the closet. A knit cap and gloves would help, too, since I still hadn't totally thawed from the icy waters.

I trudged through the darkness, making a wide, sweeping arc in the direction of Maggie's house. It was bitterly cold, and if the goat had any sense of self-preservation, it would find a place to hide from the brutal wind.

Clicking my tongue, I walked and listened for any sign of it. I found my boots and jacket, stiff from the cold. The winter air was whistling through the trees, and as I bent to gather my clothes, a weak bleat floated on that breeze. With quick, sure steps, I hustled toward the sound. The arc of my flashlight illuminated a fallen tree. Behind it, a tiny ball of fur trembled.

"Hey there, goat," I whispered, squatting low. "You caused a lot of trouble tonight." I kept my voice soothing and calm. "Don't run." I reached my hand out, slowly moving toward it as the goat looked pathetically hopeful. One touch of my hand to its head and it rose to its feet and trotted between my knees.

"There you are." The goat sniffed at the can in my hands, propping its hooves against my thigh. "You like that? It's for you. Let's go, champ."

I scooped the tiny animal in my already full arms. Its legs were damp from the snow, and its pathetic bleats insisted she was not happy about her current predicament. "I hear you." Dropping my frozen coat and boots, I tucked the goat into my jacket, zipping it inside so that only its head popped out from my collar. With my free hands, I scooped up my shit and hustled back toward the cabin.

The oats came in handy when I settled the goat into an old, sturdy doghouse. It was a replica of the cabin itself, and in the two years since Bodhi died, it had remained empty. No one could replace that dog, so I hadn't even tried. Safe from the elements and any predators, the goat nestled into a corner of the house and fell asleep. I locked the small, attached run and eased back into the cabin, closing the front door with a soft click.

My deep, heavy sigh vibrated through the cabin.

What a fucking night.

It was late, and I was exhausted in every way a man could be. Despite the ache in my legs, I leaned against the doorjamb to my room and stared. Maggie had curled herself around my blankets, one pillow tucked between her knees and her arms wrapped around it. I'd never wanted to be a pillow so badly in my fucking life.

Her chestnut hair had dried in clumpy waves and was splayed at her back. My fingers itched to smooth it from her face, but I stayed rooted at the doorway.

I couldn't help but think how different my life would be

had I only told her, all those years ago. There were times when I felt her gaze linger just a fraction too long, and I knew—I knew in my bones she felt something for me too. I could have leaned across my truck and kissed her. Spilled my guts and shared the only secret I kept from her. That I was made to love only her.

But I didn't.

Instead, I'd hesitated and she was gone. By the time I'd pulled my head from my ass to realize it, she'd moved to her aunt's ranch, and David was dead.

Shoulders heavy, I sank into the edge of the bed. I knew I should get up, walk to the couch, and give her space. I couldn't. Every time I closed my eyes, all I saw was Maggie drowning in the bitter, hazy waters of the stream. I could protect her if she was here, within eyesight. When she shifted and turned her back to me, scooting to the far edge of the bed, I lay on top of the blankets next to her.

Sleep came quickly—swirling images of hazel eyes and umber hair and Maggie in my arms consumed me as I finally accepted defeat.

～

THE SMELL and crackle of bacon exhumed me from darkness. I couldn't remember a time when I'd slept so deeply, so unaware of my surroundings, that it took a few seconds to get my bearings.

I was in my empty room, but the whisper of Maggie's scent clung to the air. I looked beside me, the blanket pulled up and the pillow adjusted against the headboard.

Swinging my legs off the bed, I rested my forearms on my knees and took a breath before standing. Facing Maggie always took considerable effort if I wanted to remain in control of my emotions. I was completely unprepared to see her in my space.

I padded from my room to the kitchen. Maggie's back was to me, dressed in the clothes I had laid out for her. Seeing her in my clothes filled me with possessiveness, and a burn spread across my chest. I knew better. She had had a traumatic night, but that didn't stop the words from rumbling out of my chest.

"You always did look better in my sweatshirt."

THIRTEEN

MAGGIE

Now

The deep gravel in Cole's voice raced up my spine and tingled down my limbs. His unexpected, rich grumble made my core tighten and go slick. I placed my hands gently on the counter and steadied my breath.

When I awoke in his bed, it was a shock. A hazy memory floated to the surface—being lifted in his arms just before I snuggled into the most comfortable bed I'd ever slept in. In the middle of the night, I gasped and startled awake. It rattled me still that I felt a deep comfort to wake up with Cole's wide, warm palm splayed across my thigh. I tiptoed to the bathroom and changed into the clothing he'd left folded on top of his dresser. The faded sweatshirt—the same one from high school I had loved to steal—smelled so good that I closed my eyes and pulled the clean and woody smell to the bottom of my lungs.

Instead of going to the couch as I should have, I climbed back into bed next to him. Cole's breath was heavy and deep, and I gently pulled the mussed covers from beneath him. I tugged them up to our shoulders as I settled in next to him. When his body sought mine, I stilled. The fire of his touch was oddly calming as I sank deeper into the comfort of the bed. When I'd shift or roll, his foot or hand or hip would find me.

When I was forced to face the man in the morning, I was completely unprepared. Morning was heavy in his voice, and its rich, thick rumble rolled through me. Determined to not freak out, I pasted on a wide smile and turned to face him.

Mistake.

A pair of gray sweatpants hung low on his trim hips, and a white T-shirt clung to the muscles beneath it. The shirt was tight enough to see the muscles beneath it coil and flex. I swallowed past the tightness in my throat.

"Good morning!" I chirped too loudly. I cleared my throat and continued. "Ha. Um, I'm making breakfast."

"Smells great." Cole walked into the kitchen and settled his large frame onto a stool by the small island.

"There wasn't much, but I figured eggs, bacon, and toast would do." I tucked a loose strand of hair behind my ear to keep from trembling. It was unnerving to have Cole be so *agreeable*. It freaked me out. "Also"—I steadied my nerves with a deep breath—"I can't thank you enough for what you did last night." Fear clawed at my throat, but I tamped it down to level my gaze with his.

Something dark and fleeting crossed his handsome face, but as soon as I'd noticed it, it was gone.

"Of course."

Knowing I wasn't going to get anything else from the insufferable *Officer Deck*, I busied myself by pouring a cup of coffee for each of us. When I slid the mug toward him, he nodded and took a sip, but he locked his eyes on mine before he swallowed.

He looked down at the cup. "How did you know how I take my coffee?"

Shit.

"Just lucky, I guess." I shrugged. He didn't need to know that I'd found out from Honey at the bakery. Guessing someone likes an exact two-to-one ratio of sugar to heavy cream—not milk—isn't weird, right? Sure.

I turned back to intensely focus on the bacon and eggs and prayed he'd just let it go. I could feel Cole's eyes at my back. The air in the small cabin crackled with tension. I'd never woken up with a man and made him breakfast. No, even when I'd dated, I kept my home life separate, and making breakfast for Cole in his kitchen felt too intimate.

Hadn't I wished for this? Domestic bliss with a man who chatted with me while I made breakfast on a lazy weekend morning. David and I certainly never stood a chance, and with Lottie, I made it a point to never have sleepovers with men I was seeing.

Pulling the carton of eggs toward me, I tipped my chin over my shoulder. "Scrambled or gooey?"

"Gooey, please."

"Two over-easy eggs, coming up."

As I cracked the eggs into the pan, I felt the heat of him press at my back. His thickly muscled arm reached next to me, pulling a toaster out of the cabinet.

"I can make the toast." His voice was low, and his breath was so close it tickled my ear. I closed my eyes and pulled a breath through my nose.

"Thanks. I couldn't find the toaster," I managed.

"Yeah, I keep it put away. Don't like much out on the counters."

I glanced around at the polished surface of the stone countertop. "I can see that. You know," I continued as I plated the bacon and flipped the eggs, "this place surprises me."

Cole popped the bread into the toaster and leaned a hip against the counter. His arms crossed over the expanse of his chest. "Why's that?"

"I don't know. I just . . ." I shook my head and turned to slide the eggs onto two plates.

A small laugh escaped him. "It's fine. You can say it."

I raised an eyebrow at him and smiled. "I thought this was a shack. Some bachelor pad that was falling down around you. I certainly wasn't expecting all this." My arms swept wide to encompass the entirety of the cabin.

It was a small open-concept space, but it was beautiful. Rough-hewn wood floors gave a rustic edge that offset the bright-white stone countertops. The kitchen cabinets were painted a soft gray, and each drawer had a textured, wrought iron pull. It somehow balanced masculinity with clean, feminine lines.

Cole lifted a shoulder in a smooth nonchalance that had my inner goddess screaming. How he could be so effortlessly sexy was the real crime here.

Fuck. Now you're thinking about his handcuffs.

"My house in town isn't anything special. I've lived there since I moved out of my parents' place. But here is somewhere I can escape." His eyes turned moody and dark.

"Escape?" I knew if I talked too much, he'd clam up, and I hadn't spoken this many words to Cole in a dozen years or more.

"Just be left alone. To be myself. Where I don't have to hold it all together all the time."

My heart broke for my old friend. He was really making it hard to hate him when he sounded so broken. Everyone saw him as Deck—strong and tough and steady. No one thought to look deeper, ask him if he was okay, or provide a safe space for him to fall apart if he needed.

Just to be left alone.

Cole's words vibrated through me. I was so desperate to see another side of him that I didn't want to hear the actual words he was telling me. He loved this place because he could be alone, and I was invading that space.

I pushed my eggs around the plate, losing my appetite. After a bite or two of toast, I emptied my plate in the garbage and moved toward the sink.

"You cooked for me. I'll do the dishes."

Please don't make this harder by being nice to me.

"Okay. I need to get going then. I need to find Sassafras. God, I hope she's alive." Fear tickled my throat as I thought about having to break Lottie's heart if I couldn't find the goat, or worse, if it were dead.

"I found her last night. She's set up in the doghouse."

I stared openly as he focused on his plate and ate his breakfast.

"You found her?"

"Yes. I went out last night after you fell asleep."

I took a step forward and reached out my hand but hovered it just above the muscular curve of his shoulder. I couldn't touch him and still maintain my composure. Instead, I curled my hand into itself and whispered, "Thank you."

Cole dragged the last triangle of toast through the egg yolk and moved to the sink. "I'll walk you home."

Dismissed.

Clearly, our intimate morning was over, and I cursed myself for trying to read more into it. I hurried to gather my clothes. The coat I'd worn last night was completely water-logged and ruined. I held the cuff of the sweatshirt I wore and had started to pull my arm through when his voice stopped me. "Keep it."

I nodded and pulled my boots over the socks—his socks —I still wore. Silently, we gathered Sassafras and trudged through the snow toward my house. Her soft fur tickled my lips, and I nuzzled her warmth into my neck, so relieved that she was safe. Once we reached the backyard, I tucked Sassafras into her pen and secured the lock. I tugged it twice to be sure it was fastened. Cole walked the perimeter, inspecting the boards and making sure that there was no other way she had escaped.

He pulled the gate to check it again himself, and when I turned to walk up the steps to the back porch toward my house, he followed. I reached under the antique milk crate I had stuffed with potted flowers and grabbed our spare key.

"You need a better hiding spot. That's the first place anyone would look." His voice was hard and riddled with annoyance.

With my back to him, I rolled my eyes. "Yes, sir," I teased.

In an instant, he was crowding the space at my back. "Careful now."

His fingers gently dug into the bone at my hip, and my heartbeat ratcheted higher. I turned and raised an eyebrow in defiance, only to be met with the smoldering dark eyes of the sexiest man I had ever seen. My breath caught in my throat. His gaze flicked to my mouth, and it opened on a desperate breath.

Suddenly, my hands were held above my head, secured by one hand. His other snaked under the baggy sweatshirt to splay across the thin skin across my ribs. My hips jerked forward, and I could feel his steel press into me. His mouth consumed me, swallowing the mewl that escaped. The kiss was rough and demanding.

I wanted more.

All the ways I'd fantasized about Cole paled in comparison to having the real deal in front of me, devouring me on my back porch. My breasts pressed into him, my nipples aching to feel the rough pads of his fingertips brush against them. When he bent to lick and nip at my neck, his body dragged against mine, and my tits bounced against his chest.

A breathy *Cole* was all I could manage. But my voice broke the spell, because as soon as it escaped me, the wall came slamming down. He released my hands and stepped away as though my presence physically hurt him. A numbness filled my chest, colder than any icy waters.

Cole turned and stomped across the snow toward his cabin.

No goodbye.

Nothing.

I knew letting Cole back into my heart was a mistake. The man was infuriating and totally unfair. He ran so hot and cold, and I couldn't afford to fall apart when whatever connection I felt between us blew up in my face. I was no longer a lovesick teenager who pined for him.

But goddamn, did he wear the fuck out of some gray sweatpants.

FOURTEEN
DECK

Now

When did I lose control? In the three weeks since I lost my mind on Maggie's back porch, I still couldn't pinpoint it. Was it when I saw the way my ratty sweatpants rolled over her hips and slipped farther down with every step she took away from the cabin? Or when my heart pinched in my chest at the sight of her cooking breakfast in my kitchen?

Damn, she'd looked perfect there.

All I knew was that the string of my control was pulled taut, and the moment the words *Yes, sir* playfully moved past her full lips, I couldn't take it.

Thank god she'd said my name and dragged me out of my delusions, or I would have truly snapped and done anything I could to take her right there on the back porch. She wanted me too—I could feel it in the way she arched her back, pressed into me as warm moans of pleasure thrummed in her throat.

Just thinking about kissing her had me growing thick between my legs, and I had to adjust myself in my jeans.

Fucking focus, dude.

I ran my palms across my face and sank a little deeper into the seat of the unmarked car. My mouth twitched around the faux hair above my lip. A knit cap sat low on my brow, and the oversize black sweatshirt felt hot and tight around my neck.

I studied my reflection in the mirror. Looking left, then right, I could appreciate the overgrown stubble running along my jawline. I'd let it go the last few days, and the scruff, combined with the fake mustache, wasn't all that bad. I looked like a badass Freddie Mercury. A goddamn stud.

More like a seventies porn star.

Okay, maybe I looked a little like a porn star, but it had to be done. The fucking Dick Bandits had tagged another two buildings in town.

In an effort to regain control, I'd avoided Maggie completely. I dove into work with more forceful attention than necessary and was determined to find whoever was defacing my town. After poring over maps, timelines, and grainy footage from Mr. Richardson's grocery store parking lot, I'd still come up empty-handed. The only thing that was clear was that it wasn't just one person I was dealing with. Likely, it was a group of kids from the community college. Maybe even the high school. My pulse hummed in anticipation.

Tonight we'll find out. Hell yeah.

My car was dark—an old Cadillac abandoned on the police lot for years. Earlier in the day, I had gotten Lincoln's brother Finn to park illegally to make sure no one took this space or the one next to it. One phone call to Finn and his monstrosity of a truck was backed out, leaving the space free and clear tonight. I parked on the side street, but with a perfect angle to get a clear view down Main Street.

My eyes swept down our small town's busy street. It was bitter cold, but our residents were used to it. Bundled up and huddled together, they held steaming cups of hot chocolate or coffee as they walked the street. Storefronts were decorated for the quickly approaching winter holidays —painted windows, twinkle lights, small speakers with Christmas carols floating onto the street.

The junker had shitty heat, but despite the cold, warmth spread through my chest. I knew the faces of every resident. Their names, how most everyone was related. Some birthdays. It was a town with a lot of heart, and I wasn't about to let some punk-ass transplant who couldn't appreciate us ruin that. I was fully committed to finding who was behind it and pressing charges.

I just had to find him first.

My eyes skimmed through the couplings of people, glancing past their hunched shoulders to look for someone, anyone, up to no good.

My eyes stopped dead on Maggie's brown waves tumbling down her sculpted shoulders and Honey's blonde strands beside her. Maggie wore a trapper hat, with fur-lined flaps to cover her ears. She looked fucking ridiculous, but I couldn't help the slow grin that split my face.

Dragging a hand over my mouth, I pressed down on the fake mustache. The damn thing was already losing its sticki-ness. Maggie slipped through the crowd, and I shoved down the burn of disappointment that rose in the back of my throat. I continued scanning the streets, watching people mill in and out of the shops as the sun dipped low behind the mountain.

A rap of metal against the glass of the driver's-side window had me straightening in my seat. I couldn't see the person's face, but I'd recognize those hips anywhere. I cranked the window down a few inches as cold air rushed in and filled the interior. "Get out of here."

Maggie was bent at the waist, her nose the prettiest shade of pink, and my heart tumbled in my chest when her bright smile spread across her face.

"I brought you something." She angled toward me, revealing a steaming cup of coffee from Biscuits & Honey.

The floral smell of her hair, mixed with the scent of the warm, nutty coffee, had my ability to hold back at its breaking point. I tipped my head toward the passenger seat, and she rounded the back of the car on a soft laugh. I looked around, making sure no one was watching us and taking advantage of my moment of weakness.

The minute she nestled into the bucket seat of the car, I knew it was a mistake. There was no way I could be this close to her without wanting to run my fingers through the softness of her hair.

"This is"—she gestured with her cup toward all of me —"quite a look you've got going on."

Maggie handed me the coffee, and I was careful to not let my fingers graze across the delicate skin of her knuckles. I took a sip, letting the hot coffee burn its way down my tightening throat.

On a sigh, I peeled the mustache off my lip. "It's a disguise."

Maggie's hearty laugh filled the car and sent a ripple of desire down my spine. "Oh, I can see that."

I stared through the windshield, unable to take in the full beauty of her face at this proximity.

"So," she continued, "what are we doing here?" Her hands slapped at her jean-clad thighs. I noticed the slim silver band she always wore on her right middle finger.

After her grandmother, Ms. Dolores, passed away a few years ago, she had started wearing it. Every day.

It was the little details that haunted me—that made it nearly impossible to stay away from her. I'd done it somewhat successfully for over a decade, but my resolve was running thin. Despite the ache that resided in my jaw every time I thought back on all the tiny missteps that had grown into the canyon between us, I didn't *want* to stay away anymore.

I wanted to know everything about this woman. To find out everything I had missed. Her quirks, her favorite song, if she'd still never let me win at cards, whether her eyes leaned more brown or green when numb satisfaction slid across her face after we were both thoroughly used up.

I swallowed a groan and focused on the street ahead of me. "It's a stakeout." I hated the pinch in my throat that sounded like irritation. On an exhale, I finally looked at her. "I'm trying to catch the bad guys."

"I'm sure you are, Captain America."

I raised my eyebrows at the nickname. A blush stained her cheeks, and I pressed my fingers into a fist to keep from dragging a thumb tenderly across the deepening color.

"Sorry. It's just something I sometimes call you. It's stupid . . ."

"Upholding the law is a duty that I take very seriously," I deadpanned.

Her eyes widened, and she rolled her lips together, trying to keep from laughing. Finally, I relented and smirked, dissolving her into a fit of laughter.

When I laughed with her, the laughter itself felt strange in my chest. As though it had been years since I'd felt truly at ease and the sound of my own genuine happiness was foreign to my ears.

"Yeah, I . . ." Shame washed over me. "I'm sorry about all that. Sometimes, I . . ." *Fuck.* I had no idea how to continue that sentence. Sometimes I saw you out on dates and jealousy made me crazy and irrational? Sometimes you looked so beautiful that it was painful to look at you, so scowling felt easier? Sometimes I'd watch you and Lottie cross the street and wish it was me you were going home to?

Instead, I stayed silent, letting my eyes drop to the cup warming my hands. When her fingers curled around my forearm, my eyes shot to her face.

"Maybe we just leave the past in the past?" Maggie spoke so softly I could barely hear her over the hammering of my own heart.

All I gave her was a hard stare until my eyes felt dry. Maggie was offering me what I had wanted for so long—to let the past stay buried down so deep that it couldn't claw its way to the surface and lay bare every mistake that had led to the chasm between us.

My agreement tasted so metallic I couldn't speak it. I felt a rusted knife in my gut at the thought of erasing all the memories we'd shared. But the carefully crafted facade of my disdain for Maggie O'Brien was so real that even my closest friends believed it. When our relationship shifted and changed, it was easier to be dismissive and aloof rather than feel the raw ache of a life without her in it. I was a fucking moron to think that protecting her from afar and keeping a watchful eye could ever be good enough.

A chance.

That was what she was offering me. A chance to forget about the mistakes of my past. Of not telling her how I truly felt about her. Of that horrible night with David. Of all the days since that I've lived a half existence.

I didn't deserve her second chance, but I was fucking taking it.

I sucked in a breath to steady myself. I needed to get this right.

"Marge-mellow"—a smirk hitched the side of her lip at the nickname—"I could never forget my past with you in it. But I am *all* for a fresh start."

My hand flexed at my side, aching to reach out and touch her. Take her face in my hands and devour her. Maggie released a shaky breath, and the delicate sound had warmth pooling between my legs.

As I shifted toward her, a flicker of movement caught my eye. Three figures skulked in the alleyway between the bookstore and Andersons' barbershop, skirting around the glow of streetlamps.

Fuck.

My eyes dropped to Maggie's plush lower lip, and I hated that my sense of duty overrode the raging hard-on in my pants.

"Hang on," I ground out. "There's someone there." My voice was harsh and low. If I wanted to punish them before, interrupting what was about to happen between Maggie and me made me want to tear them limb from limb.

Maggie ripped her gaze from mine and tracked the figures down the dimly lit space between the buildings. A small gasp clutched her throat, and her arm jerked in my direction.

Maggie's long-forgotten drink tumbled into my lap, soaking my thighs with lukewarm coffee.

"The fuck . . ."

"I'm sorry. I'm so sorry." Maggie's hands fumbled with the old door handle as her eyes pleaded with mine. "But I . . . I have to go."

Pushing herself out of the old car, Maggie hustled across the street. She kept her head down and practically ran down Main Street and out of view.

What in the hell just happened?

The black-clad figures holding spray-paint cans were long gone, but the fresh scent of Maggie still filled the car.

I filled my lungs with her scent and blew out a harsh breath. I had no fucking clue what had flipped the switch, but I knew one thing for certain.

Maggie was spooked.

FIFTEEN
MAGGIE

Fifteen Years Ago

"You look lovely, dear." My mother's soft eyes met mine in the bedroom mirror as I swished my burgundy prom dress left and right. I had scrimped and saved, and Mama had worked six extra shifts at the café so we could afford it.

A small smile crossed my lips but didn't meet my eyes. "Thank you, Mama."

"Oh, honey." She smoothed her hand over the long curls that tumbled over one shoulder. "It's just a dance. I know you hoped Cole would ask you, but David asked first, and you accepted. Just try to have fun."

"I know." Small tears filled my eyes, and I blinked them away before I ruined the makeup Mama had done for me. "I just"—I sighed—"I really thought he was going to ask. But he didn't, and when David asked, I didn't *not* want a date."

"I understand. And your friendship with Cole is very special." She squeezed my bare shoulder. "But love is a funny thing. It takes its own time to unfold. If it is meant to be, it shall be."

Her words were meant for comfort, but all I wanted to

do was stomp my foot and pout. Deep down I knew she was right. If Cole really wanted to take me to prom, he would have asked.

He hadn't.

After David asked me to prom, I'd heard from Cassidy Traeger that Cole had asked Erin O'Malley, a junior, to be his date. She was a nice enough girl and a star on the softball team, but I kind of hated her . . . just a little.

"Everyone is meeting at the church for pictures under the gazebo," I finally said. "We should get going."

Mama nodded and handed me the little gold purse she used only for special occasions. It was filled with lipstick and some extra money I knew she couldn't afford.

When we arrived at the grassy lot behind the church, it was a riot of tulle and sequins and color. Practically everyone in our small graduating class was there with their dates. Groups of girls were in wide circles, showing off their dresses and taking selfies. Guys were huddled together in little groups, looking awkward and uncomfortable in their rented tuxedos. Parents stood on the perimeter, snapping photos and asking couples to move this way and that while they documented the evening.

I scanned the crowd for my date, but David was nowhere to be found. Some of my girlfriends came up and gave me hugs, and the excitement of the day was contagious. Something about dinner and dancing and the tradition of a bonfire at the lake afterward felt electric—life changing. My mood lifted just thinking about it.

Finally, I spotted David across the field in the middle of a group of guys, telling an animated story. I frowned, just a little, when I saw that his vest was not our agreed-upon color to coordinate with my dress. Rather, his entire tux was a loud, electric teal. He saw me but offered only a smile and a nod before returning to his story. I looked down and fiddled with the slim straps of my dress and smoothed my hands across the fitted bodice.

"Wow," a deep, familiar voice said from behind me, and I turned to see Cole Decker as handsome as he had ever looked before. My heart flip-flopped in my chest, and I felt warm all over when he smiled at me in his tux.

"You look . . ." He paused. "Um. Maggie, you look . . ." He trailed off, not finishing the thought.

"You're not so bad yourself." I laughed and bumped his shoulder. "I can't believe you're wearing a tux."

"It's horrible," he said, pulling at his collar as though it were choking him. We shared a laugh, but when he looked at me again, our laughter faded, and we stood for what felt like a lifetime, just staring at each other. He was looking at me differently, somehow, as if I wasn't just his best friend who liked to hike and fish and drive with him around old country roads.

We snapped out of the moment when the moms started clucking and herding everyone to stand in a line, boys first, for group photos. I watched the guys playfully shove each other as they awkwardly lined up and pulled at their collars and sleeves.

David was among them, his teal tuxedo a stark contrast against the rest of the group. I laughed a little at his choice of color—David was always the center of attention, telling jokes and making people laugh. He was a talented artist from a wealthy family, and I figured that being loud was just a part of his personality. I wasn't upset that he'd asked me to prom. Frankly, I was glad *someone* had, if I couldn't go with the guy I wanted to.

As I chatted with my girlfriends, I let my eyes wander to Cole. It was completely unfair how his broad chest filled out his tux, and even though he was clearly uncomfortable, it looked *so freaking hot*. I swallowed hard and looked away when his eyes met mine. He was by far the hottest guy in the group—but I could never say that out loud. We were close, and while sometimes it felt like things got a little flirty, we had never *ever* been anything other than good friends.

Finally, it was the girls' turn to have the mothers *ooh* and *ahh* while they took pictures.

David stepped toward me, arms wide. "Well?" he asked, gesturing toward himself. "Pretty awesome, right?"

I couldn't help but laugh. "You're ridiculous. None of our pictures will look good, because we don't match!"

"Oh, don't say that." He put his arm around me, and I couldn't help but feel a little special, basking in his glow. "They'll all look good because you're in them, beautiful."

I warmed at his words. No boy had ever called me beautiful, and it made my heart flutter, just a little.

At the dance, David and I were actually having a pretty good time. He was vivacious and loud and everyone loved him. When he did the worm across the dance floor, people lost their minds and cheered for him. I stayed mostly on the outskirts, swaying and dancing with my friends. Truth was, I loved to dance, but David sucked up all the energy in the room, and I was fine with hanging back and looking on. When he was crowned prom king, I looked on with pride and ignored the glaring looks Ellody shot me as she danced with him, her queen sash slipping off her shoulder as they swayed.

I could use the time to sneak glances at Cole and his date. Erin looked amazing in her pale-blue dress. It was flowy and elegant against her tall, thin frame. I couldn't help the twinge of jealousy when his hands wound around her tiny waist and they swayed to a slow song. He was attentive, bringing her punch and laughing at her jokes. He looked happy and my heart sank, just a little.

Later, a large group of us changed clothes and headed out to the lake. There was a bonfire, music, and general rowdiness. The post-prom party was a well-known tradition, and as long as no one got too out of control, the parents and cops mostly ignored it. All the girls were drooling over Cole and his friends in their swimsuits and did their best to show off for the boys. I stayed quiet, but I didn't miss the contrast between David's lean body and the way Cole's arms and broad chest had filled out from sports and lifting weights.

"Girls! I think it's really happening!" Erin squealed as she huddled in a circle with us. While most of us sipped a beer, she had also been doing shots, and her heavy eyelids and lack of volume control spoke to her current drunkenness.

"I kissed Deck and he kissed me back, and I think things might get *serious* tonight!" she continued, shimmying and clapping her hands. Her eyes danced with excitement while my stomach curled.

Did he really kiss her?

I looked out over the crowd and saw Cole hanging out with our friends, Colin and Lincoln, and a few other boys from class. He didn't seem drunk, but when Erin met his eyes and waved, a big smile spread over his face, and he waved back.

He's here with her because he wants to be.

He wants her.

The conversation about Erin fooling around with Deck dulled and muted in my ears. I couldn't think straight, and the beer in my hand wasn't helping. I cared about him, and deep down I thought we might eventually end up together.

Once or twice I'd scrawled *Maggie Decker* on a slip of paper, just to see what it looked like. Those thoughts turned bitter as I realized that I had been wrong. We were nothing more than good friends. I looked at Erin. She was tall and thin and had gorgeous blue eyes and perfect hair. It was no wonder he was attracted to her. Erin bounced off toward her date, and Cole wound his arm around her shoulders.

I looked over at David, who was stalking toward us. He was fun and quirky and completely in his element as the life of the party. As he approached, I stepped toward him and accepted another plastic cup of not-quite-cold-enough beer. It was bitter and kind of gross, but I drank it anyway. David was charming and seemed interested in me, and I needed to push out any thoughts of my unrequited feelings for Cole Decker.

~

"It's fine, baby. You said you wanted this."

The memory of David's voice last night rang in my ears as my head pounded. I felt sick to my stomach, and I couldn't tell if it was because I'd had too much to drink last night, or if I was just thinking about what I had done.

My eyes were gritty, and when I opened them, the light from my bedroom window seemed to blind me. I clamped my hands over my eyes and groaned.

Flashes of the bonfire the night before ticked in time with the pounding in my brain—David's friendly smiles, too much beer, seeing Cole leave with his arm wrapped around Erin's shoulders, David urging me to take a shot of something that burned my nose and throat, more beer, David's hand moving from my hips to my ass as we danced, whispers in my ear about how pretty and sexy I looked.

No. What had I done?

I gathered my courage to sit up in my bed and immediately regretted it. My hair looked like a rat's nest—*Was that a leaf stuck in it?*—my eyes were bloodshot, and my face was sickeningly pale. I tested out my legs, but when I stood, they wobbled underneath me. There was a dull ache between my legs, and that was when it hit me. The reality that I really did have sex with David came crashing back, and my stomach roiled.

Running to the bathroom, I emptied the contents of my stomach. I felt like death, and I hated myself for what I had done. Tears burned a path down my face. When my stomach was raw and empty, I lay on the floor and let the cool tile soothe my hot cheeks.

I didn't love him, not even close. He was funny and popular and told me I was pretty, and I gave him something I could never get back. I couldn't even remember all of it. The bits and pieces that hung in my mind were hazy and broken. We'd left the bonfire in his truck, and the next thing I remembered, we were in the back seat, kissing. More compliments, more kissing, then somehow my panties were gone. I was unsure but also excited and a little scared. David's voice was soothing and urging me to keep going. Before I knew it had even started, it was over, and I felt . . . nothing. Everything was foggy after that. I only remember waking up.

Does this mean we're together now? He never actually asked me to be his girlfriend. Will David tell everyone what we did?

After I didn't think I could puke anymore, I peeled myself off the floor and checked my phone. No missed calls or texts from David. There was, however, a text from Cole.

Cole: Marge! I didn't get to say goodbye last night.

Hope you had a great prom! Let me know you got home, okay?

Fresh tears streamed down my face. Cole had left with Erin, but he still cared for me enough to make sure I got home safely. I couldn't stand the thought of facing him, knowing what I'd done. He'd think I was a slut, and he'd probably look at me completely differently knowing I'm the type of girl who would sleep with someone just because they made me laugh and said nice things to me. Shame washed over me.

I crawled back into bed, wishing prom had never happened at all.

SIXTEEN
MAGGIE

Now

"You always did have a soft spot for that boy." Mama's voice was wistful, laced with the hint of a smile.

"Trust me, Mama, he is *not* a boy."

"You know what I mean." She laughed. "To me, Cole Decker will always be seventeen and over the moon for you . . . whether he realized it or not."

I shifted the phone on my shoulder while I scrubbed the oven door and wiped it clean. It had been two days since Cole and I had shared a *moment* in the car and I ran. My house was stress cleaned from top to bottom, and I'd taken to finding the most random cleaning tasks to tackle—like the crack between the oven door and its hinge.

"He's spent the last decade making my life miserable, and you know it." I listened intently, hoping she'd disagree with me. My heart pattered in my chest.

"Just like a little boy chases the girl he likes on the playground." My heart beat faster as she continued, "Cole Decker is a man who doesn't know what to do with all those feelings. He was destined to be a police officer—trained to compartmentalize complicated feelings. His daddy was the same way when we dated."

The spray bottle clattered onto the floor. "You dated Sheriff Decker? Mama! When was this?"

"Oh, stop. It was nothing. A tiny blip in my life, not even worth mentioning. We were kids—when I was taking classes at the college. Just before your father. But his personality was part of the problem. He never could open up."

Shocked by the revelation, I stayed silent. Mama never talked about anyone before my father. When my dad left her, pregnant and twenty-five in a town she didn't know, my mother had been destined to raise a daughter on her own.

Like mother, like daughter.

My chest felt tight, and worry gnawed at me. Lottie and I were going to have a serious talk soon, and I had a sinking feeling neither of us would come out of it unscathed.

I refocused on my conversation. Mama was on another cruise with my stepdad, Keith, and she was calling me between ports. Not long after I moved back home and was settled, she'd met Keith at the café, and our families had blended together, giving me a sweetheart of a stepdad and four stepbrothers scattered across Montana and Washington.

"So what's got you all worked up over Deck, baby?"

I peeled the cleaning gloves from my hands and sat in the center of my kitchen floor, soaking in the smell of lemon and rosemary. I couldn't keep my secrets from her. I may have a built-in bullshit detector, but I'd inherited it from her. She was a master at sussing out the truth, so I'd learned early on I might as well give it to her.

"Well, we kissed. And then he ran. And then we *almost kissed?*"

Damn it. I sound like I'm sixteen again.

I lay back on the cool tile floor and closed my eyes, waiting for the judgment in her voice. Instead, she released a slow breath. "Well, then. That is something."

I paused. "That's it? 'That is something'? Come on. You *always* have an opinion."

"Darling, if it's meant to be, then it shall be."

Frustrated, I pressed my lips together. Part of me wanted to be sixteen again so my mama could tell me exactly what I needed to do.

Adulting was fucking hard.

"You just need to talk to him," she said at last.

I made a disgusted sound in my throat. "That's so . . . I don't know. *Simple.*"

"The best things in life usually are, dear."

I stayed splayed on the tile for the rest of our conversation, thinking over the night in his cabin, the tension I felt in the car, and how I could possibly talk with Cole without climbing that moody, delicious man like a tree.

ANOTHER TWO DAYS passed before I mustered the courage to seek him out. When I crept past his house in town and found the windows dark, my heart sank to my stomach. Cole may be stubborn as fuck, but so was I. I had showered and scrubbed and shaved *all of me* in order to feel like my most badass self, and that certainly wasn't going to waste.

I nodded at my reflection in the mirror and turned toward the police station.

"Well, look at you!" Ms. Arlene was packing up her purse as I approached the counter.

"Hi, Ms. Arlene. How are you doing tonight, dear?" I smiled my sweetest smile.

"Oh, just fine. Still hoping my grandson Darius gets his act together and finds himself a nice girl from church."

I smiled at the way her crepey skin crinkled around the corners of her eyes.

"Maybe I could pass along your number if you're interested." Hope rose in her voice as she patted her tight black curls, and I couldn't help but laugh.

Darius was wild, reckless . . . and twenty-one years old.

"Oh, I'm flattered, but no thank you. Actually"—I needed to tread lightly if I didn't want gossip printed about me in the *Chikalu Chatter* by morning—"is Deck around?"

With a tip of her eyebrow and a glance down her nose, I knew I was screwed.

"Well, sugar, he's not here." A wide smile deepened the lines of her face. "But I did hear him say something about spending a quiet night at home . . ."

The cabin.

I thanked Ms. Arlene and prayed she didn't spend the next hour working her way down the Chikalu phone tree.

With renewed vigor, I pulled my coat tighter to protect against the winter wind. In my car, I sped up the mountain and wound my way through the country roads toward Cole's cabin. The roads were dark, and the canopy of the forest shrouded the dirt driveway to his home. A tingle of anticipation zipped across my skin as I climbed the stairs.

I ran my damp palms across the outside of my thighs and focused on breathing. I should have brought a bottle of wine or something—anything—to keep my hands from fidgeting. As I raised my fist to knock, the door cracked open.

My clever, well-crafted, and flirtatious greeting withered and died on my tongue.

Cole answered the door looking like a damn snack. His

chestnut hair was disheveled, as though he'd carelessly dragged his hands through it. Bare-chested and barefoot, his jeans hung low on his hips, showing off the perfect V that had my eyes dragging lower and lower and lower. When my eyes could finally snap to his face, amusement danced in his eyes.

"Hey there, Magoo. Can I help you with something?"

My mind raced with a thousand things Cole could *help me with.*

"I, uh . . ." I cleared my throat. "I thought I'd see what you were up to tonight—if you want to hang out? Like old times."

Cole's jaw ticked once, as though he were thinking about whether or not it was a good idea to let me in. I squared my shoulders and gave him my most genuine smile. He dragged a hand across his chest, stopping just over his heart, and when he smiled back, relief flooded my system.

"Come on in, then." He stepped aside, just barely, and I had to squeeze past him through the doorway. He smelled like spice and fresh laundry or soap—*good-smelling man.*

Taking in the warmth of his space, I noticed the lighting was low. A fire crackled in the corner, and a half-full whiskey tumbler sat on the table beside his couch. I tucked a loose strand of hair behind one ear and risked a peek at Cole just as he dragged on a white T-shirt.

Oooofph.

The hit to my core had me clenching and swallowing a moan. I didn't know what was sexier, the cut lines of his abdomen and the light smattering of soft hair or the way the white cotton stretched across his broad chest and barely contained his biceps.

"I hope I'm not interrupting," I said.

He simply shook his head once. That infuriating man

wasn't giving me an inch. I continued to look around his space and appreciated how tidy he kept it. Cole poured another drink into a rocks glass and held it out to me.

"Whiskey, neat."

"Thanks," I said and took a sip. The warmth of the alcohol buzzed past my lips, and after the initial burn down my throat, a subtle heat spread through my chest.

Mmm, I hummed.

The silence in the cabin was painful in my ears. I so desperately wanted those tiny moments that shone with a glimmer of hope that Cole and I could find our way back to the friendship we'd once shared. But instead, most of our exchanges felt stilted and awkward.

Nosy at heart, I continued my assessment of his sanctuary, and I came to realize that it still held surprises. Masculine and tidy, but soft in unexpected places. Lining a thick reclaimed wood mantel were pictures of his family. One of Lincoln, Colin, and him from high school that I recognized from The Pidge. As I looked at his youthful face in the photograph—the face of what was once my best friend in the whole world—my heart twinged.

I needed to tell him *why* I'd freaked out and left the car. That it had nothing to do with the crackling energy between us. I had to tell him what I *saw.* I needed to trust him with the truth and believe that he would help me and do the right thing. I buried the thought. I still needed to confront Lottie and get to the bottom of it. I'd know if she was lying, and then I could figure out for myself what to do next.

When my eyes landed on a small, framed piece of drawing paper, my heart shuddered in my chest. Perfectly centered, though slightly faded with time, was a crayon drawing of a rainbow.

"What's this?" I asked.

Cole drained the remnants of whiskey from his glass. "That's, um . . . something special. From a very long time ago."

I studied the rainbow again. It was clearly a child's drawing, the lines overlapping and a riot of color. I squinted and leaned closer. It was then I saw the perfectly imperfect "C.O." in the corner of the paper.

Tears burned in my eyes. A mother knew the evolution of her child's handwriting, and there was no doubt in my mind that Charlotte had drawn that rainbow.

Had she drawn it for him? When? Why?

Based on the rudimentary formation of the letters, she couldn't have been more than five or six. Jesus, when she'd been that age, she used to go on and on about Cole and how *amazing* he was. He'd gone to her school for Career Day, and ever since then, Cole had been a hero in her eyes. My heart broke every time I refused to tell her that, so long ago, I knew him better than I even knew myself. That he was kind and funny and beneath his gruff exterior was a good, strong man. Instead, I'd let my hurt feelings and wounded pride allow me to stay silent.

"You're awfully quiet." Cole's deep, rumbling voice danced over my skin as he came up behind me. He dragged one fingertip down the curve of my neck, fire licking a path across my shoulder and down my arm.

"Just lost in old memories, I guess." I gulped the last swallow of whiskey and set it on the mantel. I turned to face him, but he was so close I had to tip my chin up to meet his dark eyes.

"Lately, some new ones have been haunting me." His voice was rich and thick as his eyes roved over my face and neck. He was stoic and overbearing and immovable, but there was also something tender in his eyes as he took me in.

I was terrified of his nearness, but my body hummed with pleasure at the same time. If Cole didn't kiss me soon, I was going to die.

SEVENTEEN

DECK

Now

Maggie was so close that I could count the flecks of moss green in her irises. She had every reason to hate me—for how I'd tucked tail and run when she told me she was pregnant, everything that happened with David that she didn't even know about, how I'd treated her in the years after his death—and yet she was standing in my living room, plush mouth open, just waiting to be devoured.

A deep and vital part of me needed her to hate me. I couldn't imagine a world where I had any right for Maggie to look at me the way she was in that moment. I carried the darkness of David's death with me like a cloak. Most called it an accident, but I knew the truth—if it hadn't been for my arrogance and inability to keep things impersonal, I never would have chased him down that highway.

The sharp bite of whiskey hung on Maggie's breath as I stepped closer, brushing the backs of her arms with my fingertips. A good man would have walked away. A worthy man would have protected her heart and kept his distance.

I was not either of those men.

One kiss. One kiss was all it took for me to let years of building walls to keep her at a distance crumble around me. I hadn't thought of much else since that kiss on her porch. It was painfully clear that we were tethered—circling each other while being drawn closer and closer.

Moving forward, Maggie mirrored my steps backward until the table dug into her ass and stopped her. "Are we friends, Cole?" she whispered.

"No."

I palmed the back of her neck and pulled her mouth to mine, claiming it in a searing, hungry kiss. Maggie opened her mouth and a small, delicate noise escaped, but I nipped and tugged at her lower lip. Her throaty moan had me deepening the kiss and leaning my large frame over hers.

Years of pent-up frustrations poured into her. I wanted —*needed*—to claim Maggie as my own. My tongue moved against hers, and she hitched a leg over my hip. I gripped her thigh hard as I pressed my erection into her.

"Tell me you don't want this." I needed her to tell me to stop, or I would tear us both apart.

She pulled her lips from mine, and fire danced in her eyes. "I won't."

"Maggie," I growled. "Tell me, or I'll be buried inside you. I'll claim you, and there's no coming back from that. You can't escape me."

"I want this." Her voice was breathless, the glass of whiskey thick in her voice, but her strong words shattered me. "I want you to make me yours."

I licked the tender skin along her throat and nipped at the base of her neck as my fingers feathered along the line of her collarbone. "I'm going to worship you, but have no doubts, doll." My tongue dipped into the hollow. "You've always been mine. You're it for me."

A low groan was all the invitation I needed.

Reaching behind her, I squeezed her perfectly firm ass and dipped lower to grab her thighs and hike her legs around my waist. I tilted her hips to center her heat around the ridge of my cock. A white-hot current sparked and balled at the base of my spine.

My hands couldn't touch enough of her skin. My fingers dipped below the hem of her shirt, and the soft skin was like an inferno against my fingertips. I raked my nails up her spine, peeling her shirt from her and pulling her chest into mine. Swiveling off the table, I carried Maggie the short distance to my bedroom.

Slamming the door closed with my foot, I spun her around and moved her hair away from her neck. I devoured her delicate skin, Maggie pressed against the door as she pushed her ass against my raging, hard length. She was pliant and willing in my arms. When I splayed her arms above her head and dragged my hands down her arms, the sensuous groans that escaped her throat had me nearly coming in my jeans. I palmed my erection, begging for release, but I was going to leave her boneless and satiated before I even thought about myself.

Maggie reached back to tangle her fingers in my hair. Every scrape of her nails sent lightning bolts through my veins. I was spiraling. I needed control. If her hands were on me, I'd never be able to hold myself together.

I gripped her sides, massaging my thumbs into the muscles. Reaching for my highboy dresser, I paused.

"Do you trust me?" I licked and kissed the shell of her ear.

"No." She lolled her head backward against my shoulder.

My cock pulsed. I needed her answer more than my next breath. "Do you want to?"

"God, yes, Cole."

Her back arched, and she turned her face into my neck and licked the rough stubble of my jaw.

"I promise I'll take care of you, baby." My inner voice screamed in my ear. If Maggie kept touching me, I was going to unravel at the seams. Palming the cold metal of my handcuffs, I dragged them across the bare skin of her belly.

Maggie sucked in a breath.

I continued a torturously slow assent up her arms. When I reached her wrists, I paused.

On a breath, Maggie gave me everything I needed. "Yes."

Flipping the cuffs open, I pulled her left wrist into the circle of metal. Carefully, I closed the loop, leaving her just enough room to move her wrist but still feel the bite of cold metal against her thin skin. I kept my hand over hers but bent lower to leave a trail of kisses up her back as I moved her right hand closer to the left. Muscle memory had the handcuff secured with barely a thought.

"Cole . . ."

"Yes, doll. Talk to me." Her arms bent back at the elbow, capturing my head within her bound wrists.

"I need you to fuck me."

My pulse hammered in my eyes, and blood surged through my veins. I sank to my knees, unbuttoning Maggie's jeans and peeling them down the full curve of her ass. Her thong disappeared between her cheeks, and I moved one hand from her knee, up her leg, and between her thighs. I dragged my fingertips across the smooth, silky fabric and pressed my face into her ass when I felt her panties soaked through.

I kissed and licked the outside of her hip as I lowered her panties to the floor. The overwhelming need to make her feel incredible was irresistible. With her arms raised above her head, Maggie dropped her forehead to the door.

I felt the smooth skin of her seam. Dipping one finger between her folds, I played with her pussy. With gentle strokes, I listened to every moan and sigh. Every intake of breath as I moved one finger, then two, deep into her heat. I could feel her core tighten around my fingers, and with the press of my palm against her clit, her pussy pulsed around me.

Her climax was hot and wet, and I couldn't help but to press my face into her and taste every last drop.

EIGHTEEN
MAGGIE

Now

I was coming, hard and fast, handcuffed and against a door as Cole Decker devoured my pussy. Honey had joked about Cole using handcuffs, but I had no fucking clue it would be as hot as it was. My legs trembled and my insides liquefied.

Cole stood, his strong chest pressed against my back, holding me up. His wide palm cupped my hip as he steadied me. I was lost in the warmth and spicy smell of his cologne and barely registered his hands circling my wrists. When he freed me from the handcuffs, I tried to protest—to tell him that I liked it and wanted more. Instead, a small moan escaped my throat and was swallowed by Cole's hungry kiss.

He scooped me up and carried me to the bed. Splayed across his comforter, I gazed up at his handsome face and saw fire swirling with desire in his eyes. He burned a path of tender, hungry kisses down my neck and across my breasts. I needed more of him. Everywhere his body touched mine was alight with a million sparks of electricity. I couldn't get enough.

I reached my hand between us and gripped the thick length of his cock. The quick inhale of his breath had me smiling and stroking, slow and hard. I teased the large vein on the underside and flitted gentle strokes across the head. A low growl rumbling from his throat sent a prickle of desire straight between my legs.

Cole reached into the nightstand and grabbed a condom. I watched as he rolled it down over his length. When he tipped his chin up, he caught me staring and smirked.

"Come here," he said as he grabbed my hips and dragged me lower toward him. When he centered himself at my entrance, our eyes locked. "Watch," he demanded.

"Yes, sir." I couldn't tear my eyes away from the point where our bodies were about to be joined.

"Good girl." My body clenched around him at his words. Never in my life would I have guessed how hot those words would be coming from Cole.

Instead of thrusting deeply, as my body was screaming for him to, Cole barely pushed past my entrance. I watched, entranced by how the thick head of his cock stretched me open. Inch by decadent inch, Cole pushed inside my slick heat. My inner muscles fluttered around him as I adjusted to his size.

"Fuck, baby." Cole sucked in, and a breath hissed across his teeth. When he was finally seated, fully inside me, his voice was tight and full of emotion.

My hips bucked, begging him to move inside me. "Move, Cole. Please. I need you to move." Cole lowered his head to mine as my arms wound around his muscular back.

He rolled his hips and began pumping into me. He set a

demanding pace, murmuring words of pleasure and doting. I could feel my rapture stack and build. His hands skimmed down my ribs and over my breasts. My nipples strained against his fingertips, and when he finally rolled them between his fingers, I came undone.

Squeezing him through my orgasm, I could feel myself coming around the girth of his cock. I had never felt so satisfied, so full, in all my life. As I came, Cole's back stiffened and he planted one final, searing kiss on my lips as he came with me. A deep, hearty moan escaped him as the waves of his pleasure rolled through us both.

I loved how vocal and enthusiastic he was. Energy radiated from the center of my chest out through my limbs. I was boneless and tingling—I had never been so deliciously and thoroughly used. Cole slipped from me and moved toward the bathroom. I had every intention of following him to clean up, but my limbs wouldn't work. I needed a minute to catch my breath and steady my heartbeat.

Cole came back into the darkened room, naked and still half-erect, looking like a Viking god come to life. He carried a small washcloth. Cole bent at the edge of the bed, kneeling beside me. I rolled toward him, tucking my hands beneath the pillow. He reached under to capture one wrist. He held it gently, examining it as his fingers brushed over the thin skin. Lines of worry etched in his forehead.

"I'm sorry, Maggie. I shouldn't have . . ."

"Stop," I said softly. "You asked. I wanted to."

"I marked you." His brow furrowed as he looked at the tiny red indents on my wrist.

"I liked it." I moved my hand to his face, forcing his eyes to meet mine. "We didn't do anything I didn't want to do."

Cole's eyes closed as he moved his face toward my hand. He looked tired and sweet and happy. Opening his eyes, he moved his focus to my naked body. With one hand, he took the warm washcloth and began wiping down my legs and at my center.

"I can," I started.

"I want to take care of you," he pleaded. It was then I realized that Cole needed this. Just as much as he needed and wanted control when we were fucking, he also needed to take care of me—make sure that I was all right, unharmed, and safe.

I lay back and allowed him to clean me. When he pulled a soft blanket over me, I tucked myself into a ball and drifted into a blissful sigh. Seconds later, his large frame was denting the mattress beside me. Cole curled himself around me, hiking my knees up so we were as close as two humans could be. He placed a gentle kiss on my shoulder, and I drifted to sleep to the sounds of his breathing and the smell of his skin on mine.

Minutes or hours later—I couldn't tell which—I awoke to the sounds of icy rain pattering on the tin roof of the cabin. The sound reminded me of nights I'd lie awake, huddled under my threadbare sheets, in the cramped trailer of my childhood. I would often think of Cole and imagine us in this exact scenario, wound around each other, breathing the same air. The soft drumming of the rain against metal was the soundtrack of my childhood, and it brought a peaceful comfort.

In the morning, I would have to pick Lottie up from her sleepover and get back to living my day-to-day life. We'd likely have to talk about what tonight meant, if it meant anything to him at all. But for now, I could be content with Cole's heartbeat thumping at my back and his strong arms pulling me closer to him.

~

Honey burst into the flower shop, scooting past a customer with a curt nod and tight-lipped smile. When she reached me, her eyes sparkled, and she was grinning. "Please tell me that you are the reason for the shit-eating grin I saw on Deck's face today."

I shushed her and wound an arm around her shoulders to lead her toward the back office. I nodded at my clerk, Ruthie, to excuse myself while she took care of the few customers we had in the shop. As soon as the door to my office clicked closed, I turned to see Honey with her hands clamped together under her chin, her bright-blue eyes dancing with excitement.

"So . . . ?" She was seconds away from dissolving into a fit of giggles.

I calmed the uptick of my heartbeat and tried to hide the smile that played at my lips. "I don't know what you are talking about," I answered coyly.

"Bullshit!" She laughed. "You two hooked up, didn't you?"

Unable to hide the truth from my best friend, I laughed alongside her. "It's safe to say that our relationship has definitely . . . changed." I couldn't help the bubble of happiness that fluttered in my belly.

"So what is this thing between the two of you?" she asked. "Just sex?"

"I'm not really sure. We had an incredible night. In the morning, we didn't really talk about the future or anything, but it feels like . . . more? I don't know. I feel like I'm seventeen again."

"You just"—she looked at me expectantly, palms up—"didn't talk about it?"

I shrugged. "Not specifically. In the morning, things felt so normal. Natural. We cooked breakfast together, had coffee on the back porch of the cottage. Then he walked me home, kissed me stupid when he dropped me off, and went to work."

I toyed at the skin on the inside of my lip. Should we have talked about it? The sex was crazy intense, but we'd both wanted it and felt great about it. There was zero awkwardness the next morning, so I rode that high until I had to come into work today.

"Look, don't sweat it," Honey said, noticing my nerves. "You're both adults, having a good time." She wiggled her eyebrows up and down playfully. "You did have a good time, right?"

I let out a breath I didn't realize I was holding and released a barking laugh. "Yeah. It was *really* good. Totally unexpected." I thought more about the emotions that had erupted from the both of us, the handcuffs, how he cared for me afterward, the intimate way he'd held me throughout the night.

"Can I ask you something, Hon?" I knew she'd keep my secrets safe, and I was in uncharted territory here. I needed her sexual experience to help me work through a few things.

"'Course." She nodded once and perched atop my desk.

"When we were together . . . god, please don't say anything to Colin about this . . ."

Her eyes leveled with mine. "Listen, we don't keep secrets from each other, but I promise you, he doesn't need to know the details of your bangfest with Deck. He doesn't *want* to know."

"Okay. So, it was intense. Passionate and fevered, and it opened me up to something I never even realized I craved."

"Yesssss, girl." Honey closed her eyes and nodded as she listened to me.

"He was demanding. Controlling, in the best way. We used his handcuffs."

At that, her eyes flew open. "I knew it! I knew deep down you were a kinky bitch like me!"

I smiled at her, and the fact that she would never judge me helped me relax as I opened up to her. "I called him 'sir,' and I freaking *loved* when he took control of my body while I was handcuffed. It was so damn hot."

Honey fanned herself and grinned. "I bet."

"I have never, *ever* had sex like that. Usually it's either regular missionary, or I'm on top. I can't think of a single time in recent history that I gave in to my partner in even remotely that way. Usually I'm very much in control. I thought I *liked* being in control."

Honey thought for a moment and then said. "Don't you see? That's probably exactly why you liked Cole being so in control. You're a bad bitch. You run your own business. You've raised an incredible daughter with little or no help. You make a thousand decisions every day and have to live with those decisions. You're the good guy and the bad guy in *every* situation."

I grabbed a bottle of water from the mini fridge for each of us and gulped down the cold liquid as her words sank in.

"It probably felt really fucking freeing and *nice* to not have to make those decisions for yourself. To be a woman and just feel and be."

Realization dawned over me. "Oh my god. You're so right."

"I figured." She shrugged as if she knew she was all along. "You're so used to being the one with alpha energy in any relationship—because that's how you live your life. But now you've got someone whose dominant energy is greater than your dominant energy, so you don't *have* to be the alpha. Because trust me, Deck is definitely an alpha."

"When I was with him," I continued, "he was taking control, and I felt like my mind just went blank. Like my bones dissolved in my body. I didn't have to think about anything." I began pacing in my office at my revelation. "I didn't have to think about whether this was a good choice or a right choice or what the long-term consequences of my actions would be. I can't tell you the last time my mind was so quiet. Now all I keep thinking about is how badly I want that again."

"Well, I have it on good authority that Cole and the boys are planning to get a few beers at The Pidge tonight. Sounds like you and I have a date." Honey hopped off my desk, winked at me, and breezed out just as quickly as she'd come in.

NINETEEN

MAGGIE

Fourteen Years Ago

"You're a whore." The words slapped me across the face as if they'd had physical power against me. Hyori Lee-Kim, David's mother, exuded wealth and power as she stood in the expansive doorway of their home. Her arms were crossed tightly against her chest, long manicured nails chiseled to razor-fine points.

Tears burned at my eyes, but I lifted my chin and bundled my tiny baby against my breast. "Please do not speak to me like that in front of her." I hated that my voice broke on the last syllable.

"I've told you more than once: you are not welcome here."

"David and I talked yesterday. He said that he was ready to meet his daughter." I clenched my jaw to keep the tears from spilling.

"David does not have a daughter."

"Are you kidding me? Look at her!" I tipped Lottie slightly toward her. A single eyebrow tipped up as she looked down her long, straight nose at us. There was no denying Lottie was David's. Her stark black hair was thick and straight. Her dark eyes the same rich carob.

Mrs. Lee-Kim blinked slowly, never indicating the sleeping baby softened her heart at all. However, after a moment, she took one step back and allowed me to enter their home. I had never been to David's house. It was perched on a bluff on the outskirts of town, overlooking the national forest. It was decadent, expansive, and remote—nothing at all like the double-wide trailer I was used to. Looking around, I realized that our tin-can trailer could probably nestle in their foyer, and we'd still have room to move around it.

"Thank you."

She turned and walked toward the back of their home. I quietly followed, shushing and bouncing Lottie as she fussed in my arms. When we reached the dimly lit media room, David was engrossed in a video game. The roar of a car engine and explosions startled Lottie into a full-blown cry, and I adjusted her weight to my shoulder.

"David." Her voice was like ice. "You have a guest."

He barely acknowledged her and kept smashing the buttons on the remote controller. I stood, bouncing a fussy Lottie and patting her bottom, unsure what to do. Without another word, Mrs. Lee-Kim turned and abandoned me in the doorway.

After an eternity, David's game ended, and he turned to me. As if he were shocked to see me standing there, he blinked a few times.

"Oh, hey," he said.

I took a deep, cleansing breath. "David, this is Lottie."

He barely peered at her before nodding and rifling through a drawer beside him. "Cool."

"Do you want to see her?" I asked.

"Nah, I'm good, man." David held up a small baggie and began tapping out a white powder. "Want some?"

Do I what?

"David, no. What are you doing? I have the baby." I turned to shield her tiny face from whatever it was he was doing.

David shot me a bland look over his shoulder. "You know, I thought you'd be more fun."

Shame burned in my cheeks. The effervescent, enigmatic David I thought I knew was nothing like the man in front of me. This David was reckless, soulless.

"I'm sorry that you don't think I'm very much fun, but I'm raising *our* baby. *Alone.*"

"What do you want? A medal? Money?"

A white-hot ball of anger flared in my chest. The visit was supposed to be a way to help him see what he was missing by not being a part of Lottie's life. I turned to leave.

"By the way, Mom says we need a paternity test."

"You know very well that you stole my virginity, and I haven't been with anyone else. Lottie is *yours*, David, whether you want her or not."

"Look," he said, anger laced in his voice as he rose from the couch. "I didn't *steal* anything. You were ripe and ready as any whore I've been with. You wanted this." David grabbed the front of his jeans and tugged on himself.

Bile rose in my throat. Shame consumed me. The truth in his words pierced my skin, and I couldn't escape fast enough. As I bundled Lottie up, the first of several tears streamed down my face.

"You may not love me. Or her. But you know where to find me if you decide that you want to be a part of her life."

"I won't."

I ran through his house toward the door, clutching

Lottie to my chest. After she was safely in her car seat, I tore out of his driveway, willing myself not to look in the rearview mirror. I couldn't count on David. If I was going to give Lottie the life she deserved, I had to be strong. I had to rely on myself.

Tearing down the mountain highway, I left Chikalu Falls behind me, and with it, the last shred of my innocence.

TWENTY

DECK

Now

The house band was rocking The Pidge tonight, and
Colin's deep voice had most of the crowd on their feet and
dancing to a popular, upbeat song. I stayed planted on my
stool, doing my best not to stare at the door. Earlier, Colin
had said that Honey mentioned her and the girls meeting
up with us tonight. Excitement had my knee bouncing, and
I tried to play it off as moving along to the beat of the music.

Lincoln walked up to me and passed me a fresh beer.
"What's new, brother?"

*Everything. My entire universe has tilted on its axis, and
it has everything to do with Maggie O'Brien.*

"Not much, man," I answered instead. "Work's been
busy."

Linc eyed me as he took a pull of his beer, and it had me
wondering how much Maggie had told her girlfriends. Had
the game of small-town telephone already made its rounds
through our small circle of friends?

"Any luck on finding who's been tagging the buildings?"

"Shit, man." I sighed. "I thought I was close the other

night. I spotted them, but something came up, and they slipped away." I thought back to Maggie's odd reaction in the car, and something scratched at the back of my skull. Brushing past the thought, I focused on our conversation. "Though now I'm fairly certain it's high school kids. Locals."

"Sounds about right," he said. "You remember that night we smeared Vaseline all over Johnny Achman's windshield?"

A deep laugh rumbled out of me. "Oh shit! I'd forgotten about that. Goddamn, he was pissed. Didn't it take, like, *hours* for him to get it all off?"

"Yeah. He didn't realize what it was and made the mistake of flipping on the wipers." A rare grin from Linc had me laughing and lost in old memories. As kids, Colin, Lincoln, and I had gotten into all kinds of bullshit. Usually Maggie stayed out of it. She was too focused on school and working to get a scholarship, but I'd always told her what we were up to, and she would roll her eyes and laugh. *Idiots* she'd always say as she shook her head.

Maggie was woven into the fabric of my childhood, and just thinking about getting a piece of that back had my heart shifting and rearranging in my chest. This morning, she'd left early, and we didn't have the lazy start to the day I had hoped for, but I could respect that she had her own life full of responsibilities that didn't include me. That fact didn't stop me from driving past the flower shop a time or two just to get a peek of her. Every time I saw her through the large glass windows, helping customers, she was smiling and radiant and gorgeous, and when I caught my reflection in the glass, I realized I couldn't remember the last time I didn't look quite so hardened.

Linc shifted in his seat, and my eyes tracked him to see

Honey and Jo working their way through the crowd toward us. My stomach hollowed out when I noticed that Maggie wasn't with them. We hadn't specifically talked about seeing each other again today or meeting up at the bar, but I had irrationally gotten my hopes up.

I scowled into my beer and took another sip, but it tasted bitter and flat on my tongue. As the women approached, Lincoln wound his arms around Jo and buried his nose in her light-brown hair. Jealousy flared in my chest, and I shifted to push it down. I had never been anything but happy for him and grateful to Jo for pulling him out of his darkest days. She had given us our friend back, and I had to stop being a fucking baby about the fact Maggie wasn't with them.

I'm such a prick.

"Hey, Deck," Honey singsonged. She smiled widely, and any doubt I had as to whether Maggie had told her we'd hooked up vanished.

"Honey." I nodded at her and leaned in for our usual friendly hug.

She sat across from me—her hands clasped and her chin resting atop her fingers—and stared at me.

Jo planted a quick peck on my cheek and settled into the nook of Lincoln's arm. After we ordered a fresh round of drinks, I finally looked at Honey.

"Just say it," I said.

Honey feigned shock, pressing a hand to her collar. "Say what?"

I grumbled into my beer and focused on the band and the crowd dancing.

"So, Jo . . . ," Honey started, "it's a shame Maggie couldn't make it tonight."

Jo eyed her sister. "Yeah, you're the one who told *me* she was staying in tonight."

"Oh, that's right." Honey swatted a hand in the air. "She's such a dedicated and incredible mother. Don't you think, Deck?"

Three pairs of eyeballs turned my way, and suddenly my skin felt too tight for my body.

I cleared my throat. "Uh, yeah. Sure. Maggie's great."

The ruse was pointless. I'd spent the better part of fifteen years grumbling about Maggie and making excuses to avoid her at all costs. The trio just stared at me as I pretended to watch the crowd on the dance floor two-step and twirl to the next song.

Finally, I set my beer on the table with a snap. "Fine."

"Oh, thank god," Honey said right over Jo's enthusiastic, "I knew it!" Linc just shook his head and laughed.

"My nonexistent relationship with Maggie has somewhat *shifted* in the last few days."

"Oh, darling." Honey smiled. "We know."

"Well, what the hell? What's with the mind games, then?" I asked.

"*We* could tell things changed between you two. But we wanted to be sure that *you* knew things had changed." Jo was grinning from ear to ear, resting her hand across Lincoln's thigh.

I let out an exasperated sigh. These women were insufferable, but I loved them, and they were as close as any family I'd ever had.

"So what are you still doing here, man? Go be with your girl."

I appreciated the humor laced in Lincoln's deep voice. Draining my beer, I tossed some bills on the table—enough to cover at least a round or two of their drinks—and gathered up my coat, leaving the bar without another word.

My confidence waned as my steps crunched up the path toward Maggie's front door. I noticed it was a little icy and made a mental note to grab some salt and put it down so she and Lottie didn't slip and break their necks. As I raised my fist to knock, I paused.

What if she doesn't want to see you? What if this is her time with her daughter, and you're intruding? You should have texted her a heads-up.

Fuck.

I went to turn and heard the lock click. Maggie pulled the door open, and when her complex hazel eyes greeted me with a warm welcome, my shoulders relaxed.

"Cole! I thought I heard a car pull up."

Nerves jittered below my skin. I felt like I did the night in old man Bailey's field—excited and nervous and a little bit nauseated.

"I, uh . . ." I steadied my nerves and steeled my voice. "I came to say hello, but if this isn't a good time, I'll go."

Her warm smile melted my insides. "Don't be silly. Come on in."

Maggie pushed open the door, and I was welcomed into her home. It hadn't changed much since the night a few years ago when I brought her home from the Sagebrush Festival. It was pretty, clean, and functional. Christmas decorations lined the mantel, and in the corner was a large, real Christmas tree. I wondered where she'd gotten it or how she had managed to haul it inside herself.

"Have you eaten? Lottie and I were just about to have some frozen pizza and watch a movie. It's not great—it's from a box—but it's food, if you're hungry." Maggie shrugged in the cutest way, and all I wanted was to gather her up in my arms. Instead, I stood stiffly in the entryway.

"Pizza sounds great."

When we walked into the living room, Lottie was sprawled on the large couch in a nest of fluffy blankets and several plush, square pillows.

"Hi, Deck!" She smiled and lifted her hand in greeting. A wave of affection rolled through me, as it always did when I spoke to her.

"Charles." I bowed my head slightly and was rewarded with a small giggle. Maggie looked at me, a bit confused, but didn't call me out on why Lottie and I were on such friendly terms. She may have spent the last fifteen years hating my guts, but Lottie and I had had an easy friendship ever since the Career Day when she'd stolen my heart. I always waved at her when I drove by, and unless she was with her friends, she'd grin and wave right back.

"Okay," Maggie said as she handed me a plate of pizza, "prepare yourself. It was Lottie's choice of movie tonight. She picked a horror flick." Maggie shuddered, but my chest bloomed at the thought of holding Maggie's hand through the scary parts.

Who the fuck am I right now?

"Scary works for me."

Maggie motioned toward the small love seat, and instead of sitting at Lottie's feet, she settled onto the small couch next to me.

For the next two hours, I stared straight ahead. My fingers itched to pull Maggie's hand into mine, but with Lottie there, I just couldn't do it. Maggie's scent was intoxicating, and every time she shifted, I wanted to brush her dark locks away from her shoulder to reveal the long line of her neck. It was the most torturous two hours of my life.

The movie was pretty dumb—a typical slasher about idiot teenagers drinking in the woods and getting trapped by a local family of serial killers. A time or two a jump scare would send Lottie or Maggie screaming just loud enough to make me jump too. We laughed and ate and talked about everything and nothing throughout the movie. A time or two I caught Lottie giving me the side-eye. I wondered what she thought of my unannounced visit. Her eyes would flick to the space between Maggie and me so I made a concentrated effort to keep a respectable distance.

I tamped down a strange wave of emotion as I sat with them. It felt so good to be there with them—talking, laughing. God, I fucking missed this. I missed Maggie's friendship more than anything. It took those seemingly insignificant moments, with the melody of Maggie's laughter floating on the air beside me, to realize just how much I've missed it. I lived with so many regrets, but losing her as a friend was by far the biggest.

When the credits rolled, Lottie had dozed off—she snored just like her mama. Maggie roused Lottie, earning her a grumble as she padded toward her bedroom. I stayed, clearing the empty cups and throwing away the paper plates and pizza box. The quiet of the house rang in my ears. I was hyperaware of the fact Maggie and I were about to be alone in her darkened living room.

Was last night a one-off? It seemed as though we weren't going back to ignoring each other, but fuck. If Maggie and I weren't on the same page with this thing, she'd scoop my heart out with a spoon, and I'd let her. Last night, it could have appeared as though I was in control, but Maggie had every broken piece of me in the palm of her hand.

Her quiet footsteps had me flexing my hands at my

sides. When she stepped from the hallway, I was struck by her beauty. *Beautiful* didn't even come close. Maggie was dressed in leggings that hugged her muscular legs and firm ass, and her oversize T-shirt hid what I knew was a trim waist and perfectly supple breasts. A wave of desire swept through me and settled between my legs.

There was something about Maggie that had shifted, grown in the years since I'd truly known her. It was a quality that no woman on the planet ever possessed. She was so multifaceted that I could spend my entire life trying and still never quite figure her out. She was strong, yet yielding. Fierce, but she radiated kindness. Lighthearted and dangerously passionate about everything she did. She had no clue how one look from her lit up my insides.

With swift steps, my strides ate up the distance between us, and I cupped the back of her neck and hauled her chest against me. A surprised gasp escaped her throat as I covered her mouth with mine. She had no idea I had waited damn near twenty years to kiss her like this, and I wasn't about to stop now. Her lips were soft and pliable as I swept my tongue against hers. The way Maggie opened for me had blood surging through my veins.

I pushed down a panicked sense of urgency. My heart twinged, emotions digging deep and taking up space behind my sternum. I wanted to be with her—here in her home— just her and Lottie and me . . .

Mine.

I poured my heart into that kiss, moving my hand from behind her head to the front of her neck. My wide palm encircled her slim neck as I moved my head back to let my eyes drift over her face. Her eyes were wild, lust swirling in their mossy depths. I kept my touch on her neck featherlight but didn't remove it. My other hand pulled at her lower back, the ridge of my cock pressed against her belly. I couldn't get her close enough. I wanted every soft inch of her to be touching every hard inch of me.

"You can't kiss me like that." Maggie's voice was heady and electrifying.

"I'll kiss you however I want."

"Jesus, Cole." She closed her eyes as her head tipped sideways. I planted wet, hungry kisses along her exposed neck and felt her pulse hammer beneath the delicate skin. "I love the way you want me. Why couldn't it have always been like this?"

Desire clouded her words, but they still landed with a swift punch. She was absolutely right. Our bullshit, however justified it had felt at the time, had robbed us of this. We had wasted so much time. My heart and soul was already fifty steps ahead, but she deserved to have someone who took his time with her heart.

I pulled back and held her perfect face between my hands. "Maggie O'Brien, I should have done this a long time ago."

Her bright smile nearly killed me, but I continued: "Will you go on a date with me?"

A soft blush stained her cheeks. "Yes."

I planted a firm kiss on her lips before she could take it back. My heart stuttered in my chest when she looked at me again and said, "I've been waiting a long time for you to ask me."

"I'll make it up to you."

"And I'll make it up to *you*."

Maggie laced her hand with mine as we walked toward the door. As much as I would have loved to allow my eyes to eat her up as my hands felt every inch of her naked body, I didn't want to ruin the simplicity and purity of tonight. It was perfect, and my aching dick couldn't ruin that.

One last needy, lingering kiss at the doorway and I was back in my truck, heading to my house in town. I already knew I'd be spending less and less time there. The cabin was closer to Maggie, and my burning need to be near her overrode the convenience of a bed closer to the station.

TWENTY-ONE
MAGGIE

Now

Something akin to unease skittered through my belly as I waited for Cole to arrive. The morning had been nearly perfect—bitter cold had given way to a sunny day that felt downright balmy compared to the weather we had been getting. Though it was just a few short days before Christmas, Cole promised that a short afternoon ride on his motorcycle would be worth it. I had my doubts as I pulled my knit hat low on my forehead.

Lottie was working at Biscuits & Honey. Lately, she was determined to make a few extra dollars, and Honey didn't mind the extra help. I sat, bundled up in my coat, boots with thick socks, and jeans. I looked out onto the expanse of my property. Part of the reason I had fallen in love with it was the shelter of the trees and the open fields to plant my cut flower gardens. While most of Chikalu Falls seeped into the sprawling flats of Montana, I had chosen to find my sanctuary up the mountain. The winding roads to my home wove through trees and bluffs that, even in the dead of winter, were breathtaking.

Space.

Something I had craved so desperately when I'd sat in the cramped corners of my room in the rickety trailer I grew up in. I wanted Lottie to have the space and freedom to explore, discover, and feel as though her possibilities were endless. I wanted her to hold on to that feeling as long as she could.

The low rumble of Cole's bike cut through the thin winter air. The sun was warm on my face, and as he pulled into my driveway, its warmth soaked into my bones. I pulled on my sunglasses and waved in his direction.

"Hey, doll."

Hearing Cole Decker call me *doll* never ceased to send a ripple of pleasure straight to my core.

"Are you sure about this?" I gestured, palms up, at the melting snow dripping from the rooftop.

"Positive. It's a great day for a ride."

"Hmm . . ." The guttural noise from my throat was reserved for when I wasn't quite believing the bullshit I was being fed.

"It's a short ride. I promise." Cole lifted a half-shell helmet in my direction. I grabbed it and unceremoniously plopped it on my head. It was heavy, and my neck wobbled under its weight.

"Where's yours?" I asked.

"You're wearing it." Cole adjusted the strap beneath my chin to secure it. He flicked the side of the helmet playfully and grinned. "I'll be fine, and there's no way you're getting on my bike without a helmet."

He straddled the bike, ending the argument I had been gearing up for. Cole may be hot as fuck, but he still had a knack for irritating the hell out of me sometimes. I supposed old habits died hard.

Resigned, I looped a leg over the motorcycle behind him and settled his hips between my thighs. Being this close to him, I could smell the richness of his soap swirling with the leather of his jacket. If I could bottle up that deeply *masculine* scent, I'd bet good money Ms. Trina could sell it at the Blush Boutique and make a killing.

The rhythmic vibrations of the bike beneath me did nothing but spur on my already aching libido. I pulled a steadying breath into my lungs and gently placed my hands at Cole's hips.

He turned his head toward me so I could hear him. "Ready or not."

At that, the bike pulled us forward, down the path that led away from my home and out onto the open country road. My heartbeat ratcheted up—nerves and excitement bubbling just beneath the surface of my skin. The crisp air burned in my lungs, but I gulped it in. I could taste the fresh, cool air. The smell of gasoline and pure pine wafted around us as we took the lazy, winding path that looped around the mountain.

Cole had been right, I barely registered the cool air as we rode. In this town, there wasn't a road I hadn't been down a thousand times before, but from the back of Cole's bike, it was breathtaking. Every cliff and bluff that gave way to an expanse of pine forest seemed endless.

My hands moved from his hips to around his waist, holding on to him as we raced over and under the hillside. Cole released one hand from the handlebar to lay his hand over mine. Despite wearing gloves, the warmth from his hand radiated up my arm and spread through my chest. The bright sun filtered through the trees, casting shadows along the road. I was lost in the dancing trees. I had never felt more *free*.

I tilted my head and rested a cheek against the leather at his back. As the world rushed past me, I closed my eyes and focused on the warmth of wrapping myself around the most complicated, confounding man I had ever known. Cole dropped one hand to reach back and cup my knee. He caressed the back of my knee—nothing terribly sexual, but my body hummed with the memory of being stripped bare with Cole. When his hand squeezed three times, I paused. Something significant hung in the air, but I couldn't place it. I lifted my head to search his face, but he was looking straight ahead, completely focused on the road.

True to his word, the ride was short. We'd wound up in Tipp, a small neighboring town I had visited. Cole pulled the motorcycle into a space in front of a quaint coffee shop named Brewed Awakening. I hadn't spent much time here, and rather than hugging the mountains, Tipp sprawled across the flats of Montana. We'd passed several cattle ranches on the way in, and rugged masculinity clung to the air. In the darkening early evening, the town had a much different vibe than Chikalu. Not bad, but the way the residents looked at us with a healthy dose of wariness and skepticism had me inching closer to Cole.

"Where'd you find this place?" I asked as he pulled open the glass door.

"Girl I went to State with had grandparents from Tipp. We'd made a connection, since it's pretty close to Chikalu."

"Oh, a *connection*." I teased and bumped my shoulder into his biceps.

Cole scowled down at me. "It wasn't like that. We were in the same law enforcement program. She was intense, driven. *Just friends*."

I smiled brightly at him. "I guarantee she had a crush on you." When he rolled his eyes, I added. "Who wouldn't?"

He answered with only a harrumph, and a tiny part of me loved that I could still get under his skin, just a bit. The small coffee shop was warm and inviting as we entered. With his arm around me, Cole led me to a small love seat in front of a roaring fire.

When he walked away, I watched his large, imposing frame step up to the counter. The eyes of the woman working behind the counter took in all of him with an appreciation that had jealousy unexpectedly flaring in my chest. I had seen Cole in town on dates with other women over the years, and I had trained my body to not react. Whatever this was blooming between us had awakened that primal part of my brain that wanted to claim him in every way.

A few moments later, Cole returned with a piping hot latte. I took a tentative sip as he eyed me.

"I'm not the only one who can find out a coffee order," he said as a playful smile tugged at his lips. I couldn't help but smile at him and settle deeply in the squishy couch.

A flicker of worry that my inner feminist should be thoroughly disgusted crossed my mind, but I tamped it down. I knew with every fiber of my being that Cole ordering coffee for me came from a place of friendship and maybe even a sense of actually *wanting* to take care of me. I hated to admit that it felt pretty incredible. Cole's large frame barely fit on the couch next to me, but I loved feeling the warmth of his muscular thigh run the length of mine.

"I have a question for you." Cole stared into the fire, and a prickle of nerves tingled behind my ears. When I stayed quiet, he continued. "What if"—my heart raced at his words and my stomach whooshed—"you become a crazy goat lady."

Laughter erupted from me.

Humor. Nothing too heavy. I can do this.

"Well, that is *never* going to happen. That goat is going to be the death of me. She escaped two more times, and I think she's tunneling out. That damn goat is smarter than me."

"Nope. That's not how this works. There's no such thing as an impossible *what-if*."

I didn't know if it was the fire or his words or how my body was in hyperdrive at being so close to him, but I warmed at his implication.

"Okay, fine. What if . . . you left the force and became a rodeo clown."

Humor danced in Cole's eyes, and he'd never looked so much like the boy I once loved than he did then. "Really? I couldn't be some stud, buckle-chasing rodeo champion? I have to be the clown?"

"You wanted to play!"

Cole reached his hand over to tickle my ribs, and I dissolved in a fit of giggles. He was playful and light and engaging. I couldn't help but think about all the years we'd lost between our friendship and today. Not wanting to ruin the moment, I stuffed those old, regretful feelings as deep as I could and focused on the complicated, delicious man in front of me as we laughed by the fire.

Our ride back to town was a bit cooler, but Cole took the short way, and before I knew it, we were walking up the steps to my home. I wanted nothing more than to drag him inside and watch his muscles flex and bunch as we tore at each other's clothing.

"Hey, Mama!"

Well, I guess panty ripping isn't happening today.

Lottie opened the door and smiled up at Cole. "Is Deck staying for dinner?" Hope laced in her voice, and I felt a twist of guilt in my gut. I needed to talk to her about so many things. My suspicions about seeing her with the vandals, whatever this was developing between Cole and me, her missing science assignment. It was all too much for me to process, so instead of handling it, I did what I had to do—pack away my feelings and check things off my list, one at a time.

"Sorry, baby, not tonight." I ignored the pain beneath my breastbone at how Cole's smile faltered fractionally.

He recovered quickly and added, "Wish I could, Char-broil, but I do have work tonight."

Lottie pouted and whined an *okay* before stomping away.

I smiled at him, silently communicating, *Teenage girls are fun.*

I straightened my spine and sighed. "Thank you, again, for an incredible date. I had a wonderful time."

Cole leaned forward, crowding my space and sending my pulse into the stratosphere. "You two stay out of trouble, you hear?"

A wicked grin toyed at my lips as I popped up on my tiptoes to kiss his cheek. "Yes, sir," I whispered in his ear.

A low growl formed in his throat, and my body hummed with pleasure. I didn't have the freedom to let Cole take me whenever the mood struck, but damn if I didn't wish he could ravish me in the doorway and feel that growl rumble through me.

I watched him walk away toward his motorcycle and wondered . . .

What if he was always meant to be mine?

～

Me: I've got something planned for this weekend.

Me: I think you'll like it.

I stared down at my phone and held my breath as the tiny bubbles popped up and disappeared. My finger tapped the back of my phone.

Captain America: Oh yeah?

Me: A date. Lottie is spending the weekend with a friend's family in Butte. After I deliver flowers for Bob Stadler's funeral on Saturday, are you free?

Captain America: I can make that work.

My smile grew as excitement built for another real, adults-only date with Cole. I hummed along to the radio beside me as I continued working on the floral arrangements at my worktable. My phone buzzed again.

Captain America: I don't like sitting at work when I could be at home doing filthy things with you.

My eyes bugged at his words, and I reread them twice to make sure I wasn't just fantasizing. I pressed my thighs together. That man was naughty and I loved it.

Me: Officer Decker! What would Ms. Arlene think if she found out our beloved detective sergeant had such a dirty mouth?

Captain America: Worth it.

Me: I have you saved in my phone as "Captain America." You're supposed to be the good guy.

Captain America: You're gonna want to change that, doll. I'm not the good guy.

I was supercharged with desire as my mouth went dry. Cole had a way of making me feel desired, powerful.

Me: Fine then. Go on.

Captain America: A challenge? I like it. I want your breath on my skin when I make you come tonight.

I swallowed a moan and looked around my empty shop. It was the middle of the day, and someone could walk in at any moment. The mere thought of Mrs. Coulson, the sweet lady who owned the local café, walking in while my cheeks were flushed with desire had my pulse rabbiting.

Captain America: You'll be begging me to fuck you.

Ho-ly.

Shit.

My breath was coming fast as my nipples hardened and tingled.

Me: Oh my god, yes. Keep going.

Captain America: Are you already wet for me, doll?

I looked around the shop again and dipped my hand across the front of my jeans. My clit screamed for more pressure. I wanted him. I was desperate.

Me: Yes.

Captain America: I am so fucking hard right now.

I thought of Cole's long, hard dick pressing against the zipper in his pants. I wanted to palm it and feel it twitch beneath my touch.

Me: I wish I was there right now. I could feel just how hard you are for me.

Captain America: Baby, if you were here, I'd have you on my desk with your legs spread.

My hand fisted, my nails biting into my palm.

Captain America: Pick up the phone.

A second later, my phone was vibrating on the countertop.

"Hello?" I answered, my voice husky and thick.

"Slide your fingers over your pussy." Cole's voice was commanding, intense, and laced with desire.

"Yes, sir," I purred. Not giving a *fuck* about where I was

or that someone could come in, I moved my hand over my jeans.

"Good girl. I'm stroking my cock right now, wishing it was your mouth I was fucking."

"Oh my god, Cole. Yes." I flipped the button of my jeans and shimmied them down my thighs.

"Are you fingering yourself right now? Tell me."

"Yes," I whimpered. My hips rocked as I teased the slicked seam of my pussy and imagined it was his mouth on me.

"I wish I could taste that pussy. Keep going until you come."

Pushing my fingers inside myself, I hit all the spots I knew could bring me to the edge. "I'm already close."

The heavy, ragged breathing on the other end of the line pushed me to the brink as I envisioned Cole stroking his cock, getting it ready to slide inside me. I pictured him in the uniform that hugged his broad chest and always made my fantasies spark to life.

In the background I could hear the sounds of Cole inching closer to the edge of his own orgasm. My body coiled tight. "I'm right there, Cole."

"Do it. Do it, doll. Come for me."

I imagined his release, in tandem with mine, as his cock pulsed and my core tightened. On a cry, my release exploded. A grunt tore from his throat, and I knew he was right there with me. My body was on absolute fire, and instead of the languid numbness after release I'd hoped for, I was more amped up than ever.

"Jesus, Cole. That was . . ." I didn't even have the words.

He was breathing hard, but his voice was more relaxed. "I don't deserve you. You're incredible."

The tinkling of the front door bell had me diving below the counter, yanking my jeans back up.

"Shit! Fuck!" I scrambled to rearrange my clothes without whoever just walked in seeing me. "Someone came in. I have to go!" I hastily disconnected the call and ran a hand through my disheveled hair. I'd call Cole back later, but right now I had to scrape together any shreds of my dignity.

When I popped back up and saw Honey striding toward the back, I sighed in relief.

"Hey!" she chirped. "Wanna do lunch?"

TWENTY-TWO

DECK

Now

Jerking off to the sounds of Maggie's moans on the other end of the telephone was not the most professional moment of my life—that was for damn sure. When Maggie's flirtatious texts hinted that I might get an *entire weekend* alone with her, I couldn't resist. My body ached for her, and when she cracked that door, just a bit, I'd kicked the damn thing open.

Unfortunately, hours later, I was still getting hard just thinking about it. I kept busy with menial tasks and drove around Chikalu, checking in on some of our senior residents. One in particular, old man Bailey, hadn't been around town in a while. I rarely worried about him anymore —he and Lincoln took care of each other. Lincoln had purchased his property a few years ago, and Mr. Bailey still lived out there in the cottages. Still, that ornery old man was a staple in this community, and it was my duty to make sure that he was still kicking.

I drove down the winding gravel drive toward Linc and

Jo's home. They'd remodeled it, reclaiming it from the elements and turning it back into the beautiful farmhouse it deserved to be. I thought of Maggie and how she deserved a house as big and welcoming as theirs. She'd done it, too, all on her own. I pulled my squad car past the Big House and down toward the small cottages that dotted along the river.

The old man opened the door to Cottage Four and stepped out just as I was exiting my vehicle.

"What do you want?"

"Nice to see you too, Mr. Bailey." I held my hand out to him.

"Hmm," he grumbled, but took my hand in his for a firmer-than-expected handshake.

"I was just making some rounds. Seeing that everyone's doing all right. That no one needs anything."

"Deathwatch, you mean." He was a piece of work, that old man. "Well, I'm fine. What with Jo and Honey always up my ass and making me eat dinner with them. Trust me, when I die, they won't let me go peacefully. I'm sure those two will raise hell over it."

"They are some strong-willed women. I'll give you that."

I had turned to leave when he motioned toward the warm fire just inside his cottage and added, "Word is you've been running around with that O'Brien girl again."

Intrigued, I stepped inside and sat with him at the small kitchen table. I stayed silent as he poured two cups of strong-smelling black coffee.

"She's a niece, of sorts, you know."

I eyed him skeptically.

"Niece through marriage twice removed or some other bullshit," he continued. "Her piece-of-shit father skipped town when Denise was pregnant with Maggie. Didn't have much of a family connection to speak of, though little Lottie was named after my late wife."

"I didn't realize," I said. My thoughts layered one over the other as I mused about our quirky town and its many facets. Mr. Bailey rarely spoke of his late wife, but the girls had once swooned that it was a great love story. I'd take their word on it.

"She's too good for you. You know that, right, son?" His steel eyes bored into me.

"Yes, sir."

"Well, at least you're not also a dumbass."

I chuckled, and we fell into a companionable rhythm. We talked about Lincoln and Jo, the property and how it was changing, how things in a small town are always changing but still seem to stay the same. Once my second cup of coffee was through, I stood and excused myself. Old man Bailey walked me to the door, and as I stepped out and placed my cap on my head, I shook his hand in farewell.

"I may not own it anymore, but next time you want to take that girl out on the back field, ask first."

A smile cracked across my face at the memory. "Ah. Thought I got away with that one."

"Anyone who wasn't stone-deaf could hear your dually from a quarter mile away. I'm no fool."

I nodded and shook his hand again. "Well, I appreciate you not telling my dad."

A smile crinkled the thin skin around his crystalline eyes. "Nah. The look of sheer terror on your faces was enough. Figured I'd scare you straight. For a minute, at least."

After leaving, hope continued to bloom in my chest that

Maggie and I could finally have our second chance in the town that held so much of our lives. While I would never forgive myself, if I could find a way to atone for the sins of my past, we might just have a shot.

TWENTY-THREE

DECK

Fifteen Years Ago

"Do you think he'll notice?" Colin eyed the bottle of my dad's Maker's Mark. It was dusty from sitting untouched in the cabinet for so long.

I shrugged. "I doubt it. He never touches it."

The guys met up at my place because my parents were out of town for the weekend. It was the end of summer, and our last night with us all together, so we were determined to make it count. I was headed off to State for a criminal justice degree. It was only a two-year program that I didn't think I needed, but Dad had insisted I take it.

After a case of Shiner, we started rifling through the barren liquor cabinet. I passed the bottle to Lincoln, who eyed it and took a tentative pull while Colin got some glasses from the kitchen. We were all sitting on the edge of the back porch, lined up and legs swinging, looking out onto the expanse of my yard as music pumped from the speaker next to me.

"Are you nervous?" I asked Lincoln.

"Nope."

Lincoln was headed off to basic training. He'd decided that joining the Marines was a better deal than trade school around here. He'd always been big and quiet, and I didn't expect a different answer, but deep down, I think he was most nervous about leaving his family behind in Chikalu for the first time.

As a song ebbed from the speakers, Colin pulled his acoustic guitar across his lap and started playing along. "With you two idiots gone, I guess I'm leaving too."

Colin slayed with the ladies, and since learning to play the guitar, he had been determined to make it in music. He was a rock star in the making, and with his crooked smile, I was sure he'd do it too.

"Nashville?" I asked.

"Nah. I think I'm going to try Texas. There's a good scene there, and I think I've got a shot."

"Hell yeah, you do," Linc said.

We clinked our glasses as a silence settled over us. Nerves were simmering just under the surface, but none of us were willing to admit that we were all scared shit-less. So instead, we sat around bullshitting and smoked cigars that Colin brought with him. We laughed until dawn, and then the red sunrise peeked over the horizon. When it was time to leave, I hugged them both and tried not to cry.

~

MY HEAD HURT like hell the next morning, but I had one thing left to do before I left for State. After prom, I'd kicked myself so many times. I should have grown the balls to ask Maggie to the dance, but every time I had the chance, I froze. By the time I mustered the courage to do it, David had already asked her.

He was loud, a show-off, and he liked to run his mouth. I knew Maggie forward and back and couldn't see them together. I also fucking hated how he looked at her—like he was about to devour her anytime she walked in the room. For a few weeks after prom, they were together, and David was the jealous type, which meant my time with Maggie was pretty much over. She spent her days after work with him, and I saw her less and less.

But word got around that they'd called it quits, and I wasn't about to make the same mistake twice. I was determined to tell her the truth—tell her that I thought I was in love with her and that I wanted to be her boyfriend. Maggie had earned a scholarship, and we were both going to State. It was finally going to be perfect.

Earlier I'd texted Maggie, and she'd agreed to hang out. When I pulled my truck up to the front of her home, a sense of unease wrapped around the base of my skull at seeing her. Her eyes were downcast, and she looked kind of pale.

Maybe she's still upset about the breakup. Fuck.

I wanted to be able to tell Maggie that David didn't matter. I would be a better man, do anything to make her happy.

"Hey, Margie!" I called out the open window and grinned at her like a fool.

She offered a small smile, and even though she looked tired as hell, she was radiant.

"You're dumb." She offered a quiet laugh, as she always did when I called her stupid nicknames. Maggie climbed in my truck, and the cab filled with the floral smell of her perfume. I hoped it would linger awhile after she left so I could smell it again once she was gone.

"I want to take you somewhere."

Her eyes met mine, but they were different somehow. I swallowed hard and stared ahead as I pulled the truck onto the road and headed toward the high school. I parked out by the football field, where I knew no one would see my truck and we could be alone. The entire ride, Maggie was quiet, and I wanted to know exactly what she was thinking. She seemed a little moody and distant, but I'm sure that was because she was also thinking about leaving for school. When I parked, she raised her eyebrows at me.

"Do you trust me?"

Her eyes got a little watery. "Of course." She smiled, but it didn't reach her eyes, and for a second I almost told her we should forget it and I'd take her for ice cream or something. Instead, I steeled my nerves and forged ahead with my plan.

"It's locked," she whispered.

I winked and pulled back the part of the chain-link I knew was busted. She finally—finally—smiled a real smile and ducked under my arm to hug my waist.

"Go on. Go," I urged.

Maggie slipped through, and I looked around once before putting the fence back in place. We found a spot high in the empty stands and looked out over the football field. Every time the team and I took the field, I looked up in the stands to find her. She probably didn't know that, either, but I could tell her. Every game she smiled, jumped up and down and cheered, waving wildly at me, and it was the fuel I used to play my fucking heart out.

I scrubbed my sweaty palms against the thighs of my jeans. My chest felt tight, as though my heart was shifting around, and my pulse was skittering. I shifted my body to look at her. She was painfully beautiful—her brown hair falling in soft sheets against her pale skin. She hated the little mole that was on her jaw, just under her ear, but all I could think about was kissing that very spot.

I rested my hand on hers. Over the years I had touched Maggie a thousand times, but never like this.

Soft. Intimate.

"Mag, I . . ." I cleared my throat. "There's something I want to talk to you about." My pulse hammered, blood surging through my veins.

"I'm not going to State," she blurted.

My brain sputtered and paused.

What the fuck?

"Uh . . . ," I managed.

"Cole," she started. I loved that she always called me Cole, even though everyone else called me Deck or Decker, but there was wariness tightening her voice. I searched Maggie's eyes as they filled with tears, clinging to her long, dark lashes. As one spilled over, my world shattered.

"I'm pregnant."

Two words and my stomach dropped; the earth fell away.

"David?" I worked my jaw, recalling how he and I had nearly come to blows last month when I'd overheard him talking about *popping Maggie's cherry*. It had taken both Colin and Linc to keep me from knocking his fucking teeth out.

Her face twisted with hurt. "Of course it was David. I'm not a whore."

"No, I didn't—" I scrubbed my hands across my face.

You're fucking this up, dude.

The future I'd built in my mind—the one where Maggie

and I went off to college together and started a life, where I took care of her and she would never have to live in a trailer park again—broke apart. My mind splintered in a thousand directions. I was angry—at her, at him, at myself. Hurt and wounded pride bubbled to the surface.

"Didn't he wear a condom? Jesus, Maggie."

"It was prom, and I had too much to drink. I . . . I don't remember." Shame washed across her face, and it was too painful to look at her.

Stay. Stay with her and help her. You don't need to go away to school, and you can be here for her. You can still be together.

I almost said it too. I almost poured my heart out and told her that even though she was seventeen and I was eighteen and the baby wasn't even mine, I didn't care. I would stay and help her, and we could figure it out. I could get a job, and maybe eventually we could get an apartment or something. I didn't have the answers, and I didn't know the details, but I knew I loved her and that I would do whatever it takes to protect her.

The unanswered questions between us hung heavily in the air, neither of us willing or able to move.

"So what are you going to do?" I finally croaked out, still unable to look over at her.

In my peripheral I saw her lift her chin and steady her jaw. "Mama said I had *options*. But I told her that I was keeping the baby. I'll get a job and try to save money until I have the baby—" A sob racked her as the words tumbled from her trembling lips.

"Fuck." I released a whoosh of breath. "Listen, I'm sorry I got angry. I'm still trying to wrap my mind around it." I looked down at her flat belly, still not believing that she was growing an actual human in there. She wrapped her arms around her midsection, and I looked away.

"It's fine. I just needed to tell you before you left."

"Look, maybe I don't need to go. I can go to the community college if Dad still insists I get a degree."

"What?" Her brows crinkled, and her eyes searched my face. "Cole."

I took her hand again, but she pulled it from my grasp. "No, Cole. I didn't tell you this so that you could stay or rescue me or anything like that. I just . . . needed you to hear it from me before you left."

She doesn't want you. She doesn't want you to stay.

I steeled myself against her words. The hope that bloomed in my chest withered and decayed. I had misread all the signs. Maggie had never seen me as anything other than a friend, and we'd never be anything more. Especially now that she would be having a baby.

"I could stay—" I started again, refusing to believe that there wasn't something more between us.

"No." Maggie stood and started to place a hand on my shoulder, but stopped herself. "Goodbye, Cole."

I watched her rush down the stadium stairs, never looking back. I should have rushed after her. Demanded to talk through it a little more so we could figure it out. I wasn't ready to let her go. Fuck State. I didn't need it—didn't want it. I wanted *her*.

But I didn't go after her.

I sat in the stadium like a fool, staring out onto the field for over an hour. I don't even know how she got home, and I don't remember the drive back to my house. I felt like a zombie the rest of the night, replaying all the things I should have said to her. But none of that mattered. Maggie didn't see the same future I did.

The idea that I could manage to stay *just friends* with Maggie was ridiculous, and yet I knew I'd willingly do it. I would have spent every day being tortured by the fact that she wasn't mine. But she said no, and that was where it ended for me.

The next morning, I loaded up my truck for State and drove away.

TWENTY-FOUR

MAGGIE

Now

"You're being weird today," Honey said as she popped a french fry into her mouth.

"I am not." I threw a fry, landing it directly in the little red basket in front of her.

"Is it something with Deck?" A flutter erupted in my belly, thinking of how steamy things had gotten between us earlier.

"I don't know." I pushed my basket away. "Things are good, I think. But sometimes I wonder . . . are we moving too fast?"

"Maggie, I wouldn't call a relationship with someone you've known your entire life *fast*."

"That's the thing," I started. "How are we going to make this work? We have so much history. So much time in between when we were best friends to now. I spent more than a decade telling myself that I hate him for being moody and irrational and kind of a prick."

"To you he kind of was," she admitted.

"Now I'm second-guessing everything. Is he really that person? Was I wrong this whole time?"

"I think he takes the small-town cop thing a little too seriously, but he's always loyal to a fault."

I nodded and peeked at her through my lashes. "I heard a rumor once that he tried to stay home from State, but his father wouldn't let him." Honey's eyes grew wider and I pressed on. "I had no idea if my being pregnant was the reason, but I don't know." I shrugged against the invisible weight that pressed across my shoulders. "At the time it kind of felt like it. I couldn't stand the thought of him throwing everything away, pissing the sheriff off. Plus, the rumors around here were incessant. I knew going to my aunt's ranch was the best decision. For both of us."

Honey covered my hand with hers. "You were left with impossible choices. I know as well as anyone that you can't look behind you. Only forward. I know you two will figure this all out."

My lips thinned and I nodded. "I'm trying to make the right choices. Not just for me, but for Lottie too." Honey's hand squeezed mine in solidarity. "I know the bone-deep ache of growing up without a dad," I continued. "I just *does something* to a little girl. What if I bring Cole into our lives and we can't make it work? I can't imagine doing that to her." My sigh came out more like an aggravated grunt as I blew a stray strand of hair from my face. "Sometimes I just wish I could actually hate him."

Honey clicked her tongue. "You're too good to truly hate anyone."

"It was so much simpler when he irritated the shit out of me. Did I ever tell you about the time at Mr. Richardson's grocery store? He was taking up an entire aisle with all his beefiness." A smile cracked at the corner of my mouth at the memory of how good he looked. "I tried to move my cart past his, and instead of getting out of the way, he just stared at me as I fumbled to move my cart around his. It was infuriating."

"Did you get him back?" A visible thrill ran through her, and she grinned.

"I started giving out his phone number if anyone asked for mine—guys at the bar, online sign-ups, rewards cards. For months."

Honey laughed. "That must have driven him batshit crazy."

"It was so worth it." I grinned back, already feeling my tension dissolve. There was just something about confiding in Honey that helped ease my mind. "There was always something slightly satisfying in knowing he couldn't forget about me. That we still had some sort of connection . . ."

"Maybe this is just the new-and-improved version of your relationship," she said. "I think you at least owe it to yourself to try to find out. Give him a real chance. What's the worst that could happen?"

I stared at her. "He shatters my heart into a thousand pieces? Lottie gets her hopes up that she'll have a father figure around and it turns to dust? I do have more than just my heart to think about."

"You're the most levelheaded person I know. You make good choices, and if Deck is one of them, trust that. Go with your gut . . . and maybe also your pussy."

I laugh-snorted into my Diet Coke, feeling the fizz burn through my nose as my eyes watered. "Oh my god, you will not believe what happened just before you came into the shop . . ."

After sending Lottie off with her best friend's parents, I hurried through the house to straighten and tidy everything up. I fully planned on inviting Cole back to my house after our date—a house that we'd have all to ourselves. Some strategically placed candles, some fresh flowers and greenery, and it would be perfect.

The floral delivery for the small funeral at the church took a bit longer than I'd anticipated. Bob Stadler was an elderly rancher everyone hated. Truly. He was gruff and often offensive. Rough around the edges but lacking the wisdom and charm of, say, old man Bailey, our other resident grump. Once the floral sprays were arranged, my heart sank to see only a handful of Chikalu residents in attendance. I stayed through the opening service, paid my respects, and hurried home.

Once there, I cranked up some new country music and sang my heart out as I cleaned. By the time the house was organized and I was dressed and ready for our date, my blood was tingling, my pulse in a frenzy. I was as hopeful and excited as any teenage girl could feel. Steadying my breath, I reminded myself that I was a grown woman. Sure, Cole had just done something to liquefy my insides, but there was no need to swoon.

As soon as the doorbell rang and I pulled the door open, my eyes ate up the length of his legs, across his chest and neck, and stopped at the smile that tilted on his chiseled face. He looked relaxed, happy.

I did it.

I swooned.

"You're staring, doll." His smile melted into a cocky smirk.

Blinking at him like a cow looking at a new gate, I had to shake my head to snap back to reality.

"Hi!" I said, an octave too loud. I gently cleared my throat. "Sorry. Hi. Come in. I just have to grab a few things."

I stepped backward through the doorway, and as Cole advanced, his arms wound around my waist and pulled me closer to him. His mouth hovered just a whisper from my own.

"I missed you," he said.

I loved the way his voice grew thick and sultry when I was in his arms. I tipped my chin, just enough to close the distance between us. He kissed me lazy and slow and deep. I savored every taste, and when his tongue delved deeper, my hips bucked toward him instinctively.

I tracked my hand up his neck and scalp and laced my fingers into his hair. The moan that vibrated from his throat urged me on. I lifted my leg to feel the pressure of his thickening length exactly where I ached for it. Cole's hand gripped my thigh and squeezed.

I reluctantly broke the kiss. If we didn't stop now, we'd never leave my house. "Mmm. Remind me to let you miss me more often," I teased.

"Don't you dare." His eyes flared, and it sent a throb straight to my core. I had no idea why I loved when he was so demanding, but it seriously worked for me.

I gathered my coat, hat, and gloves. I eyed Cole standing in my entryway, wearing jeans and a black Henley that stretched across his chest. "Did you bring the things I said you needed?"

"It's all in the truck, but I don't know why I would need all my snow shit."

I leaned my body into his and whispered, "That's the surprise." As I did, I reached my hand into the front pocket of his jeans and dragged my thumb against his hard length as I grabbed his keys. "Let's go!"

Cole groaned and adjusted himself. A swell of pride laced with desire twisted in my chest as I stomped into my boots and headed toward his truck.

"I'm driving. Get in!" I called as I rounded the garage toward my own truck, Peppermint. "I need to get something, but no peeking!"

Cole just shook his head and crammed himself into the passenger seat of his truck. I gathered everything we needed, and I couldn't help the giddy yelp that escaped me as I climbed into the driver's seat. He was so tall my legs barely reached the pedals.

"I have to be annoying and move your seat and mirrors. Are you gonna cry about that?" I narrowed my eyes at him.

"I'll live."

I smiled to myself again, made the adjustments, and eased out of the driveway and onto the highway. After a short drive, just out of town, I pulled the truck into a parking space on the side of the road.

"This is the Devil's Flume."

I bounced in my seat and clasped my hands together. "Yup."

The Devil's Flume was a source of legend around Chikalu Falls. In the summers, people all over the county would flock to the stairway and climb the 293 stairs as a grueling workout. Every year, the Chikalu Falls Fire Department teamed up with the police to raise money by having the cops and firefighters do laps on the stairs. Shirtless, of course. It always drew a crowd, though I could never tear my eyes off one particularly yummy officer.

Next to the stairway was a one-hundred-foot bluff. In the winters, it was reserved for only the bravest, or stupidest, to go sledding. It was dangerous and reckless and freaking awesome. It wasn't crowded save for a small group of boys taking turns shoving each other down the hill and laughing.

"Are you ready?"

Cole looked at me and shook his head before closing his eyes. He sighed, and I knew I'd won. His deep sense of responsibility sucked all the fun out of his life. He needed to let go. Laugh a little. Be a little stupid.

As he tugged on his snow pants, parka, hat, and gloves, I pulled the large toboggan sled from the bed of the truck. Snow crunched under Cole's boots, and he helped me haul the sled to the edge of the bluff.

"You do realize once we go down, we have to walk all the way back up, right?"

"Uh-huh." I grinned.

I nestled the sled into the snow, rocking it back and forth to be sure it was smooth. I gingerly stepped onto the sled and inched toward the front, leaving room for Cole to nestle his legs around me. We barely fit, but I was tucked between his arms and legs. I scooted my bottom, inching us forward as he held on to the rope.

"Sometimes you have to let someone else be in control."

He stared at me, unbelieving. "You're going to break your neck."

"Of course not." I shook my head and fastened my hair into a ponytail. "You might break yours, but I'll be fine. I have you to cushion the fall."

He barked out a laugh and adjusted my hips so that I was tucked tightly against him.

"All right, Mayhem. Let's go!"

The air whooshed out of my lungs as the winter wind whipped against my face. Together we weighed significantly more than Lottie and I, so the speed itself had my stomach bottoming out. Tears sprang from my eyes as the trees blurred past. Years ago, the county had removed the pathway trees so it was a straight shot down the run. Within seconds, we were coasting to a stop.

My breath was hard and fast. My pulse was skittering out of control. Behind me, Cole's laughter filled the air. It was rumbling and warm, and I wanted to crawl inside it. I plopped myself to the side, trying to catch my breath.

Cole lay beside me as snowflakes drifted across the bluff. I barrel-rolled away from him and spread my arms and legs wide. Up and down I moved my limbs until I made a perfect snow angel. I had grunted to haul myself up—it was no easy task in the layers upon layers of PrimaLoft snow gear—when a snowball smacked me right in the chest.

"Dick!" I yelled and brushed the snow from my front. Then I scooped up the biggest snowball I could manage and launched it at Cole's face. I missed, and instead, the tightly packed snow hit a high school–age kid right in the back.

"Dude!" The kid turned and looked at me with anger. I put both hands up and did my best to bite back the giggles that threatened to erupt from my chest.

Cole stepped in front of me. "All right, son. It was an accident." Recognition floated over the kid's face as he looked Cole up and down. Cole bent down slowly and scooped snow into his gloves. "But this isn't."

Cole launched a second snowball at the kid, and all-out pandemonium erupted. The group of high school boys whooped and hollered as they gathered and threw snowballs.

A battle cry pierced the icy air: "Get Officer Deck!"

"I will protect my lady!" Cole hollered as he charged the group. I dove for cover behind a pile of snow. Stockpiling snowballs, I did my best to defend my position. Cole's police training kicked into overdrive when he vaulted a snowbank, hammering two kids with snow midair.

We laughed and screamed and feigned death. When the ruckus settled, I was out of breath, half-freezing, and completely, idiotically, head over heels in love.

TWENTY-FIVE
DECK

Now

The six-mile drive back to Maggie's house felt like a thousand. From the driver's seat, I couldn't help but look over at her every few seconds. Her cheeks were flushed from the cold, and her hair was hanging in damp waves. She rubbed her hands together and held them in front of the hot air pumping out of the vents. Another sideways glance in her direction had the flush in her cheeks deepening.

"What?" she asked.

I stared down the road and tried not to smile. "Not a thing."

Being with Maggie felt as easy as breathing. In the short time we'd been spending together, I couldn't fathom how I'd managed to stay away from her for so long.

We bounced down her driveway, and I was consumed with thoughts of *what if*.

What if we made a home together?

What if we didn't have to go through life alone?

What if I could prove to her I was worth the wait?

The devil on my shoulder whispered rotted, oily words

of skepticism, and I steeled my gaze just above the steering wheel as we stopped.

"Hey," Maggie spoke softly, her hand finding my thigh. "Come back to me."

I looked at her, lost in the depths of anger and self-hatred. Her large round eyes flitted between mine. She was clearly confused, lost by my ping-ponging moods.

Don't ruin this for her.

Planting on a smile I hoped reached my eyes, I said, "I'm here. Let's get warmed up."

Inside Maggie's house, the tension melted from between my shoulders. Enveloped by the warmth and comfort food wafting in the air, my stomach growled.

"I'm glad you're hungry." She giggled, patting my abdomen. "I've got beef stew ready to go for us. If that's okay?"

"Okay? It smells amazing. Thanks, doll." I gathered the wet, dripping outerwear in my arms. "Mudroom?"

"Just off the kitchen, to the left."

When I tracked back to the kitchen, Maggie had put on a radio, and the soft beat of country music hummed from the small speaker. Her back was to me, and I allowed myself to appreciate her every curve. Closing the distance between us, I pressed my frame into her back and swiped the sheet of her hair off her neck and over her shoulder. I laid a soft kiss on her skin, and a ripple of pleasure rolled through her.

Recognizing the popular song, I turned Maggie to face me. Starting slow, I swayed left and right, humming the melody. Her body reacted to me, leaning closer and melting into mine. Gaining confidence, I rolled my hips and moved into a subtle two-step. With a gentle twirl and dip, we were lost in the moment, dancing barefoot in the dim lighting of her kitchen.

I ended the song with a kiss, leaving her breathless.

"I wished for this," she said as I brushed a strand of hair out of her eyes. "I always thought dancing in the kitchen was the most romantic part of all those movies Mama would watch."

Maggie had a way of stealing the words from my mouth. I dropped my mouth to hers, pouring my very soul into that kiss. Like a spark, the air crackled with energy between us. No longer hungry and cold, I was inundated with thoughts of consuming only her.

Her weight shifted forward, urging me to step backward. I stayed rooted to the ground, holding on to the only thread of control I could grasp. My hands found her hips, and I lifted her to the uncluttered countertop.

"Nice try, Magellan," I teased. My hands tangled in the silken strands of her hair as I tipped her head back, exposing the lean line of her throat. "But when you're with me, like this, I'm in control." My mouth found the pulse point in her neck and sucked. "Do you understand?"

"Oh . . ."

I paused my assault and looked at her, waiting for her answer.

"Yes, sir."

My smile grew and my heart pinged. "That's my girl."

Maggie's eager response to my words had every part of me wanting to be buried deep inside her. When she raked her nails down my chest, a breath hissed across my teeth. She tugged at my shirt, lifting it over my head and tossing it on the floor.

"You are so fucking hot." Delight laced in her voice, and pride swelled in my chest as Maggie appreciated my bare skin under her hands. I wanted her. Craved her in every way. I squeezed her ass one more time before hauling her up and over my shoulder. With a playful thwack on her ass, I stomped toward her bedroom.

She squealed with delight and continued to run her hands up and down my back. "Left!" she hollered when I almost went into the wrong bedroom. I pivoted, and once we were inside her bedroom, I tossed her on the bed. Immediately, I covered her body with mine. My kisses were hungry, and my hands itched to palm every last inch of her. We pulled and tore at clothing. Desperation hung in the air.

"I need to feel you. Feel this." She stroked my rock-hard cock through my boxer briefs. With one hand, I found the edge of her panties at her hip and yanked them down her thighs. With the pad of one finger, I teased her slit, caressing her wetness in lazy circles.

I fisted my cock and squeezed the base. I wanted nothing more than to rail her, hard and fast, but Maggie deserved more. She deserved to be taken care of, and I'd be damned if I let my own lust-fueled haze trump that. Hitching an eyebrow, I brought my finger to my mouth and sucked.

A moan tore from my chest. "You taste so fucking good, Mag."

Shock melted into yearning as Maggie's hip bucked forward, craving any kind of friction her greedy little clit could find. She was hot and swollen and ready for me. I trailed wet, open-mouthed kisses down her body. Maggie's knees moved up, spreading herself wide, ready for me. I dove in, gently at first, licking and tasting every drop of her desire. She was soft and warm on my tongue.

My body raged and ached to come. I steadied my breathing and focused on listening to the cues Maggie was giving me. With every hitch of her breath, sigh, and tilt of her hips, I could devour her in exactly the way she needed.

When I reached a hand up to palm her breast, I could feel the tight tip of her nipple, and I gently pinched, rolling and teasing. She tightened, on the brink of unraveling.

"I want to feel you come around my cock. Is that okay, baby?" I needed to be surrounded by her when she pulsed through her orgasm.

"Cole. I'm close."

I continued to stroke and tease, waiting for my answer.

"Yes."

The word was barely past her lips, and I slipped inside her, long and deep and hard. Taking Maggie bare, feeling her silk wrap around the length of my cock, was an unbearable pleasure. I moved my hips to feel my entire length slip in and out of her folds. Capturing her lips, I delved into her mouth as I continued to fuck her over and over.

"I wish I could control myself when I'm with you." My breath was ragged as I leaned my forehead against hers.

Maggie clung to me, her nails raking across my shoulder blades, around my shoulders and down my chest. The sharp bite of her nails only heightened my pleasure. I was charging headfirst into my own release as pressure built at the base of my spine.

"Where do you want me to come? In you or on you?" I gritted through my teeth.

"Oh, Jesus, Cole . . ."

"Say it," I demanded.

Maggie exploded around me, hot, slow ripples down my cock as her body went rigid. The deep, rolling pleasure forced my own orgasm to follow just behind her, and I slipped my cock from her to paint her smooth belly. Long, hot ribbons crisscrossed against her abdomen, claiming her as mine. When the roaring waves of my orgasm stilled, my eyes met hers.

"I, uh . . ." I cleared my throat, and shame swept over me. "I'm sorry. I should have made sure that was okay."

Humor danced across her eyes, crinkling them in the corners, and a smile lit up her face. She brushed her hand back through her hair and laughed—a deep, hearty laugh that wrapped its fist around my heart. "Are you kidding me? That wasn't even something I knew I was into, but damn. That was hot."

Relief washed over me. When Maggie shifted to get up, I placed a gentle hand on her shoulder. "Stop. Let me."

I ate up the distance between the bed and the bathroom with quick strides. I had to rummage through only two drawers before finding a washcloth, and I let warm water run out of the tap. I stared at myself in the mirror.

You are such a piece of shit.

I filled my hands with water and scrubbed my wet hands over my face. Angry red lines tracked down my chest —Maggie's nails. She was wild, adventurous.

More than you fucking deserve.

I braced myself against the bathroom counter and allowed one steadying breath before I tentatively walked back to Maggie. She should be angry, horrified that I'd taken us both to the brink without making sure that my actions were something she was comfortable with. In the moment, she seemed really into it, but in my postrelease clarity, nerves chittered under my skin.

As I walked in, Maggie's arm dragged up the sheets in one long, languid movement, welcoming me to the bed. "Hey, gorgeous."

"Gorgeous?" A smile tugged at the corners of my mouth.

"Definitely." Her toes pointed, and she stretched as I took my time wiping and cleaning her belly and between her legs. I was careful to smooth and kiss after every swipe of the warm cloth. "Mmm," she moaned. "I've never been taken care of like this. It feels so . . . decadent."

I tossed the rag in the hamper and curled myself around her. Maggie turned toward me, her fingertips tracing the red lines across my chest. Her eyes went wide, pupils dilated, as she looked at me. "I'm sorry, Cole. I didn't mean to hurt you."

"You can't hurt me, doll." My voice was rocky, huskier than normal. I kissed her hair and bundled her closer to me.

It was a lie. The dirtiest one I could tell. Because the truth was, Maggie was the only human on the planet who could do more than hurt me. She could tear my heart out of my chest with her bare hands, and I'd willingly come back for more. Maggie lived in my bones, soaking down deeper every moment, with every touch.

Maggie's breathing grew soft as her fingers brushed through my hair. "Do you ever think about what would have happened if we'd gotten together in high school?"

"No." I owed her too much to lie. "I don't let myself."

Her silence was oppressive. I didn't have the words to help her understand, but I also couldn't have her misconstrue my meaning. "I learned to redefine what something was so I wouldn't go crazy not having it."

"We've really been assholes about this, haven't we?" Tears thickened her voice, and I felt the bridge of my own nose burn. I blinked hard, steeling myself against the emotions tugging on my chest.

I let out a sigh. "Somewhere along the way, it got out of hand. I made the choice to push you away." I framed her face in my hands and tracked my thumb over her cheekbone. "I won't do it again."

~

In the morning, the intensity of the night before lifted, but only fractionally. With a lazy start to the day, I awoke with Maggie's tongue tracing the lines of my abs, sinking lower as I moaned in appreciation. We made love—over and over until we both were starving, laughing, and delirious.

I moved clumsily in her kitchen, not sure where anything was tucked away. Maggie smiled over her coffee cup as I fumbled through her cabinets.

"I can help you, you know."

I pinned her with a glare, and she laughed, shaking her head into her coffee.

"I like taking care of you," I said at last.

Maggie's eyes stayed focused on the countertop. "That's new for me. It still feels a little strange."

I rounded the island to plant a kiss on the top of her head. "You'll get used to it."

I gave her my best smirk and watched as a pink flush started at her throat and eased its way to her cheeks. Resigned to not being able to help, Maggie plopped onto a stool, pulled a stack of mail in front of her, and began sorting it. When she paused on a simple white envelope, my chest stung as though scorched with a branding iron.

She opened it and fingered through the cash. After a soft, sad sigh, she must have felt my gaze on her because her head popped up and caught me staring. The red in her cheeks deepened as though she'd been caught doing something wrong, or as though she were embarrassed.

"I get these every once in a while."

I nodded once but couldn't find my voice.

"I don't even remember when they started coming," she continued. "I think they're from David's family. The only way they ever show they remember her, let alone care." Her voice was laced with venom.

I knew I had to tell her the truth. I wanted to be the kind of man who deserved to breathe the same air as Maggie O'Brien.

"April eighth, just after you came back from living with your aunt," I said, my eyes hesitant to meet hers.

"What?" Her nose crinkled in confusion.

"That's when you started getting them."

"What? Wait. How did you . . . ?" Realization dawned on her as her doe eyes went wide.

My stance was strong, but I couldn't hold her gaze for longer than a heartbeat. I could hear her soft breathing and the crackle of the bacon on the stove.

"Cole, all this time? It was you?"

I nodded once.

"But"—she smoothed her hands across the envelope—"I don't understand."

Guilt.

"I cared about you and wanted to make sure you and Lottie were taken care of."

Also, the guilt.

"That wasn't your responsibility . . . and you *despised* me."

"I never hated you. Quite the opposite, actually." I dragged a hand through my hair and flipped off the burner —the bacon was already ruined. "I didn't know how to handle my feelings for you, but I also couldn't *not* help you two if I could."

Oh yeah. I am also the reason Lottie has no father and you had to raise her alone.

"Cole, I'm not sure what to say. All those times we picked at each other . . . I never knew there was more to it."

"When you live with a secret as long as I have, you'd be amazed at what you can hide." I pushed off the counter. "If you need time to process all this, I can go—"

"What? No."

I paused to finally look at her. Tears pooled in her eyes as she furiously swiped at them. "I don't want you to go. Come here."

I stepped close to her, tucking my hips between her knees. Maggie's hands brushed the hair at my temples before sliding around to my neck.

"I'm paying you back. Every dollar." Maggie's sweet hazel eyes bored into mine.

The sheer ridiculousness of it nearly had laughter bubbling out of me until I realized she was serious. "Magpie, no. It was a gift. I wanted to do it."

"It's too much." She shook her head, and something akin to sadness crept into her eyes. I couldn't stand it.

"Fine, then, I found it on the side of the road." I needed us back on solid footing, to hear happiness laced in her voice.

Her gaze flicked up as she shot a dull look in my direction.

I smiled my cheesiest smile at her. "Buried treasure? Mysterious drug bust gone wrong? Long-lost billionaire relative?" I wiggled her in my arms, and she cracked a smile. "Look, it doesn't matter where it came from."

"You didn't need to do that, and if I'm being honest, I feel really weird about it. All this time I thought it was David's family."

The mention of his name cast a shadow in the room. I pressed my lips together and nodded.

"It's monumentally pathetic that I thought it was from them."

"Not pathetic," I said, tipping up her chin with my knuckle. "Hopeful."

She nodded and pressed a kiss to my lips. "The truth is, there were times when we *did* need the money. I was too prideful to ask for help, and it paid the bills or got Lottie something fun. You did that."

Lottie's sweet face swirled in my mind, and I had to press my tongue to the roof of my mouth to keep my emotions in check. I cleared my throat with a rough grunt. "I'm just glad it helped."

"Thank you, Cole. We're good now, though. You know I can't accept any more." Maggie's eyes searched mine, but I gave only a soft grunt in response.

"I'm serious—no more." Maggie wrapped her arms around me again, and I clung to her, gripping my forearms around her back.

Maggie sighed. "You're a good man, Cole Decker."

The moment was too good, too pure. I didn't have the heart to tell her. I would, just not today. If she knew the truth about David, she could leave, and I would turn to dust.

TWENTY-SIX

DECK

Four Years Ago

Sparks and embers rose around the plumes of smoke as I thumped another log onto the fire.

"Careful with that or we'll have to call the fire department over, and I can't get into a fight tonight." Lincoln watched me toss another log on the fire.

"Shit." I laughed and stretched my arms wide. "You're in with the law, son!" Lincoln just shook his head and relaxed a bit more in his chair.

Mission accomplished.

Chikalu cops and firefighters had a friendly, half-hearted hate toward each other. Each division thought they were the coolest, baddest motherfuckers in town. Truth was, outside of a few tussles here and there, we left each other alone. Ever since my dad retired, I was the only Decker man on patrol, and the familial expectation to hold that position with honor was heavy. Dad was the best of the best, and there were many days when those shoes felt impossible to fill.

I dug a fresh beer out of the cooler and tossed it to

Lincoln. He caught it and popped the top, and I got a good look at him while he drank. Finn was worried about Lincoln, and if I was being honest, so was I. It had been two years since he'd gotten back from Afghanistan, but Lincoln was a changed man. Though he'd always been intense and a little quieter than most, he was holing up out there on old man Bailey's property. We'd go weeks without seeing him, and that was hard to do in a small town, even for him.

Out on the property where Lincoln rented a cottage, I glanced at the copse of trees in the distance and rubbed under my breastbone, where a hitch always formed when I allowed myself to think about that night with Maggie. All I'd had to do was open my fucking mouth and tell her how I felt. I was a chickenshit—too afraid she didn't feel the same way. Pushing away the memory, I reached in my bag, needing something stronger.

"What's up, fellas?" Finn stood at the open door of his truck and banged a hand on the roof. His enthusiasm for life radiated from every pore and was acknowledged only by a grunt from Linc. Colin pulled his truck behind Finn's and ambled out with his acoustic guitar strapped across his back. They dumped more beer into the cooler, then pulled the old folding chairs closer to the fire.

I shook their hands, and Colin clamped a hand on my shoulder before doing the same to Lincoln and settling into a chair. Finn pulled me into a hug and lifted my feet off the ground.

"I never see you anymore, man!"

He set me down, and I playfully pushed him away. "Dad retired and I got thrown on second shift. How's that for a fucking promotion?"

"Shit," Colin piped in. "Sooner or later you'll be running the place. This is just the next step." He tipped his bottle toward me. Colin always had a way of seeing the good in other people. Something I needed to learn how to do.

I needed to be better and not let my demons ride shotgun. Hell, half the time, it felt like they were behind the fucking wheel.

We moved into a steady rhythm of drinking and bullshitting. Colin plucked at his guitar and sang a bluesy rendition of "Freebird." Finn sang along—loud and totally off-key —while Lincoln stared into the flames.

As one song bled into another, the conversation was easy. Natural.

"Lot of changes at the bar, brother," Finn said around a pull of his beer.

Colin nodded. "I'm trying. Trying for it not to be such a shithole."

After his brother had died, Colin left behind his career as a musician and bought the run-down townie bar. He'd busted his ass to clean it up, and his connections in music helped bring in some talented bands. The Dirty Pigeon was slowly becoming a place people actually chose to eat, drink, and dance on a Friday and Saturday night.

My new shift schedule meant that sometimes after work I could head over and shut the place down. By the time I rolled in, it was well past midnight. Mostly I'd find a space near the bar where Colin and I could shoot the shit. Rare occasions that Maggie got a night away from being a single mother, she would be out with her friends, and I worked hard to ignore the way men stared at her ass or clumsily twirled her around the dance floor. On the bad nights, I nursed a beer and left. On the worst ones, I got a hair up my ass and chose someone who could pass as her in the dark and filled a need.

I felt a poke under my ribs just thinking about it, but I figured a second-rate Maggie was better than no Maggie at all. At least that was what I told myself.

Finn laughed as Colin told him a story from his time on the road, and I couldn't help but look around at my closest friends in the world. Finn's eyes were bright and playful while Colin told an animated story. Even Lincoln looked comfortable, at ease.

My chest pinched with a strange sensation. Gratitude, I assumed. I was grateful that so long ago we'd formed a bond that stayed steady through time and distance, personal demons and petty disagreements. It was us. The four of us living our lives and doing our best not to fuck it up too badly.

Around that campfire, our bond felt unshakable.

"You gotta come out on Saturday, Linc," Colin started. "The Kyle Pritchard Band is playing a sold-out show. Besides, we need to get you laid."

"Shit, man." Lincoln laughed quietly into his beer. It would be a feat to get Lincoln into the bar on a crowded weekend night. He was struggling with his PTSD, and we all felt a little helpless, but we never gave up on him. "I'll leave the ladies to Finn."

We laughed. Finn never had trouble meeting women or making friends. The flicker of a strange expression crossed Finn's face, but my eyelids were starting to get heavy, and my mouth felt a little numb.

I was definitely getting fucked-up tonight.

When Finn abruptly got up and walked into the darkness toward the creek, the conversation died.

"Well, fuck," Colin said, grunting as he stood from his chair. He steadied himself on his feet. "I gotta take a piss too. I'll make sure he doesn't get lost."

I looked over at Lincoln, whose attention was lost in the fire again.

"You ever make it back to your uncle's place? Where you bagged that monster elk?"

He shook his head. Lincoln used to live for hunting, but even that had lost its appeal since he'd gotten back from Afghanistan. He and Finn were running a fishing guide service, but it was really Finn doing the guided tours while Lincoln took care of the business end. It allowed them to make money—Finn was definitely the more personable of the two—while Lincoln could hide away in the office.

My head buzzed, and the alcohol made my limbs slack. Images of Maggie and shitty choices and everything else I'd managed to fuck up in my life swirled in my gut.

"Man," I whispered, "sometimes I think I should have joined you."

Lincoln turned toward me. "Joined me?"

"Yeah, man. Enlisted." I shrugged.

"Maybe," he said. "You'd've made a good Marine. But you had people here that needed you."

I was sure he meant my parents, but I couldn't help but think of my Maggie.

Stop that shit. She isn't your anything.

"You know one of the worst things?" He took a deep glug of cheap whiskey and passed the bottle to me. "We all went over thinking we were doing *good*."

The alcohol burned down my throat. "You did a lot of good. You did what most can't."

He nodded. "I know it. I know it's true but . . . sometimes I don't know if that was enough."

Lincoln opening up was a rarity, so I kept my mouth shut and looked into the flames.

"Some days it felt like the more we helped, the worse it

was. Like the more we did, the worse it got for people in the end. Not every day, but some days . . . fuck. Be glad you don't have to deal with shit like that."

He scrubbed his hands over his face, and a well of tears burned at the corners of my eyes. I knew *exactly* what he was talking about.

Knowing that you tried as hard as you could but only made it worse.

I cleared my throat. A heaviness blanketed my shoulders.

"I need to tell you something." The words were out of my mouth before I could stop them. Alcohol made my tongue feel thick, and I could tell I was shitfaced, but in that moment, I couldn't hold it in any longer. I knew Lincoln had made a few deals with the devil in Afghanistan, and he was living with the fallout from that. I knew he could handle what I was about to tell him. He'd keep it and relieve me of having to carry the burden alone.

"Can you keep a secret?" The words were fucking dumb, but I was drunk. Of course he could. Instead, he just stared at me and nodded once.

I opened my mouth to tell him. Unload everything and unburden myself.

And pile your burden on him.

A wave of shame washed over me. I was so tempted to tell him everything and allow him to carry the load of the truth with me. But why? What good would that do other than weigh down his shoulders with my shit? Lincoln was a good man and a great friend—he didn't deserve that. He was dealing with his own issues and didn't need mine to deal with too.

"Listen, man, I . . . ," I said, starting to backpedal.

Just as I was about to back out of that conversation, a

shout and howl came from the creek. We both jumped from our chairs and clumsily raced toward the creek bank. We came across Colin doubled over, laughing his drunk ass off.

Finn had been taking a piss and lost his balance, pissing all over himself and falling into the shallow creek. This time of year it was less than two feet deep, so while he was soaked, he was fine. We dragged his soggy ass up to the bank, collapsing in a drunken heap.

The heaviness of my conversation with Lincoln dissipated as I watched laughter actually meet his eyes. I knew that not telling him was the right choice.

I didn't need an excuse to ease my pain. From that moment on, I never once—ever—told anyone what really happened the night David died.

TWENTY-SEVEN

MAGGIE

Now

Tiptoeing into Lottie's room in the darkness, I sank onto the edge of her bed. Her deep breaths indicated she wasn't getting up anytime soon. I peeled the sticky hairs from her face and looked at how young and innocent she seemed. Time was going too fast. I blamed myself. So many nights I wished she'd be a little older. That it would be a little easier. Recently it felt like time was spinning out of control and there wasn't anything I could do to stop it.

So I would steal those quiet moments. Take them and tuck them away and let them fill the cracks of my damaged heart. Lottie looked so much like David, which was fine by me. She was always the best parts of him anyway—vivacious and friendly, with a wicked sense of humor. He may have been absent, and he had succumbed to his own demons, but I had won. He had given me the greatest gift I never knew I needed, and I would always find a way to be thankful for that.

Deciding to let Lottie sleep a little longer, I dragged the

laundry basket from her room and headed toward the washer. I never bothered to separate darks and lights.

Who has time for that bullshit?

I pulled a hoodie from the basket, digging through the pockets to make sure another rogue lip gloss didn't ruin our clothes again. Finding nothing, I went to toss the hoodie into the tub, but something caught my eye. Stark against the black cotton fabric were tiny droplets of hot pink. I pulled the hem of the sleeve closer. My nail scratched against a smattering of paint. Nausea roiled in my stomach, and I *knew*.

The night of Cole's stakeout, I had recognized Lottie in her jeans, and seeing the paint-splattered hoodie finally confirmed it. Somehow she was involved with whoever had been tagging dicks around town. Cole was determined to find who was responsible and punish them. He was going to arrest her.

I needed to talk with her. What she'd done was wrong, and I had to get to the bottom of it. Was she just at the wrong place at the wrong time or—*shit*—was she more involved? This prank had been going on for *years*. There was no way she'd been in on it from the beginning. Lately, I'd been so wrapped up in the newness of Cole that I hadn't been paying enough attention. How could my good, sweet little girl be wrapped up in something so serious?

I knew Cole had a deeply rooted sense of honor. He wouldn't be able to let this go, and he wouldn't be able to ignore it just because it was me and just because it was Lottie. It felt like everything was crumbling around me. The shaky foundation we had just started building rotting and falling to nothingness.

It had become abundantly clear over the course of my life that I didn't deserve to have everything. This was just another way for the universe to tell me I couldn't have a man who loved me and be an attentive mother to my perfect and sweet daughter. I couldn't be a mother and a woman. I would have to choose, but in reality there never was a choice.

I would always be a mother first.

I CASUALLY AVOIDED Cole for three days, letting the hustle and bustle of Christmas serve as the perfect excuse while I tried to get my bearings. I desperately tried to find a way to have a serious conversation with Lottie without having her completely shut me out. I watched her like a hawk, driving her everywhere myself and not allowing her space to talk with her friends on the phone without me being within earshot.

I was *that* mom.

Unfortunately, I had already agreed to let Lottie attend the school lock-in, and I couldn't afford to lose the footing I'd gained with her lately. Backing out of my permission for her to go would have caused the mother of all arguments. The day after Christmas lock-in was a rite of passage in Chikalu, and having gone to many myself, I knew it was fairly well supervised.

As we waited on the porch for her ride, I gnawed at my bottom lip, gathering the resolve to be direct with her.

"Listen," I started. "I expect you to be responsible and make smart choices tonight."

Her eyes rolled up into her skull. "I know, Mom."

I set my hands on her shoulders. "I'm serious, Lottie. No getting into trouble. I know you've been . . . having a little too much fun." I pinned her with a stare.

Lottie's dark eyes went wide, and the throb of her heart-beat in her neck pulsed—she never did have a poker face.

"I found your sweatshirt in the wash. It has spray paint all over it."

"Well . . . I—"

I threw a hand up, cutting her off. "Look, I don't want to hear it. It's over. You're busted."

Lottie threw her arms around my waist. "I swear, Mama. I had no idea they were going to do that."

I squeezed her back, relief flooding through me at real-izing she had simply gotten caught up. That she wasn't some terrible teenager and I'd royally fucked her up. "You promise? I need to hear it won't happen again."

"I promise," she whispered. I gave her one last squeeze as her ride pulled into the driveway. I reminded myself I needed to trust her and kissed her hair before she trotted down the steps and headed into the darkness.

I stepped inside to grab my purse and car keys. Lottie's overnight stay in the school library also meant that I didn't have any excuses to not see Cole. I suggested a postholiday group date to Honey and Jo. My stepbrother, Hayes, owned and operated Pronghorn Brewery, just outside of town. It gave me the opportunity to see Cole and our friends but also avoid quiet, too-personal conversation with him that would have me spilling my guts.

By clearing the air with Lottie, I was confident that I could put it behind me. Lottie had simply found herself in the wrong place at the wrong time. I trusted her, and my heart swelled that she'd promised it wouldn't happen again. It was a blip on the radar—one I wouldn't have to share with the hyper-observant Officer Deck.

When I arrived at Pronghorn Brewery, pride swelled in me, as it usually did. We may have been young adults when our parents met and married, but Hayes and his brothers had accepted me into their fold as though I'd been there all along. I wished the four of them lived closer to Chikalu. The brewery was upscale, with heavy wood and iron accents. Where The Dirty Pigeon had the small-town charm of a dive bar and dance hall, Pronghorn was intentionally upscale. The entire back wall opened up like garage doors during the spring, summer, and fall months, facing a breathtaking pine forest. Firepits with cushy seating dotted the exterior. Inside, a large, double-sided fireplace roared to life, and we moved high-top tables together.

"Maggie!" Hayes called over the crowd and dropped his towel to weave through the patrons and say hello. Behind him, I spotted his younger brother Scotty, and my eyes went wide.

"Hey, you!" Delight rippled through me at seeing the twosome. "What are you doing here? Guys, you know Hayes, but this is his younger brother, Scotty."

"*Our* younger brother," Hayes corrected, and I stuck my tongue out at him.

Scotty scooped me up in a hug. His tall frame lifted my toes several inches off the ground as I laughed. "Your mom didn't tell you? I couldn't make it in time for the holiday, but I'm back."

"You're moving back to Montana?"

"Yeah, not too far from here. Tipp."

"What a coincidence!" I threw my arms around his shoulders again. "I just visited the cutest little coffee shop there with Cole."

Scotty eyed Cole before looking back at me. "Just make sure you call before you randomly drive over. I'm still getting my bearings in that town. It's a little . . . quirky." Scotty was often protective, even though I was older than him, but his words held weight. They seemed a bit like a warning, and tiny little alarm bells went off in my brain. I glanced back at Hayes, who chatted with Jo and Lincoln before sending me a wave and disappearing behind the bar.

I'll have to drag it out of him later.

Refocusing on our group, I couldn't help but smile—the first genuine smile that had spread across my face in days. Lately, I felt as though I would crack from the tension, and sitting here with our friends felt so *normal*. I wished it could always feel like this. My eyes flew to Cole, and I considered what he would think when I told him about my suspicion regarding Lottie.

Will he help me? Will his duty outweigh his feelings for me? How can I even ask him to choose?

Cole stood as stiff as an evergreen, and when I angled toward him, he took my brother's hand in his own and nodded. "I'm Deck. It's nice to meet you."

"Scotty. You too." Scotty looked between Cole and me before planting on a cheesy grin. "I like this one. You can't trust a man that can't squeeze your hand. Good handshake there."

I rolled my eyes between the two men standing with their chests puffed out.

"Law enforcement?" Cole asked Scotty.

"Government securities."

A nod and a *hmm* was the extent of Cole's response. Guys were so weird sometimes—like they were nonverbally assessing the other right out in the open. At least most women had the audacity to use their words to dig straight to a person's core.

"Will you hang with us?" I asked.

Scotty eyed Cole again and then surveyed the group. "Not tonight, Maggie. I'll let you get back to your friends.

Will you be at your mom's house next week for Sunday supper?"

"Sure will!" I hugged him again and added an extra squeeze. My heart lifted at the thought of him having a place closer to home. His presence tonight made his absence seem that much harder, and I was thrilled to see him again.

I smiled into the beer that was set in front of me.

"Your family makes you happy." Cole's warm voice trailed up my neck, and I couldn't help but lean into the warmth of his frame.

"They do. We became close once Mom married their father. I didn't have a choice—you'd think they had always wanted a sister."

Cole's voice dipped lower, barely above a whisper. "Were you avoiding me this week? Is this about the money?"

I peeked at him but shook my head. "Everything's all good. Just busy with Christmas and dinners and floral orders."

It was a small lie. I wasn't *avoiding* him, really. I just didn't trust myself to be alone with him until I figured out a way to tell him about my suspicions. I planted my lips to his, successfully ending that line of questioning.

When Cole's mouth was on me, I couldn't think a single coherent sentence. Thank god my mind went blank instead of letting dangerous words like *There's something I have to tell you* or *I may be falling in love with you* tumble out. When we parted, under the table, his hand gripped mine and squeezed three times.

"What is that?" I asked.

His devilish grin had my toes tingling. "If you can't figure it out, I'll tell you. Someday."

I playfully bumped my shoulder into his and turned to our group, who were more family than friends.

Colin glanced around the brewery, surveying the clean, elegant space. I called over the table to him. "Thanks for agreeing to hang out here, Colin."

"Traitors." He glowered and we all laughed. "Nah," he continued, "I think Hayes has done a great job with this space, and his beer is phenomenal."

Cole tipped his beer in agreement. "Aren't you doing a collab for the winter fest?"

Colin took a deep pull of his beer and nodded. "Sure am. Pronghorn is working on a special brew for it, I've got musicians lined up, the bakery and the bar are working out food. There'll also be food from all over town."

"Tables for everyone from the O'Sheas to the Khatris to the Friedmans—everyone's got a booth with food and games and music," Honey added with a smile. As one of the younger members of the Women's Club, Honey had a finger on the pulse of *everything* in town.

"I'm proud of our little town!" Jo quipped as Lincoln wrapped his arm around her, nuzzling his nose into her hair.

"Pronghorn has its place in Chikalu," Colin circled back, winking at me, "just like The Pidge."

"Different vibes, for sure." Honey smiled up at her husband. "Sometimes it's nice not to have a beer spilled on your favorite shoes," she teased.

Lincoln sprang to Colin's defense. "The Pidge has a rustic sort of charm. If hearing the best music in the county, let alone the state, means having a little beer spilled on your shoes, then so be it."

"Or wear sensible shoes!" Jo added in on a laugh, holding up her Converse-covered foot.

Honey tipped her elegant heel out and tossed her curled hair over one shoulder. "Never. Gonna. Happen."

"Okay, you two argue about heel heights," I said. "I'll go get us another round!" I swiveled on my stool to move toward the bar when, midstride, Cole caught my elbow.

"I'll go."

"I've got it," I said as I pulled my elbow from his gentle grasp. He bristled, but I pushed forward toward the bar and had another round sent to our tables.

The rest of the evening with Cole was off. Uneasy. On the surface everything looked fine, but tension hung in the air and laced through our conversations. Cole's posture was stiff, and several times the muscles in his jaw caught my attention as they flexed. It was like something was gnawing at him, and despite his efforts to turn it around, he just couldn't manage it.

Finally, on the car ride back to my house, I'd had enough. "Are you okay?"

He barely glanced in my direction. "Just tired."

I narrowed my eyes. "Yeah, no. That's not going to work for me."

"What? Me being tired?" Indignation laced his rough voice.

"No. You totally shutting down on me." When he finally looked at me, I tipped up an eyebrow. *That's right. I'm not fucking around, buddy.*

When he still couldn't look at me, realization dawned on me. "This is about something else, isn't it?

Staring at the road, he blew out a breath. "At the bar, it kind of hurt my feelings that you wouldn't let me help you."

I had a hard time recalling specifically what he was talking about. "What time at the bar?"

"You went to get drinks, and I wanted to help. You shot me down."

"Oh. Wow. Okay . . ." I thought back to that exchange, and at the time I hadn't thought anything of it. "I never meant to hurt your feelings."

"You don't have to do everything yourself." Now I understood the one-eighty in his attitude at the bar, so I just stared at him. When I didn't speak, he took a deep breath and added, "I'm sorry. I want to take care of you, but sometimes I feel like you don't let me."

I pinched the bridge of my nose. *Is this our first argument? What is happening?* I continued, "I think maybe I'm just used to doing things on my own."

"I know," he added, his jaw once again flexing and grinding with tension.

As his truck pulled up to my driveway and stopped, I paused on the door handle. I should have invited him in. We could talk about this like adults and work it out. I could share with him my concerns about Lottie and get his perspective on what to do.

I didn't do any of those things.

Instead, I thanked him for a fun evening out with our friends. I placed a gentle kiss on his lips, and when he moved to deepen it, I pulled away and kissed his cheek. I ignored the pang in my chest at the confusion that clouded his beautifully dark eyes.

And with slow, measured steps, I ran.

TWENTY-EIGHT

DECK

Now

Maggie and I were off kilter, and I *fucking hated it*. For years, I'd spent every ounce of extra energy I had ignoring the feelings I harbored for her, and now that the floodgates were open, I couldn't dam them back up.

We were finally together. Things were supposed to be perfect. Easy.

What the fuck is going on?

I also didn't understand why I'd felt so hurt when she wouldn't let me help her at the bar. It was just ordering beers, for fuck's sake. But it did. I hated that I'd fallen into a shame spiral over all the help she'd needed and never got. All the times that life taught her the only person she could rely on was herself.

I wanted to give everything to her—to support her, help her, protect her—but she didn't seem to need it. Or want it.

Women are damn confusing.

I needed to refocus on work and not the shaky ground of my fledgling relationship. Getting nowhere on the vandalism case, I called up my dad, and we were set to meet and go over the details. I could use a fresh set of eyes on it. Dad was the best—everyone knew that.

Being the son of the beloved Sheriff Decker came with certain concessions. I would always live in his shadow. If there was an unsolvable case, Dad could solve it.

Pulling up to my childhood home always gave way to a dichotomy of feelings. I had a happy childhood. I was fed and loved and provided for. I also knew exactly what rigid expectations were set for me.

I was to be an officer—like my dad and his dad before him. Only once or twice growing up had I *ever* considered something else for myself. Our blood ran blue, and that was the end of it.

Sitting in his rocker by the window, Dad even rocked with military precision. I climbed the stairs, knocked once while opening the door, and made my way to him.

I shook his hand. "Sir."

"Son." Dad set down his novel, something that looked to be about a sailor lost at sea. "Your mama's down at the Women's Club organizing something for the winter festival. She'll be disappointed she missed you."

I nodded. "I'll be sure to come around later in the week."

"You do that. So what do you have for me?"

I flipped open the manila folder containing pictures and my notes and passed it to my father before I sat.

"You mean to tell me you haven't solved a simple case of vandalism?"

"No, sir. Not yet."

He rubbed a wrinkled hand against the slight stubble on his chin. "You'd think it'd be cut-and-dry."

"You'd think," I conceded.

Dad flipped through the pages, his index finger skimming under my notes, and paused. "So give me your theories."

"Well," I started, "I've moved away from thinking it was a college prank. Definitely not outsiders passing through town. I think it's a kid. I had a visual on one or two of them a few weeks back that looked very suspicious—and they were young, high school age."

Dad stayed silent, only nodding for me to continue.

"However, given how long it's been happening and how random the timing of the taggings, I believe there to be more to it."

He continued to flip through the pages and paused on one photo in particular. "Did you notice something here?"

I leaned closer to examine the photograph. The spray-painted penis should have been funny—it was posed to look like a rodeo cowboy with an impressive championship belt buckle hanging just above its very enlarged ball sack.

I shook my head to keep the bubble of immature laughter from erupting, and I briefly thought back to Maggie and her what-if about me becoming a rodeo clown. I scrubbed my hand across my jaw to hide the smile that crept onto my face.

Dad flicked to another page. "And here?"

"From what I can tell, most of the designs are completely different. Some have artistic skill, while others are more rudimentary."

"And what does that tell you?" Dad asked.

It confirmed my gut feeling. "Different taggers. It's not the same person."

"Exactly," he said with a stern nod. "Gang activity."

I shot him a bland look. "Not a *gang* per se, but possibly something akin to one. Bored country kids who dare each other to tag a building. An initiation of sorts." When he simply stared at me silently, I continued, "It's a working theory."

Dad wasn't known for being the most warm-and-fuzzy father, so I had let go of the hope of receiving praise a long time ago, but as he flipped the file folder shut, a switch in him flipped as well. On a dime, he could turn off *Sheriff Decker* and suddenly just be *Dad*.

He smiled at me as though he were seeing his son for the first time today and clamped a hand on my shoulder. "Well, then. Tell me what's new and good."

"Well"—I shrugged—"it's a lot of the same. You know how it is here."

Dad took a sip of the black coffee on the table beside him. "That so?" he asked through the steam swirling above the mug.

"Look, if Mama sicced you on me to get some information, just come out with it."

At that, he laughed—deep and hearty. "Son, she's just trying to see if the rumors are true. Word around town is you and that little O'Brien girl finally came to your senses."

"Dad, she's thirty-two years old. She's not *little*."

He swatted the air between us. "Ah. To an old man like me, you and your friends will always be punk kids. But you have to give me something. I can't go back to your mama empty-handed. She'll tan my hide."

I laughed at that. Mama was the only one who could ever manage to *handle* Dad. I had no doubt she'd give him an earful when she heard I'd dropped in and he didn't get at least one morsel of gossip she could share with her friends.

"Fine," I said as I rose. "Why don't you tell her that I'll bring Maggie and Lottie around for supper next week, and she can get an eyeful herself."

I shook Dad's hand to leave and chuckled as I walked

out the door. Only later did it occur to me that Maggie and I probably needed to have a conversation with Lottie about our relationship.

Unsure how to navigate that, I thought about what it meant to be a father. I had a good one, but if any semblance of fatherhood was in the cards for me, I knew I'd want to be just a bit *different* from the man in front of me.

Open to whatever she wanted to do with her life.

More affectionate, maybe.

I swallowed the guilt lodged in my throat, tugged my dad into a quick hug, and went back to work.

I WAS GOING to nail their asses tonight. I don't know how I knew it, but I did. Something electric—a charge in the air—told me that sooner or later, these kids would screw up. They weren't going to get the best of ol' Deck for much longer.

I glanced at myself in the side mirror of my truck. I ditched the mustache, and instead of a complicated, drawn-out plan, I simply parked myself at the end of Main Street, settled in with a big-ass thermos of coffee, and waited.

The streets were quiet in Chikalu. Whipping wind and plummeting temperatures ensured that the sidewalks remained clear except for the few people who bustled in and out of the local restaurants and The Pidge. Heat pumped from the vents, and I zipped my black coat up to my chin.

I'd much rather be snuggled with Maggie, watching a movie with her and Lottie-tot. That's for damn sure.

The unease I'd been feeling earlier seemed to have been a figment of my imagination. When I'd spoken with Maggie on my way to the stakeout, she'd offered to wear a fuchsia wig and thick-framed glasses to keep me company. We'd joked and laughed, and all felt right in my world again.

Hours ticked by, and as each second dragged on slower than the last, I started second-guessing myself. There was no rhyme or reason to the taggings. No pattern. I'd thought long and hard about that too. No semblance of repetition or alignment with moon cycles. It didn't appear as though the teens of Chikalu were turning into werewolves who liked to spray-paint giant dicks all over town.

I rubbed my eyes and laughed at myself and how loopy I was getting by just sitting—bored off my ass. The police radio in my truck crackled to life.

"Deck, you on?"

I lowered the volume and responded: "Sure am. What's up, Francis?"

"I've got a report of a 10-66 down at the elementary school parking lot. I can send a squad car, but Ms. Arlene mentioned you were posting up tonight."

Energy hummed beneath my skin as my heartbeat ticked faster. "No, it's all right. I'll swing through and see what I can see. Thanks, man."

"Ten-four."

I pulled my truck out of the parking space and took the back road toward the elementary school. Intentionally parking a block away, I pulled my black knit cap low on my brow. Holstering my gun at my hip, I checked my utility belt to ensure I had anything I might need if things went south unexpectedly. I'd learned a long time ago to never assume and never be unprepared.

Minutes later, I realized that I could never have prepared for what I was about to walk into.

I cursed the snow that crunched under my boots as I

intentionally lightened my steps. The harsh, blue-white lighting of the single lamppost illuminated the blacktop at the back of the school. I peeked around one corner.

Empty.

Hugging the side of the brick building, I slowly moved my way down the north wall. I paused when voices floated on the winter air.

Kids.

Sure enough, when I glanced around another corner, three kids stood at the side of the building. One shook a can of spray paint, and over the rattle of the metal ball, I stepped wide, revealing myself.

"That's a poor choice." My voice echoed against the night sky.

Without notice, all three children took off in a sprint. One can clattered against the asphalt. I charged after them, choosing one to pursue as they scattered. As my eyes became laser focused on the figure in front of me, I began cataloging everything I could from the scene.

The electric-teal spray paint. Black hoodie. Red cap. Black hair.

Black hair. Stick-straight black hair.

I rounded the playground equipment, not giving up my chase. I surveyed the figure in front of me as I rapidly closed the distance between us.

Small frame. Female.

Lottie.

My heart plummeted and I stopped dead. I stood to my full height. "CHARLOTTE." My voice boomed, and she skittered to a halt as if the sonic wave of it had struck her. Her shoulders heaved as she tried to catch her breath—her back still to me.

Slowly the girl turned, and my stomach dropped to my

feet. The large, dark pools of her eyes stared back at me. Fear stole her voice as her lower lip trembled, but she stayed rooted to the ground.

"Get over here," I said.

Her chin tipped in defiance.

"Now!"

With slow steps, she dragged her feet across the wood chips on the playground toward me.

"What the hell do you think you're doing?" I demanded.

Tears welled in her eyes, but they didn't fall. I was putting on my best *scary cop voice*, and she didn't flinch. The girl was tough—I'd give her that.

"I asked you a question." I waited for any kind of answer. When she still refused to speak, I added, "Does your mother know you're out here?"

That earned me a disgusted sound at the back of her throat as she harshly swiped at the tears that broke free.

"Let's go." I moved forward, placing my hand around her upper arm. Lottie ripped it free. "We're going home."

"*My* home. Not ours!" she exploded. "Not yours! You're not my father." She spit venom, her words dripping with hurt and blind fury. Hardened as I could be, they cut me. Slicing me open and spilling my guts onto the snow. I hadn't meant it like that, had I?

Fuck.

I knew damn well I wasn't about to throw Lottie, a child, in jail, but the truth of the matter was that she was tangled up with whoever was tagging property around town. This couldn't go undocumented. But first I needed to get Lottie home and talk to Maggie so we could figure out a game plan.

"Walk," I choked out. Emotion clogged my throat, but I

had to keep my head. In true teenage fashion, Lottie stomped toward the parking lot, but she didn't try to run. When we got to the truck, she was shivering. I blasted the heat and Lottie sat, arms crossed, and stared out the window.

Dread pooled in my stomach. Maggie was not going to take this lightly, and I had to navigate my relationship with both of these women *and* my duties as an officer of the law.

Fuck my life.

TWENTY-NINE
MAGGIE

Now

I glanced at the clock and then back at my phone for the thousandth time, my frown deepening. Lottie was thirty-seven minutes late, and she hadn't texted me. She *always* texted me if she was going to break curfew. Bile rose in the back of my throat, and I swallowed it down as I punched out a text to her.

Me: You better have a good reason.

I tried to sit, but waiting was making me crazy, so I paced through the living room. When I heard more than one set of boots pounding up the stairs to the front door and the knob turning, I was rushing toward the door. Relief evaporated as I took in the scene in front of me.

Lottie's eyes were rimmed red, and tears stained her cheeks. Cole could barely look at me, and a deep furrow cut across his brow.

"What's this?" I asked as I pulled Lottie inside. "What's going on?"

She pushed past me and stomped toward her bedroom.

"Excuse me, young lady. I'm speaking with you!" Her back stiffened, and she turned toward us. The harsh look of indifference was a facade, barely held in place. I could read her body language and knew her heart was hammering; her fingers twitched.

I turned toward Cole, seeking answers. "I'll ask again. What is going on?"

Cole raised an eyebrow and lifted a wide palm toward Lottie, encouraging her to speak the truth.

Lottie cocked a hip. "I was hanging out with my friends."

I glanced at the clock, unease rolling through my belly. "Is this about curfew?" My words were choked and stilted.

Please be about curfew.

Please.

"You knew." Cole's voice was hard and demanding. Even without his police training, he could read me. As if I'd physically struck him, his shoulders tightened.

I opened my mouth to speak—to find the words to tell him I wasn't *sure* but had suspicions and that I had no fucking clue what to do about it.

"You knew," he repeated without giving me a chance to talk, "and you didn't talk to me about it? Damn it, Maggie!"

"No." I pointed a finger at him. "How dare you raise your voice at me, let alone in front of my daughter. You don't get to do that."

Cole raised both palms, seemingly realizing he'd let emotion get the best of him. I turned to Maggie. Tears streamed down her face. "Is she under arrest?" I asked Cole.

"Jesus, Maggie, no." I couldn't stand the pity laced in his voice.

I turned back to Lottie. "Get cleaned up and go to bed."

"But, Mama—"

"Now!" I rarely raised my voice, but barely contained, raw emotion was erupting out of me. Lottie sniffed and quietly sobbed her way to the bathroom.

The silence in the living room burned in my ears. This whole situation was royally fucked-up. Lottie probably should have been arrested. Taken down to the station for questioning at the very least. Cole's involvement with us—with me—tainted his honor. That simple fact made me sick.

Cole broke the silence. "We could have figured something out. Talked to her together."

Shame and embarrassment flared on my cheeks. "I don't need your help!" The swirl of emotions was uncontained, and with Cole the only other person in the room, he received the brunt of it. Fifteen years of confusion, hurt, and irritation boiled out of me.

"I've been doing fine on my own." I crossed my arms in an effort to protect my heart.

"If this is your idea of fine, then yeah. You're doing fucking great," Cole scoffed. The ugly, hurtful words slid past his lips so easily. Despite the instant look of horror that crossed his face, he'd done it. He'd spoken the words.

"Fuck you." I spat the words in his direction. I meant them with every fiber of my being.

Cole took one step toward me, and I bristled. "Maggie, I didn't—"

"Get out of my house."

"Maggie-May, let's back up."

"I said get out. Now." I stormed past him and yanked the door open wide. The harsh winter air blew in, matching the frigid temperature of my glare.

Cole's nostrils flared, his lips in a firm line. Before he

turned toward the door, he added, "Bring Charlotte to the station tomorrow morning for questioning. Eight a.m."

Before a sob could break loose, I slammed the door behind him, rattling the frames that hung on the wall. Behind the door, I sank to the floor and wept.

~

AFTER THE SOBS racked me until I felt used up, I wiped the tears from my face. I showered and let the warm water wash away the dumpster fire of a day. Once my nerves were steeled and I was confident my voice wouldn't break, I tiptoed into Lottie's room.

She was still awake, quietly crying. I sat at the edge of her bed and stroked her hair. I was so pissed at her, but I couldn't deny her the love and affection she so needed.

"I'm so sorry, Mama." Lottie's voice was so low she sounded much younger than her fourteen years.

"I know, baby."

"Are you mad?"

"Oh, I'm more than mad. I'm furious. And disappointed. What were you thinking?"

"I don't know, Mama. They were all doing it. I didn't think we'd get caught."

"You promised me." The reality of my daughter's broken promise lanced through my heart. "Tell me you were just in the wrong place at the wrong time."

Lottie's silence had my anger creeping up again, and I took steadying breaths to reel it in.

"Lottie . . . you need to be honest with me. How long?"

She sniffed and wiped her drippy nose along her sleeve. "A few times."

I closed my eyes and tipped my head to the ceiling.

"This is serious, baby. You can get in a lot of trouble for what you've done."

"Are you going to send me away?"

"Never. But there are consequences. For starters, you're grounded. No phone. No friends. No winter festival."

"What!"

"We'll figure out the rest of your punishment." I rubbed the heels of my hands across my brow. "We also have to meet with Officer Decker in the morning to sort this all out," I continued, unfazed by her guttural protests.

"Cole." Lottie rolled to look at me. "You mean Cole. You never call him Officer Decker. Not even Deck, like everyone else."

I smoothed her hair away from her face. "Don't you worry about that. We'll talk with him in the morning and sort this all out."

Lottie's tears continued tumbling over her lashes until she finally fell asleep. I was wrung out and collapsed beside her in the bed. I held on to her and prayed that I was strong enough to face him in the morning.

By 7:30 a.m., Lottie and I were sitting in my car, ready to walk into the Chikalu Falls Police Department. Her eyes were still rimmed in red, puffy, and tender from a long night of crying. Mine were hard. Determined to protect my baby.

Lottie stared at her feet as we waited in the foyer for Ms. Arlene to tell us Cole was ready to meet. The pity that masked her face told me she knew exactly why we were here, and it was only a matter of time until the entire town was talking about it. Her desk phone lit up, and she grabbed it, speaking softly into the receiver.

"He's ready for you. Right this way." She stood to escort us back to his office.

As she turned to leave, she placed a slim hand on my shoulder. "It'll all be okay."

I warmed fractionally to her. I hated the sympathy but could appreciate her intention. When my eyes landed on Cole, my kind feelings evaporated. Cole had a commanding presence in his office. He stood there with a scowl, arms crossed, looking—*gorgeous, irresistible, masculine*—completely aggravating.

"Ladies, please take a seat." He motioned toward the two chairs in front of his desk.

I tipped my chin, choosing to be obstinate. When he rounded the desk and leaned against it, then gave me *that look*, I sat, pressing my thighs together and cursing the pleasure that pooled there.

Lottie sat silently, refusing to look anywhere but to pick at the chipped purple polish on her nails. I carefully secured a mask of indifference. If he knew how lost I was, how much I needed help, my carefully constructed world of order, pride, and independence would come crumbling down. I'd managed to handle whatever life threw at me, and this could be no exception.

"Lottie," I spoke sternly, "do you have something to say to Officer Decker?"

He straightened at my formal use of his name.

Tears welled in her eyes and thickened her voice. "I'm sorry, Deck."

Cole's large frame softened as he turned to her. "I'm sure you are, Lottie, but there could be serious repercussions to what you've done. Businesses in this town have lost money because you and your friends have vandalized their storefronts. Unfortunately, you're the only one who has been caught . . . which means the punishment is yours to bear."

I steadied my hand on her knee. She wouldn't have to face this alone.

"And what will that punishment be?" I asked coolly.

"The Chikalu Falls Police Department is not formally pressing charges." Relief whooshed out of me. "However," he continued, "I am recommending that Lottie serve some community service hours in order to clean up the graffiti on the school building and give back to the community. Do you understand, Lottie?"

"Yes, sir." Her voice was small but clear as she lifted her eyes to meet his. She was afraid, but strong, and I filled with pride.

"I'll need some information about who else has been involved."

Horror crossed Lottie's face at the prospect of tattling on her friends. Cole recognized it instantly and continued, "I don't need specific names. But we have to find a way to end this."

His heavy sigh cut through me. He was tired, weary, and seeing this small moment of vulnerability made me want to crawl into his arms and offer him comfort.

Don't you dare.

I gripped Lottie's hand to steady myself and infuse her with courage.

"It's the art club."

"What?" he asked.

"The art club. At school. It might be a stupid thing to you, but to us it's *art*."

Instead of scoffing, as I wanted to, Cole simply shook his head. "Understood. Thank you for that information."

After a beat, I stood. I needed to escape the stifling walls of his office. "If that's all, Officer."

Lottie walked in front of me, her shoulders slumped in

shame. I didn't dare look at him, but as I turned to leave, Cole's wide palm caught my elbow, sliding down to capture my wrist. "Maggie-May . . ."

I looked down my nose at his hand in feigned disgust, ignoring the pang of affection that coursed through me at his touch.

"Goodbye, Officer Decker."

THIRTY

DECK

Now

A riot of emotion swirled in my gut.

What the fuck is happening?

I stayed silent while *stay, stay, please just stay* banged around in my head. Fifteen years of repressed longing raged to the surface, but I couldn't get my feet to move. Maggie left my office, hurried her daughter out into the cold, climbed into her car, and never looked back as she pulled out of the parking lot.

I rubbed a knuckle against my eyes. They burned from lack of sleep. I had tossed and turned all night, unable to reconcile the events of the last twenty-four hours.

I was disgusted at the words I'd chosen to spew at her. The hurt that crossed her face when I'd questioned her parenting was clear as day. I hadn't meant the words, not really. My long-practiced disdain for her was a facade, but it still tended to hover on the tip of my tongue.

So I chose anger.

Anger at myself for not being the man Maggie deserves.

Anger at Lottie for making dumbass teenage choices.

Anger at Maggie for never allowing anyone to pitch in and help her with a damn thing.

So fucking stubborn.

Anger was safer. I could feel it, hold on to it as it tore through my veins.

Control it.

Logically, I knew all relationships had ups and downs, and arguments were inevitable, but I'd never *lived* it. My previous relationships were casual, mutually satisfying, and never long-term.

Maybe there are reasons you're not built for the long term.

The familiar voice felt oddly foreign in my head. Over the last several weeks, in the quiet moments when I stared at my Maggie in the dark, I had let myself start to wonder what it would be like if she and I finally let go of our bullshit. Took our shot.

Permanence.

Dread lurched through me. Maggie didn't need me. She didn't need anyone—that much she made abundantly clear. I was the reason that she had changed from the soft, bright-eyed girl I'd fallen in love with and become fiercely independent. Maggie had had to raise a child with little support. David could have gotten his shit together, helped, and been there for Lottie too.

But sooner or later we would both have to face the truth.

I was the reason David was dead.

"Ooooh, ʜᴏᴏ ʜᴏᴏ." Honey brushed a hand across my back as I sat at her and Colin's kitchen table, staring at the playing cards. "You sure screwed the pooch."

I shrugged her off and concentrated on the shit I had in my hand.

"Oh, please. Don't act like you're not dying to ask me," Honey teased as Colin helped her into her down coat. Poker night was at their house, and Honey was having a night out with the girls.

"Cut him some slack, Hon." Colin moved the hair out of her collar and gripped the back of her neck, leaning in for a kiss. I shifted in my seat, not wanting to see their easy affection. Jealousy raged through me.

As Honey moved toward the door, I finally asked, "Did she say she was still upset?"

"Worse." Honey looped her purse onto her shoulder. "She didn't say a damn thing."

After dropping that bomb, Honey was gone, and I couldn't concentrate on anything besides the fact that Maggie could so easily turn her emotions off.

Twenty minutes went by, and I was still pouting into my beer. Apparently Finn couldn't stand it anymore. "Dude. What the actual fuck?"

"What?" I scowled at him and dug out another beer from the fridge.

If I was cut loose, I might as well tie one on.

"You need to talk about your bullshit—you and Maggie," he said.

"Nothing to say. We got into it over Lottie. We both said some things."

"Everyone fights," Colin added. "Hell, sometimes Honey and I pick at each other just for the makeup sex." He grinned his lopsided grin, and I wanted to punch him in the fucking mouth, just for being so goddamn happy with his life.

Awesome. I'm a shitty friend too.

"It's complicated," I continued. "I found out about Lottie, and she freaked out."

Finn shook his head. "I still can't believe the Dick Bandits were a bunch of high school kids from the *art club*." Humor and disbelief laced in his voice. "When did those kids get cool?"

Lincoln shot him a look. "Hey. I was in the art club."

Finn responded with a jab to his arm, sticking out his tongue in an exaggerated *ha ha*.

Colin added, "And Lottie, man. I didn't see that coming."

"That's the thing." My voice rose an octave. "She knew. Maggie knew and she lied about it. She didn't trust me with the truth." My anger stacked and built the faster I gave voice to my thoughts. "She chose to keep it a secret."

I flexed my fists at my side, holding on to my anger rather than the helplessness that dug at my core.

"It's her kid," Colin said. "What would you expect her to do?"

"Is she the only one with secrets?" Lincoln eyed me and my skin felt hot. He knew all those years ago at the bonfire that I was hiding something. I was so close to telling him everything. Afterward, I'd hoped he'd forgotten or was too drunk to remember in the first place. I should have known better.

Finn's and Colin's eyes were on me. A spotlight that felt harsh and demanding. It wasn't like Lincoln to push, but he wasn't letting it go.

"We all have secrets. Demons." I gestured across the

table, encompassing all of us. "You know that just as well as I do."

Lincoln nodded slowly. "Yeah. And we've also learned that they'll rot you from the inside."

I shook my head and pushed away from the table. They were *my* friends. They were supposed to have my back. Take *my* side, not call me out.

Finn stood with me and clamped a hand on my shoulder. "Dude, I'm gay." He held his palms up and owned it. "I know how secrets decay your insides."

"What-the-fuck-ever. I'm not doing this. Are we playing or what?" I couldn't breathe. I wasn't about to sit around like some sad sack and spill my guts. I'd contained the truth for far too long to have it exposed because I couldn't contain it any longer.

Colin shared a pointed look with Lincoln, but the topic was dropped. Tension radiated off me, and I couldn't relax enough to enjoy myself.

Instead, I drank.

And drank.

And drank.

I awoke on Colin's couch with a raging headache and an empty wallet, and I moped my way home—but not before taking an extra loop through town and down the road by Maggie's house, just hoping to get a glimpse of her.

I was rattled.

Unhinged.

But a night away with the guys brought some clarity. Things needed to go back to the way they were.

The relentless need to tell her the truth, lay it all out for her to see, was unbearable. I couldn't stand walking around all day feeling like a chunk of me was missing. She'd eviscerated heart, and I couldn't stand it. I had to tell her the full truth. If I didn't tell her, I could convince myself to let it stay buried in the past.

Forgotten.

I could pretend that it never happened. Wrap my arms around Maggie, beg for her forgiveness, and kiss away the hurt I'd seen in her gorgeous eyes. Hurt that my harsh words and demanding tone had caused. With her in my arms, I could fix it.

No.

She needed to know so she could hate me as much as I hated myself.

THIRTY-ONE

DECK

THIRTEEN YEARS Ago

Sheets of rain pounded the windshield. I adjusted my vest and tried to get comfortable in the seat of my squad car. Still getting used to the clunky fit of my vest, utility belt, and uniform, I squirmed in the leather seat.

I promised Dad two years at State to get my associate's degree in criminal justice. I had my share of college fun, but to be honest, I couldn't wait to get back to Chikalu. To Maggie. It was a feat to keep secrets in our small town, so keeping tabs on her while I was gone wasn't all that hard.

She had moved in with her aunt, and it stung to not see her pretty face around town. A few times I'd see a girl walking and my heart would beat faster, thinking it was Maggie, but inevitably her hair wouldn't be the right shade of brown, or her walk wouldn't have the same swing of her hips. Maggie became a ghost in Chikalu.

When I heard she'd moved in with her aunt, it made my life easier and harder all at the same time. Easier because I could focus my thoughts on work—serving my hometown, attempting to live up to my father's reputation. Harder because memories of Maggie were enmeshed in this town, and her absence was glaringly obvious.

Rumors about how David had all but abandoned Maggie fueled my hatred toward him. She wasn't a girl you just walked away from. She was different. Special. She left scars on your heart and left you begging for more, but he didn't see that. Instead, he became a small-town cliché and turned to alcohol and drugs to pass the time while Maggie was forced to deliver her baby without a partner to support her.

David had a rap sheet long enough to prove all the time he'd done, and I couldn't wait to nail his ass to the wall. My badge kept me from beating the shit out of him when he walked past me on the sidewalk or the time or two he had been arrested on petty drug charges. Chikalu may be a rural, quiet town, but we weren't immune to the darker sides of small-town living either.

Maggie deserved better. Hope took root inside me when I thought about me being back in town. I could be patient, wait until the timing was right before I sought her out. Sure, things had changed, but I wasn't ready to give her up.

Not yet.

I didn't care if her baby wasn't mine. It was a part of Maggie, and I knew I would love that kid just as much as I could my own.

Lost in my thoughts of a future with Maggie and a child, a blur of orange streaked past me. Recognition was immediate.

Fucking David.

Same shitty truck, painted obnoxious orange, as he drove in high school. I pulled out of the nook along the road behind him as he sped out of town. I bumped the wailers to try to slow him down, but instead of pulling over, the truck took off.

I slammed my foot on the accelerator. He had a lead on me, but my squad car barreled toward him. Adrenaline coursed through me as I wiped fatigue from my eyes, trying to focus and see through the rain that beat down on the windshield. My headlights cut through the sheets of rain. My grip tightened on the steering wheel.

Up ahead, David's truck took the winding corners much too quickly, weaving across the center line.

Thank fuck it's late and no one is on the road. He's going to get someone killed.

I called in—reckless driver, officer in pursuit—through the radio on my vest, giving dispatch my badge number and location. Seconds later, Dad's voice came on the radio.

"This is Sheriff Decker. Do not give chase. Units on the way."

Ignoring him, I continued my pursuit. I knew it was protocol to not give in to a police chase. It was dangerous and reckless, but this was personal.

This is it. I got you now, fucker.

The need to punish David was palpable—hot and thick on my tongue. It was my chance to right all the wrongs he'd done toward Maggie and Lottie. How everything was so fucked-up and it was his fault.

Around a wide bend that hugged the riverbank, I lost visual on the truck. Stomping the gas again, I scanned the blackened highway ahead of me. Rain pelted the road, and the reflection of the moon made it look coated in oil. As I rounded another bend, my adrenaline peaked.

I slammed on the brakes, and my squad car lurched forward, skidding and hydroplaning on the slick asphalt. David's truck was flipped over in the floodplain, his back wheels still spinning in the air. I silenced the sirens but kept the lights flashing as I slammed the car into park.

I rushed forward. Skid marks and upturned earth spread across the ditch by the road. By the looks of it, the truck must have rolled more than once, tearing up the ground as it tumbled toward the water.

"Eleven-eighty on Route 126 just past Runner's Road," I barked into the radio at my shoulder.

The smell of a hot engine and burning oil coated my lungs. Rain beat down, deadening any other sound, drowning out my screams as I called to him.

"David!" I yelled his name over and over as I approached the truck. Smoke and acrid fumes burned my nostrils. I waded through the knee-deep water, pushing my way toward the wreckage.

The glass of the driver's-side window was shattered and the truck's frame mangled. The cab was submerged under murky water. I yanked on the door handle, but it was stuck. I shined my flashlight around the scene, looking to see if his body had been thrown. The harsh light illuminated the sheets of rain. I frantically wiped at my eyes, peering into the darkness.

Unable to see him, I peered back into the truck. Beneath the murky water, I saw a flash of denim. Reaching through the shards of glass, I felt for any sign of David. Broken glass sliced at my forearm as I fumbled through the water. When my fingertips landed on what felt like wet cloth, I gripped it tight, trying to pull the mass toward me and out of the water. It moved, but only fractionally.

Trying the door again, I braced one foot on the side of the upturned truck and leaned all my weight backward. The metal groaned but didn't move. Panic skittered through me. A yell tore from my throat as I tried again and again, pulling with my full force at the door. With one final pull, the door came loose, careening me backward until I was splayed out, flat on my ass. Despite the knock to my skull and the ringing in my ears, I lunged forward through the cab.

The rising water made it impossible to see. I felt the life-less mass crumpled against the upended roof of the truck. If he were alive, he would drown if I didn't get him out of the water, so regardless of any additional injuries, I hauled him out of the truck. David's body was lifeless, leaden. I carried him on my shoulder. My thighs and lower back burned as I struggled up the side of the hill, out of the water and toward higher ground.

"I got you, man. Come on!"

When I reached the shoulder of the road, I tipped David off my shoulder, and my stomach curled. I'd never seen a dead body before, and his lifeless eyes bore into me. I looked away and fought to keep from vomiting. Despite knowing he was gone, I pressed my fingers into his throat, feeling for any kind of pulse.

I knelt over him and began performing CPR. I couldn't look at his torn-up face. The rain hid the tears that burned a path down my cheeks. Chest compressions kept in time with the raging voice in my head.

Fuck.

Fuck.

Fuck.

Fuck.

A helpless, incessant loop. The wails of sirens cut through the pounding rain, and I continued my best efforts at reviving a dead man.

Police, fire department, ambulance. They came onto the scene with full force. The emergency medical services team scooted me away and took over examining David's body. I sank back on my heels. My lungs burned and my limbs ached.

I watched, helplessly, as the EMS team shared a solemn look. One barely shook his head, and I knew.

David was dead.

"What the hell happened?" My father's voice was sharp with anger. I raked my fingers through my hair and flicked the drops from my fingertips. I was soaked through. Numb.

"Officer Decker. What happened?" he asked again.

I sighed, trying to figure out exactly where to start. "The vehicle was speeding. Reckless driving. I used lights and sirens in an attempt to pull him over." I barely recognized my robotic, procedural voice. "The vehicle accelerated."

"And you pursued."

"Yes, sir."

"What made him take off like that?"

Me.

He waited for my answer, but I only dropped my gaze.

"You pursued despite my direct order to the contrary." My father's voice dripped with anger and disbelief.

I stood, silent, before making a devastating choice. "I do not recall an order to cease pursuit."

His eyes flicked down my body, stopping at my shaking hands. "And then what?"

My body straightened, and I widened my stance in false confidence. "I came upon the accident. His truck appears to have rolled and landed in the floodplain. I called it in and located Davi—the body. I immediately attempted life-saving measures."

I pressed my tongue to the roof of my mouth to maintain my composure. Falling apart now would only disappoint him more, if that were even possible.

"What a fucking mess." The words were barely audible under his breath, but they stung nonetheless. "Go home. I need to notify next of kin."

"Yes, sir."

There were still hours on my shift, but I needed to get out of my soaking-wet clothing. I looked down at my hands and uniform and couldn't tell if the blood was mine or David's.

Did it even matter?

I knew that being a cop meant seeing a lot of awful shit, but I was wholly unprepared for this. I had never seen a dead body, let alone one that belonged to someone I'd grown up with. Sure, I hated the guy, but I never actually wanted him *dead*.

I was disgusted at myself for every negative thought I'd ever had about David. On the cold, soggy drive home, I couldn't help but think of Maggie.

David had been a shit partner to her and an absent father, but there was no coming back from this. Maggie's child would grow up without a father. Maggie wouldn't ever have his support.

You did this. Maggie would hate you if she knew.

Even Maggie, with her beautiful, golden heart, would never be able to forgive me if she knew the truth. In one night, any hope I'd ever harbored to make Maggie O'Brien mine died in that truck with David.

THIRTY-TWO

MAGGIE

Now

I stared at Cole's profile as his words hung in the air. He had come to the flower shop after hours and pounded on the glass until I walked from the back to unlock it for him. I was still angry and mumbled a shitty comment about his timing, but I immediately regretted it. Cole just stared at me.

His eyes were wild—dark, swirling pools of chaos as emotions splayed across his sharp features. Cole gripped my arms, and I warmed at his touch. When he told me that there was something important he needed to talk to me about, the night David died was not what I was expecting to hear.

An apology? Maybe. Lord knows I owed him a few for holding on to my hurt and wounded pride for far too long.

He didn't look at me when he told me what happened. His voice was clear but detached as he went through the events of that evening so many years ago. When he finished, he looked at me as though I was supposed to glean exactly why he was at my shop and spilling these secrets. I struggled to process the information—to reconcile the facts I knew surrounding David's accident and this new information Cole was giving me.

"I already knew you were there that night."

He worked his jaw. "Not just there. My actions set it in motion."

"But David was driving his truck intoxicated. He chose to speed away."

"I was given a direct order by my supervising officer—*my father*—and I disobeyed."

"But you tried to save him." I took a tentative step toward him, but he went rigid, and I stopped.

"There was no saving him." Cole's strong voice was quiet and wavered—years of repressing a painful memory woven into his words.

"That's it, isn't it? That's why you pushed me away?"

He only nodded, then reached into his pocket to pull out a familiar white envelope. Anger crept up my back.

All those years. All those years. Gone. Wasted.

"I don't want your money! I came to you," I sputtered. "I tried to be friends again when I moved home."

"I needed distance. I couldn't risk you looking at me and seeing the truth. Knowing what I did to you and Lottie."

"Don't you dare put this on us. Lottie lost her father long before he was dead. You made a choice to push us away."

Cole's shame morphed into stone. He turned from me and stalked toward the glass door.

"Why do you do that? Why do you shut everyone out?" I yelled at his back, emotion betraying my voice.

"Because it needs to be done."

The door clanged shut, and the only trace of him was his scent, lingering on the winter air as the cold seeped into my bones.

~

THE TIPS of my fingers burned as I scrubbed and picked at the black char around my stovetop. Funneling all my confusion, hurt, and anger meant that my house was incessantly clean. The more I cleaned, the angrier I got, because I couldn't seem to scrub away the confusing feelings swirling inside me.

I was still reeling from Cole's revelation. He'd filled in so many heartbreaking details surrounding David's death. Mrs. Lee-Kim preferred to think that Lottie and I didn't exist. I was met with disdain and sideways glances when I shed true, genuine tears at his funeral. Tears for what could have been, tears for him and his family, but the most tears for my daughter and the father she would never know. I was wholly unwelcome there, but as Lottie slept in my arms, I held my head high, paid my respects down the receiving line, and placed my hand on his closed casket one last time.

I saw with striking clarity how the pieces of the night of David's accident had unfolded. Fresh tears burned in my nose—this time for the horror that young, innocent Cole had gone through. For the burden and guilt that he'd carried alone all this time.

But he didn't understand my acceptance. His misplaced guilt clouded his judgment, and instead of *listening* to the words I was saying, he shut me out, hardening right in front of my eyes.

That's my signature move, jerkface.

I wasn't used to feeling so vulnerable, so completely exposed. I opened myself up to Cole in a way that I had long convinced myself was dangerous, and I was right. I knew better. But something nagging scratched at the base of my skull. Deep down I knew Cole was too important. We could give each other space, but whatever this was between us couldn't be over.

Not that easily.

I knew Cole and I would have to burn each other's world down—let the flames and ash consume us before either could ever be completely done with the other. Even then, it felt impossible.

Giving up on the baked-on stovetop, I threw the dishrag in the laundry hamper and grabbed my coat. I had spent too much time cooped up, thinking about Cole Decker.

"Grab your coat," I called to Lottie. "We're going out."

"I don't feel like going anywhere," she grumbled.

"Hey, you're the one that's grounded. If you wanted freedom, you should have made better choices."

Part of Lottie's punishment meant that she didn't get her phone or spare time alone to get into trouble. I had set out her consequences before realizing that also meant that *I* couldn't have a moment alone.

Lottie trotted glumly behind me. I didn't say a word, but she was going to be real pissed when she found out I was putting her to work.

We pushed through the door of Biscuits & Honey and pleasure immediately swam through my veins at the smell of coffee and baked goods. It was busy for a Sunday, and I let the warmth of the shop seep into me as we waited in line. Honey was behind the counter, her blonde hair piled on her head with a bandanna headband holding it back.

"I need carbs," I said as I reached the front of the line. "Also, Lottie's here to work."

"What!" Lottie scoffed with that disgusted hack in the back of her throat.

Honey gave me a sharp nod and tipped her head toward the kitchen. "Dishes in the back. Get to work, babe."

I grinned at Lottie's back. A little light manual labor for Lottie would be a good thing. Help round out her character and *hopefully* give me five seconds of reprieve to sulk.

"Anna," Honey called to the waitress on the floor. "Cover for me?"

When Anna agreed, Honey piled a plate high with more pastries than we needed and found us a quiet corner. Ms. Jean, Honey's mother-in-law, was meeting with a few members of the Chikalu Women's Club at the table behind us. We smiled at the ladies and tucked ourselves into our seats just as Anna dropped off two hot lattes.

"I'm worried it's really over," I said into my mug.

Honey stayed quiet, wide-eyed and listening.

"I just don't know how we get past this," I continued. "It's like a mountain of *shit* just piled on top of us. It all feels like . . . too much, ya know?"

"You two have been through a lot. You've got years of confusion and hurt feelings and some heavy stuff between you. I'll give you that."

"It just sucks, though. I let my love for him go a long time ago. Then I spent forever thinking he had turned into *such* an asshole. Then he goes and shows me this complex, kindhearted, amazing person he's been hiding, only to steal it away again." I tore into a cinnamon bun and stuffed it into my mouth. Endorphins flooded my system. Carbs really were a comfort.

"Deck's always been that man. He's the town's go-to guy. Everyone relies on him—even more than the sheriff. He's dependable, and I think that's probably a lot to carry around all the time."

I narrowed my eyes on Honey. "Whose side are you on, anyway?"

She smiled, lifting both hands in the air. "I am wholeheartedly Team Maggie and Deck. Which is why I'm sure you'll figure your shit out. Though it does seem like it would have been a hell of a lot easier had you both just gotten together in high school," she admitted.

I tore into a cruller. "Right?! I mean . . . he did go to prom with Erin O'Malley, though. She was the hottest girl in school. Every guy was drooling over her. Cole was no exception. I didn't stand a chance."

Just then, Ms. Jean leaned over and tapped my shoulder. "I'm sorry to interrupt, darlings."

"It's okay, Mom. What's up?" Honey smiled.

"I couldn't help but overhear your conversation. It's a shame you and Deck are having troubles, but you're wrong, my dear."

My face twisted, not understanding her meaning.

"That boy has been over the moon for you for a long, long time."

Her words lanced through my heart. Teenage me had pined *hard* for Cole. Wishing on every star that he would look at me as something more than the nerdy girl who made him laugh.

When I didn't respond, Ms. Jean swatted the air between us as she began to dig through a large envelope in her lap. "Oh, well, proof is in the pudding, my dear."

She gestured between her and the other women at the table. "We're going through old photographs for the winter festival. A particularly interesting one caught my attention. Ah, here it is."

Ms. Jean pulled an old five-by-eight photograph from the stack and showed it to us.

"Oh! Look at that!" Honey crooned and reached for the photo. Pointing to the picture, she asked, "Is that Colin?" Her voice was giddy with delight.

The photo was a large group shot, taken at prom by the gazebo. Warring emotions raced through me—nostalgia, longing, regret.

In the picture, most pairs were coupled off, smiling at the camera. David was off to the right, roughhousing with some other boys from our grade. I was standing on the opposite side, smiling brightly toward the camera.

"I don't understand . . . ," I started.

Ms. Jean pointed to a boy in the background, standing taller than most of the other boys his age.

Cole.

Tucked under his arm, Erin was flawless. Her dazzling smile radiated happiness.

"He might have gone to the dance with Erin. But who is he looking at?" she asked.

My mouth hung open in a tiny O. My heart banged against my ribs. I tracked his gaze in the photograph. Instead of looking at the camera, Cole's eyes were laser focused.

On me.

Emotion swirled in my chest, and my limbs went tingly. One finger tracked down the photograph across Cole's features—we both seemed so young, the promise of our whole lives stretched out in front of us.

"I—I don't know what to say."

Ms. Jean smiled softly. "There's nothing to say, dear. Some things just *are*. I think you two are the only ones in this whole town who haven't realized that you're meant for each other."

Honey reached across the table for her hand and squeezed, wiping away a misting of tears at the corner of her eye.

"Here," Ms. Jean said, "keep it." She pressed the photograph into my hands and winked at me before returning her attention to the women at her table.

I stared at it, over and over, as I looked at the emotion so clearly evident on his face.

How could I have been so wrong? Missed so many signs? I'd let my hurt and pride and stupid arrogance get in the way of truly *seeing* what was right in front of me.

"You okay?" Honey asked, her hand covering mine.

"Yeah, I . . . Wow." I swallowed, trying to dislodge my heart from my throat.

THIRTY-THREE

DECK

Now

My fist rammed into the boxing bag with a crack. I'd put more force behind it than necessary, but I wanted to feel the impact of it radiate up my arm. Over and over I pounded until my biceps burned and my arms felt heavy. I needed my lungs to burn and my mind to clear.

"I see you're not feeling any better." Colin strode up behind me, unwinding the tape from his knuckles. We worked out together a lot, and in the winter months, we spent most of that time at the MMA gym in Canton Springs.

"Fuck off." My fist slammed into the bag again, and Colin steadied it.

"I would, but *your* shit is affecting *my* shit." My eyes met his. "Whether you like it or not, Honey and Maggie are friends, so now I get to hear *all about* what's going on between you two."

"Talk shit all you want. I don't give a fuck." I was brushing him off. I couldn't let myself think about Maggie.

If I did, I'd cut and run and do whatever it took to find my way back to her.

"It's not like that and you know it. We're all just worried. That's all."

"Don't worry about me. I'll be fine."

"Is this fine?" he asked, gesturing to all of me.

"Fine enough." I focused all my attention on the bag, ignoring the look of pity he shot my way before moving toward the locker room.

I hated that my argument—breakup?—with Maggie was seeping into our other relationships. It further proved that getting involved with her in the first place was a mistake— the lie I kept telling myself soured my stomach.

I tamped down the relentless voice that sparked hope inside me. The voice that told me there was sadness in Maggie's eyes when I'd admitted to what happened the night David died. And not just sadness.

Was forgiveness laced in there too?

I desperately wanted to believe that we could find a way to move past it, but I just couldn't seem to figure out how to do that. It could be easier to go back to the way things were. My mind raced through the possibilities.

My random work schedule would make it so that I didn't have to run into her. I could work social time with our friends around when she was with them. Go back to allowing myself only glimpses of her when she walked down the sidewalks in town.

Fuck that noise.

"Colin," I called and took off after him. "Man, I'm sorry for being a prick. I do need your help."

∽

A QUARTER PAST ELEVEN, I parked my squad car in front of Maggie's house. Lottie was due for some good old-fashioned community service, and I wasn't going to miss my chance to talk with Maggie.

I cut the engine, but before I could get out, Lottie bounded out of the house and down the steps. As she hurried out of the cold and into the passenger seat, my eyes tracked behind her, glued to the front door.

"She's not here, you know." Lottie's dark doe eyes stared at me.

"Right." I cleared my throat, started the car, and pulled the car down the driveway.

"What do I have to do today?" she asked.

"Soup kitchen with the Women's Club. We're helping to serve, handing out fresh blankets, offering support for anyone who might need it."

Lottie picked at her nails and nodded.

Driving through town, she sank lower in her seat, hoping no one would see her. I slowed fractionally as we passed the flower shop, and I sneaked a sideways glance at Lottie, only to catch her rolling her eyes at me.

"You two are *so dumb*."

"Dumb? I'm not the one stuck with community service hours," I shot back.

She stared at me over her lashes. I could practically hear her scoff, *Really*—sarcasm dripping from the word.

"You're right, though," I admitted as I pulled into the parking lot to the building that housed the Women's Club. "We are being dumb."

She offered me a small smile. "She misses you."

"I miss her too." Heat bloomed in my chest. It felt damn good to say those words out loud. I had been pushing it down for too long, and I couldn't do it any longer.

"What happened?" Her curiosity was genuine. I wanted to be honest with her but also knew the *details* of the conversation I'd had with Maggie were about her father. It wasn't my place to tell Lottie everything.

"Well," I offered, positioning my body so that I could face her in my seat, "we had an argument. It happens. I said some things that I didn't mean, and I think your mom did too."

Lottie nodded but stayed quiet. Finally, she peeked at me. "I said some things I didn't mean either."

I pitched an eyebrow up and tried to ignore the tug in my chest.

"When I yelled at you and said you weren't my dad," Lottie continued. "I was just mad. I didn't mean to be such a *bitch*."

My eyes widened at Lottie's curse, but I chose to not call her out on it. Instead, I nodded. "I understand. No one will ever replace your dad. But your mom and I probably should have talked to you about what was going on between us sooner."

At the stoplight, I looked at her and chanced a gentle squeeze on her forearm. Lottie didn't pull away. Instead, she looked at me and gave me a small smile. I cleared the emotion lodged in my throat. "I'll do better. I promise."

Lottie toyed with the skin at her thumb, then leaned in as if she were spilling a secret. "Mom told me that you were very good friends, and then you weren't anymore. She told me once how that makes her sad."

I nodded, thinking about how foolish we'd been for so damn long. "It makes me sad too. But we had a lot of growing up to do."

"You're grown up now," she said plainly.

"You're right. Which is why an argument doesn't mean

that I'm going to give up on our friendship. I care about your mom. With my whole heart."

A smile split Lottie's face. "I knew it!"

A deep, genuine laugh rumbled out of me. "Yeah, it's hard to hide when it feels this good, I guess."

"So what are you going to do?"

I shrugged. "Talk to her, I guess. I need to say I'm sorry."

Lottie's face twisted up and reminded me so much of young Maggie—exactly when she was about to call me out on my bullshit. "No."

I raised my eyebrows.

"You can't just *talk* to her. That's boring."

I tried to hide my smile. "Okay, and what would you suggest?"

"A romantic gesture. Like in the movies she loves so much!"

"That's, uh"—I couldn't help but laugh a little—"that's a little out of my wheelhouse."

Lottie perked up in her seat. "I can help you! It will be perfect!"

God, I had loved this spunky little girl for her entire life. The raw emotion of it pinched in my chest. She was funny and kind and generous, just like her mama.

"That's a deal, Sassafras."

She smirked in my direction at the nickname. "Does that mean I don't have to do my hours?" she asked.

"Fat chance." I pushed my way out of the squad car. "Let's go."

Now

"There is something I need to say." I shifted my stance, peering down at the frozen ground. Thick winter clouds hung in the air, and icy whips of wind nearly stole my breath. Steeling my nerves, I started again.

"David, there is something I need to say to you." My voice floated aimlessly into the afternoon air. My only companion was a raven that cawed in response. My head dropped, and emotions rose to the surface. "Fuck, this is hard."

I cleared my throat and tried to gather my resolve. "I forgive you. For the choices that you made. For whatever struggles you had that made getting clean impossible. For choosing drugs and alcohol over a relationship with your daughter."

I thought the words would taste bitter in my mouth, but I was surprised at how clear and true they felt. David was a small-town kid who got in over his head, and rather than get help and pull himself out of it, he'd leaned deeper into his affliction.

"Thank you. For Charlotte. She is the most amazing gift, and there's so much goodness in her." Tears welled in my eyes, and I let them fall freely. It had been years since I'd cried over David. I buried my feelings so deep that they couldn't find the light of day. I focused on raising Lottie and pushed everything else aside.

I took a cold breath to continue. "David, I feel so sorry— so deeply sad—that you'll never get to know our incredible, complicated, wonderful daughter. But I hope you know that I am doing my best to honor your memory. I celebrate all the best parts of you that you gave to her. She's funny, like you. She's also an amazing artist. It's gotten her into a little bit of trouble—also like you—but she's a good girl, and I think she's going to turn out okay."

I turned my eyes to the pewter sky.

God, I hope I'm not fucking this up.

I closed my eyes, and, burying my hands in my pockets, I smiled a bit to myself. Speaking these words aloud, whether David could hear me or not, was cathartic. Fears and angers and worries that I'd bottled up for so long spilled out of me.

"There might always be a hole inside her. I tried so long to fill it, but I realized that I can't. Like me, she grew up without a father, and that's shaped a lot of her life, but we also have some incredible people in our lives. People who take care of us. People I need to let help us."

My voice dipped. The guilt and shame I carried for not being able to do it all, be everything, was difficult to let go of. It would take time, but giving voice to it was a tiny step toward doing better. Being better, for everyone in my life.

"I never loved you the way I should, but I think you knew all along. Maybe you always knew I was holding my heart back for someone else."

The chilly air crept up my neck, but I stood at David's grave site and allowed myself to grieve. I cried for him, for Lottie.

For myself.

~

"Do you think there's ever such a thing as *too late*?" Lottie asked, sitting across from me on the love seat.

My thoughts immediately flew to Cole. It had been almost two weeks since our argument, and we still hadn't spoken. Dread pooled in my stomach. I was one run-in away from grabbing him by the police vest and shaking him until he came to his senses. Unfortunately, he'd all but disappeared. Holding firm on her punishment, Lottie and I had rung in the New Year with a sad bucket of popcorn and a bowl of ice cream.

"Hmm," I answered. "Is it too late? I guess that depends on what you're talking about. Is it too late for me to become an Olympic gymnast? Yes, probably."

Lottie grinned at me and threw a piece of popcorn in my direction. She was still grounded, and although tonight was the winter festival—Chikalu's final celebration to ring in the New Year—we were cooped up at home. Stripped of the opportunity to go, this was the final consequence for her involvement with the town vandalism.

Lottie scooched closer and rested her head on my shoulder. "I meant too late for people to love each other."

"Is this about a boy at school?" I asked stiffly.

"No. Just something I've been thinking about."

Me too, sweetheart. Me too.

My chest pinched, and my heart rolled around in my chest. "I hope not." I sighed.

"I think," Lottie said, "if it's really love, they'll always find a way back to each other."

I smoothed a hair away from her face, pulling her close to me. "When did you get so grown-up, huh?" I planted a kiss on the top of her head and squeezed her shoulders. Her words swam in my brain.

"Does this mean I'm not grounded anymore?" She peeked up at me with a sly smile.

"Ha!" I squeezed her shoulders again. "Sorry, kiddo. You're still on the hook."

Sagging against me, Lottie accepted defeat. "Fine. But let's do something other than movies."

"What are you thinking?"

"Can we do makeovers?"

I laughed at the thought of Lottie using her heavy hand with black eyeliner on me. Though the idea of a night of pampering did sound like fun.

"I think that's a great idea." I booped her nose and padded toward the bathroom to dig out long-forgotten nail polish and random skin care samples I had in a basket under the sink.

"I want to do your hair and makeup first!" she called from behind me.

Oh boy. This'll be interesting.

I couldn't help but share in her giddiness. Her youthful enthusiasm was contagious.

An hour later, my hair was softly curled and my makeup set. I'd successfully avoided the electric-blue eye shadow she must have gotten from Ms. Trina, and I requested that she keep the black eyeliner subtle. I didn't look half bad.

Our toes were painted black—my one concession at

Lottie's insistence. But I had to admit, the diversion from my usual pink did look kind of cool.

Getting Lottie's hair to take a curl was nearly impossible, so instead, I was twisting it into a simple chignon when a loud knock at the door made me jump. I pressed a hand to my chest. My heartbeat was jumping through my skin.

Lottie's giddy laughter had a nervous chuckle zip through me. I eyed her as I walked toward the front door and peeked through the peephole. I pulled open the door to find Jo and Lincoln huddled on the doormat.

"Well, hey!" I moved aside so they could get in out of the cold. "What brings you here?"

Jo moved in for a hug as Lincoln stomped his boots and closed the door behind him.

"We're taking over Operation Lottie's Lockdown." Jo held up a long bag with a hanger. Lottie playfully stuck her tongue out at Jo, and they both laughed.

"I don't understand . . ."

"The festival!" Jo continued, lifting the garment bag higher. "Honey is lending you a dress. You're going to go, have a great time, and Linc and I will hang out with Lottie."

"Oh, I . . . I don't know. I couldn't ask you to do that."

"You're not asking," Lincoln added. "You're doing me a favor. I hate crowds."

"It's true." Jo shrugged.

"Besides, Mama, your hair and makeup are already done!" Lottie blinked her dark eyes, and the realization hit that the idea of *makeovers* was definitely part of this scheme.

Before I could protest again, another knock came at the front door. Lincoln pulled Jo under his arm, and they both smiled. Panic coursed through me. I steadied my hand on the knob before turning it. Hoping—praying—I knew who it was on the other side.

"Hey, doll." Cole Decker stood on my porch. He was the most handsome man I'd ever laid eyes on, with a dark charcoal suit, vest, and tie. My eyes gobbled him up, and they took in the way the suit jacket formed around his thick arms and broad chest. The vest, perfectly tapered beneath the jacket, hugged his hips. And his thighs? *Oh, his thighs.* I knew exactly how those muscles corded and flexed, and desire rippled through me.

I brought my hand to my throat, unable to find words.

"I have something I've been meaning to ask you." His voice was rich and thick. It wrapped around me, and my heartbeat ratcheted higher. "Can I come in?"

"I'm sorry, yes." I bustled him into the entryway and closed the frigid winter air out behind him. "Cole, what are you . . . ?"

He reached out, capturing me at the elbow and gliding his hand down to hold my hand. "There has always been a tug—a longing for you I couldn't explain. It scared me and I shut you out, but I can't do it, Maggie. I can't go another *minute*, let alone another fifteen years, without you."

Emotions clogged in my throat as his words washed over me. "I should have done this a long time ago," he continued. "It may not be prom, but will you be my date to the winter festival?"

His voice shook on the last sentence, and I threw myself into his arms. "Yes! Cole, of course, yes."

His nose buried into my hair, and he pressed my body into his. We held each other for what felt like a lifetime. When I looked at him again, I captured his face in my hands and was lost in his caramel eyes. "I'm sorry for being so hardheaded."

A smile played on his lips, but he remained serious. "There's a lot I have to be sorry for." His eyes lowered. "But I want to start by saying that I'm sorry for not talking to you. For panicking and shutting you out."

"I forgive you. Of course, I do. I've given it a lot of thought, too. I can't imagine what you went through the night of David's accident—seeing that as a young officer . . . " My voice tailed off, aching sadness for what he experienced crept in. "No one should have to go through that."

I took a deep, cleansing breath. "I hate to admit it, but I also understand why you felt that keeping your distance for all that time was better." I bit my lower lip before looking him in the eyes again. "But, are you sorry for disappearing on me all week?"

"Absolutely not." He laughed.

I scoffed and he gestured toward Lottie. "The winter festival was her idea. She told me I had to stay away so I wouldn't blow it."

"It's true," Lottie added. "I could tell that if you saw each other, you'd get all gooey, and it would ruin the surprise!" Her self-satisfied grin had me laughing, my heart bursting.

"Okay," Jo jumped in. "Let's get you ready for a dance!"

Jo, Lottie, and I hurried to my bedroom before I could protest. With the dress hung on the back of the door, she carefully lifted the plastic to reveal a stunning black midi-length dress. It had a deep V in front that met the cinched waist. The full skirt had inverted pleats that gave the dress gorgeous fullness. Jo held the fabric in her hands and moved it. A subtle shimmer danced in the light.

A perfect match to his charcoal-gray suit.

"Wow," Lottie said.

I swallowed thickly. "No kidding." My eyes were wide as I took in the most stunning dress I'd ever seen. A dress that I was about to step into.

"Honey knows a lot of things, and fabulous dresses are one of those things. Once we told her about the plan, she said she had the perfect one."

I toyed with the inside of my lip. "I hope it fits."

"It will," Jo said with a firm nod.

She took it off the hanger, and I undressed and stepped into it. The zipper slipped up my back like a dream. It nipped my waist, and the full skirt hid the extra five pounds that being on the wrong side of thirty had given me. The V of the neckline was subtly sexy, and I was shocked at how it seemed to make my chest defy gravity.

"Shoes." Lottie pointed to my perfect black toenails.

I smiled and lifted my eyebrows. "I have the perfect pair."

The box was hidden in the back of my closet—a guilty impulse purchase I'd made once when I was shopping in Butte. I'd had them over four years and had never worn them, but I'd also never had the heart to give them away. Completely impractical for winter, the shoes were peep-toe stilettos in matte black leather.

"Mom, you look hot!" The three of us dissolved in a fit of giggles, and I felt sixteen again.

Brushing a hand down the full skirt, I took a deep breath. Together we walked back to the living room, where Lincoln and Cole were talking on the couch. As soon as I entered, Cole shot to his feet. His gorgeous eyes went wide as they roamed all over my body, lighting every inch of me aflame.

"Maggie, you are stunning."

I dipped in a little curtsy. "Thank you."

He held out his arm to me, and when I tucked in beside him, he pressed a kiss to my ear.

"You two have fun!" Jo plopped on the couch next to Lincoln and began searching through the television for a movie.

Cole's breath hitched in my ear. "I worked it out with Lincoln and Jo. They're staying the night here, if we want them to."

I stared ahead, my stomach clenched, and desire pulsed at the tender place between my legs as I grew wet. I clamped down on my lower lip as we walked out the door.

THIRTY-FIVE

DECK

Now

Entering the gymnasium at Chikalu Falls High was surreal. On my arm was the prettiest woman I had ever known, and I couldn't help the shit-eating grin that spread across my face. Maggie's delicate fingers wrapped around my bicep, and I covered it with my hand—no way I was letting her go now.

We still had a lot to work through. Unresolved guilt lingered at the edges of my mind, but I was confident that she and I were going to be just fine. I had waited fifteen years to call her mine, and that had to stand for something.

Crepe paper and twinkle lights hung in swags across the gym. The entire place was transformed into a cozy and inviting winter wonderland. On the stage, a band was playing holiday music interspersed with classic rock and country tunes. A door led into the school lunchroom, and there were rows and rows of catered food. Thai, Indian, Mexican, Italian—a whole host of options representing the multicultural backgrounds of our little town. Circular tables draped in white had beautiful floral centerpieces.

"You did beautiful work," I noted to Maggie, tipping my head as we passed a large bouquet.

"Why, thank you, Officer Deck. I buried myself in work this week to get it done and *not* think about a certain someone," she teased.

"Cole," I said as I spun her in a gentle circle toward the dance floor. "For you, I'm only Cole."

A warm smile spread across her face as she tipped her head back and laughed. "Yes, sir," she purred, and my entire body lit up. Before I could do anything about it, Honey and Colin pounced.

"Damn, girl!" Honey called across the room, garnering a sea of wide eyes in our direction and a sexy blush to creep up Maggie's neck and stain her cheeks.

Colin popped his typical crooked smile and shook my hand. "Glad to see it worked out."

"Thanks for standing with me even when I was a prick."

He shoved my shoulder and it was dropped. That was all it took for us to be fine again, and I couldn't be more grateful for such a solid friend.

"Oh. My. *God*," Honey gushed as she took in Maggie. "I knew it would look good on you, but wow!"

"Honey, I can't thank you enough. I feel so glamorous."

"It's stunning." Honey popped her hands on her hips, and the tulle of her red dress crinkled. "That's it. It's yours now. I could never wear it again knowing you were its true owner."

Maggie smoothed her hands down the front of the skirt. "Oh no. No, I couldn't. It's . . ."

"Bup, bup, bup." Honey closed her eyes and shook her head. "Let's not worry about it right now. Just enjoy the fact that you look *so fine*!"

The women giggled, and a strange warmth tingled up my neck.

Is this what it feels like to have everything fall into place? To drop the bullshit, the facade, and just be?

Before I could lose myself too deeply in the thought, Maggie and Honey were dragging Colin and me out onto the dance floor. The song was an upbeat two-step, and I reveled in the fact that I would be able to push her around the dance floor and show off my girl. The rhythm was smooth and easy, and Maggie was fluid and graceful in her heels.

Pure joy erupted from her in a laugh, and it took every ounce of restraint for me not to gather her in my arms and beg her to marry me. I was going to, that much was certain. I hadn't quite worked out all the details, and we'd have to talk to Lottie about the fact our family dynamic was going to shift, but there was no doubt in my mind that those two girls were stuck with me.

"Thank you for this." Maggie's face held a warm glow beneath the twinkle lights.

"Thank you for not giving up on me." I tipped my face down to press my lips against hers. They were soft and warm, and I ached to deepen it. Assuming Maggie didn't want me to maul her in front of our closest friends and neighbors, I settled for the soft moan that hung in the air between us when I leaned back an inch.

"Well, Miss Maggie!" Ms. Trina swayed her hips as she danced past us. "I'm so glad you and Deck finally worked it out! Don't forget to come by the Blush Boutique. I got some *new items* that I think will be perfect!"

"New items?" I asked.

Maggie glanced away. "Ms. Trina has a specialty for, um"—she blushed—"special garments."

An eyebrow tipped up. "Oh, really? So the rumors are true?"

"Oh, definitely. Apparently she has a knack for choosing the perfect set to make a man melt at your knees."

"Apparently? She's never worked her magic for you?"

Maggie leaned backward in feigned shock. "My, my. That's not jealousy I hear, is it?"

I smirked. "You're damn right I'm jealous."

Maggie's hand found the back of my neck and kneaded the muscles there. "No. I've never had the chance—never wanted to. Until you, of course."

The music shifted and we stood apart. "Can I get you a drink?"

"That would be fabulous. Champagne?" We moved together through the crowd. Knowing smiles and nods led the way toward one of the makeshift bars. After an impossibly long line, I walked up to her sitting beside old man Bailey, looking as though he'd rather be anywhere else.

While he didn't appear happy about it, his pearl snap shirt looked freshly pressed, and his jeans had a crisp crease down the middle. Even his worn boots looked as though they'd been freshly oiled and buffed.

"Evening, Mr. Bailey."

"Son." He nodded. "I see you got your head out of your ass."

I sat beside Maggie and laid my arm across the back of her chair. "Appears so."

"'Bout damn time. Shoulda grabbed this one years ago." He mumbled something that sounded an awful lot like *idiot* under his breath.

Maggie laughed and laid her hand on my thigh. I warmed at her touch.

"You know"—Mr. Bailey groaned as he shifted in the

white folding chair—"I'm getting real tired of figuring your shit out for you kids."

We looked out onto the floor to see Honey and Colin oblivious to the rest of the world. They were deeply in love, and instead of feeling the usual pang of jealousy, only appreciation stood in its place. Mr. Bailey was right, though. At one point or another, he'd had a hand in each of our relationships. He was a pillar in this community and one of the many reasons I couldn't imagine living and working anywhere else.

"Hey," Maggie's quiet voice tickled the hairs on my ear as she whispered. "Can I show you something?"

When I looked at her and saw mischief dancing in her eyes, a hot ball of desire ran straight through me. "Let's go."

Maggie stood and grabbed my hand. We wove through the crowd, not stopping for idle chatter. Instead, she made a beeline for the back of the gym. Pushing through the doors, we exited to a hallway. Looking left, then right, her heels clacked and echoed in the darkness.

"Where are you taking me, doll?"

"You'll see."

I ran my hands up her arms, aching to feel every soft inch of her skin. We reached a darkened classroom, and Maggie looked around again. The classroom was tucked in a darkened corner, and my body tightened at the image of Maggie beneath me, her dress bunched around her hips as I drove into her. My pulse kicked up, and heat crept up my neck.

The smell of lemon cleaner and pencils hung in the air. The steady bass of the music down the hall was the only sign of life outside the darkened classroom. I had reached for a chair to block the doorway when Maggie grabbed my wrist.

"Don't." A sly grin spread across her face.

"My dirty girl. Do you want to get caught?" I planted my palm against her neck and laced my fingers in the hair at the base of her neck. My body covered hers, eliminating any space between us. My tongue delved into her mouth, tasting and teasing her.

Maggie's moan vibrated through me and shot straight to my cock. I pressed my hips forward, hating the material between us. I sank to my knees and dragged my hands down her smooth calves. One by one, I removed her shoes and set them aside. Feeling her smooth skin, I swept my hands up her legs and around the outsides of her thighs. Maggie's breath came in gasps as I looped my fingers around the edge of her underwear. Maggie gathered the skirt of her dress in her hands, exposing the black lace concealing her sweet pussy.

"Fuck, doll. You smell so sweet." I leaned forward, teasing the edge of her panties with my tongue. I licked and sucked at the sensitive skin where her muscular thighs met her pussy. She groaned, and I sat on my heels to look at her. "Ah-ah. Quiet now."

With one hand still holding her skirt up, her other hand clamped across her mouth. Her panties slid down easily, and I tucked the scrap of lace into my pocket. I hitched one thigh over my right shoulder and massaged her leg as I leaned forward again. I had to get my mouth on her—taste her—before I exploded.

One hand tangled in my hair, and when she made a fist, the sharp sting only amped up my desire. Over and over, I devoured her until her thighs were quaking and her core was tightening. She was close, and I couldn't wait to taste her orgasm. Dragging slow circles around her clit with my tongue, I slipped one finger, then two, into her. I wanted to fill her.

Completely.

Maggie cried out and pulsed around my fingers, and I pumped them into her.

I stood and turned, her arms bracing herself against a teacher's desk. I flipped her skirt up, pooling it around her waist as I unzipped the front of my slacks. My cock surged in anticipation and strained against the tight fabric of my boxer briefs.

"You're going to take this cock."

"Yes, give it to me."

Pulling my cock out of my briefs, I dragged the thick, swollen head through the wetness between Maggie's legs.

"Wait," she breathed.

I immediately stilled, pulling back. Maggie locked eyes with me over her shoulder. "I want to see what I taste like on your cock."

"Oh fuck." I took one unsteady step backward.

Maggie turned and settled onto her knees before me. She licked her lips and pressed an open-mouthed kiss on the glistening head of my dick. A pulse ran down my length, and I had to grip the desk behind her head to steady myself.

A heady chuckle passed her lips, and she dragged the flat of her tongue along the vein on the underside of my cock. There was no questioning who was in control now. With long pulls, Maggie sucked me to the back of her throat.

"Doll," I ground out. "You better stop or I'm going to come before I get to feel your pussy wrap around me."

I backed up and helped Maggie to her feet. I turned her again, gently placing my hand at her back, tipping her forward across the desk. I raked my nails up the backs of her thighs as I pushed her skirt up and over her ass.

Centering myself, I teased her entrance and the sensitive line up to her tight little ass. Maggie pushed back gently, and my fingers curled around the bones in her hips. I wanted nothing more than to surge forward into her pussy and claim her. Instead, dipping into my pocket, I grabbed a condom and made quick work of rolling it down over my cock.

I palmed her ass and squeezed as I entered her, one agonizing inch at a time. When I was fully seated, my hips pressing into hers, Maggie tipped her head back. Her mocha hair tumbled down her back, teasing me. I pulled the length into my fist and stilled, questioning.

"Oh yes," she responded. "Don't stop."

"You like being bent over a desk—ass in the air, knowing anyone could walk in and find us—don't you?"

"Yes, sir."

God, this girl.

"I want you to take me. Don't let me think. I just want to *feel*."

Tightening my grip, I held Maggie's hair as I claimed her. I pumped my cock into her slowly as she went slick around my cock. I couldn't believe what we were doing—fucking in a dark classroom where anyone could walk in and discover us.

I didn't fucking care. I needed to stake claim to every inch of Maggie. Reading her cues, I could tell she was close.

Mine.

"You're going to come for me, do you understand?"

Maggie moaned and rolled her hips. Releasing her hair and running my hands down her back, my voice hardened. "I said, do you understand?"

"Yes, please yes, Cole."

Together, we tumbled over the edge. Over and over, I filled her as she pulsed around me. Maggie's forearms shook under her weight, and I braced her as we both came down from our high. My limbs tingled, and my heartbeat was out of control. I slipped from her and steadied my arms on either side of her as I tried to catch my breath.

"Goddamn, baby." I was light-headed and dizzy.

Maggie turned in my arms. Her skirt settled, and despite the light sheen of sweat on her skin, she was perfect. Radiant. I struggled to catch my breath.

Voices filtered down the hallway toward us.

"Shit!" Maggie moved past me and bent to grab her shoes. When she turned, a giggle erupted from her as she took in the sight in front of her. Pants at my ankles, my cock bobbing and still mostly hard, I panic-laughed. We quickly used the sink in the classroom to clean up as best we could, and I buried the condom at the bottom of the garbage can.

Maggie clicked the door closed behind us. Walking down the hallways, I couldn't help but look left and right to see if we'd been discovered. The faint music from the gymnasium was muffled, and a soothing calm enveloped me.

"How do I look?" Maggie whispered as we hurried out of the building. I pressed against her back and snickered against her ear. "Guilty."

THIRTY-SIX

MAGGIE

Now

After a quick text to Jo that we'd be spending the night at the cabin, I was pleasantly surprised to see she'd packed an overnight bag and left it on the cabin's porch for me. Jo was always thoughtful and considerate like that. After slipping on the sweater and leggings she'd packed, I hung Honey's—now *my*—fancy dress on a hanger and slipped it into Cole's closet. For such an elegant and expensive gown, I couldn't help but think it looked best when it was shoved up my hips or pooled on the floor.

The fire crackled, and warmth began to fill Cole's cabin. Wrapped in a warm knit blanket, my legs were tucked under me as I watched him walk toward the kitchen. We managed to make a hasty exit from the festival without running into too many other people, but the stern look of disapproval from Gretchen Williams, our town librarian, had me questioning whether we'd actually gotten away with our little tryst.

"Irish cream in your coffee?" Cole held up two steaming coffee mugs from behind the kitchen island.

"Mmm, yes, please." I moved to stand and help him.

"I got it. You just relax." Cole's buttery voice washed over me. He may like his sex rough and demanding, but the man has some *seriously* wonderful aftercare skills. No matter how insistent I was, he wanted to take care of me, and *fuck* that felt good.

I readjusted the blanket and was entranced by the pop and crackle of the fire. Cole handed me a warm mug and leaned to kiss the top of my head before nestling into the couch next to me. Despite the plummeting winter temperature, I was warm.

Cozy.

Taken care of.

Cole's large frame sprawled across most of the couch. The tiny, rustic cabin suited him. I'd never seen the inside of his place in town, but I could hardly imagine him there. Cole needed space. Room to breathe. I watched his throat bob as he sipped the spiked coffee.

"You're staring." A smile played on his handsome face.

"I am," I confirmed. "Actually, I was just thinking how this place suits you. It's so different than I thought it was, but it's perfect for you."

He tipped his head toward me and smiled. "It's my hideaway, but I like you in it."

When he leaned forward, our lips met and the nutty, rich taste of the coffee combined with his purely masculine scent was intoxicating. Though the tenderness between my legs was still fresh, my mind immediately jumped to dirty, naughty places. Cole also had a way of bringing out my absolute, insatiable lust for him. He forgot about his coffee mug and wrapped me in his arms.

We fit together perfectly.

Cole's gentle hands ran down the length of my arm and over my hips and outer thigh.

"Was I too rough?" His voice was laced with concern.

I smiled. "I like when you're rough." Cole brushed my hair to the side, his fingertips barely grazing the thin skin along my collarbone. "I trust you, Cole."

"I'm broken." A bit of sadness seeped into his voice.

"Not to me." Stubbornness hardened my voice more than I'd meant it to.

Cole released a deep breath. "What if I can't give you all the things you want? I won't survive losing you."

I smoothed my palm down his cheek and tracked a thumb across his cheekbone, forcing his eyes to meet mine. "You've already given me everything. More than you know."

"Maggie, I spent years in love with you, but not actually loving you. Not being the man you deserve."

"And I did the same," I reassured.

"I won't let you down again." Cole took my hand. His wide palm gripped mine, and he squeezed three times.

I looked at our joined hands. "What is that? You've done that before—what does it mean?"

A faint smile pulled at his lips. "It's something my mom used to always do. Kind of like a silent signal. Three squeezes." Cole pumped his hand around mine. "I love you."

A fresh wave of emotion surged over me.

Cole Decker loves me.

I threw myself at him, straddling his lap and wrapping my arms around his neck. "Say it again." I looked at his stupidly handsome face and watched the fire reflect in his dark eyes. "Say it again so I know it's real."

"Maggie O'Brien." Cole brushed my hair from my face

and held me in place on his lap. "You drive me up a fucking wall sometimes, but I am hopelessly, desperately, inescapably in love with you."

"I love you too, Cole. I always have." He was brooding and layered with complexity, but he was *mine*. No one understood his heart the way I did, and I would guard it fiercely. "I want you to know you're safe with me. No matter what, I'll always protect you."

EPILOGUE

Deck

A FEW YEARS later

"I can't believe you actually let her get a donkey." Humor laced through Colin's voice as we watched Lottie stroke the coarse fur of her new pet.

We sat, looking out onto the backyard. After a year together, Maggie and I had talked with Lottie, and I moved into their home. We still kept the cabin, but now that we were married, it was all part of the same property. Mostly the cabin remained empty, but it came in handy when we had out-of-town guests or when I hosted poker night. Maggie and I also used it for impromptu date nights when we were feeling nostalgic.

I pressed my lips in a thin line and shook my head and looked at the derpy donkey. "Yep. They ganged up on me."

Colin swallowed a mouthful of beer to keep from laughing. We watched from our chairs on the back deck as Lottie led the donkey around in a wide path. He was slow and kind of sad looking. I couldn't help but laugh with Colin.

"But dude," Colin continued. "It's a *donkey*."

"Those girls could have wanted a fennec fox and I wouldn't have stood a chance. At least a donkey won't gnaw my face off in the middle of the night."

Colin chuckled beside me.

"Dad! Look!" Lottie's sweet face radiated happiness as we both glanced at her. More often than not, to her I was Deck, but my chest pinched every time she called me *Dad*. They were the sweetest words she'd ever spoken to me—ever since I'd fallen for her charms at Daddies and Donuts all those years ago. She might not have my smile, but that never bothered me. Maggie and I were married, and in another week, Lottie and I would be standing in front of a judge, and she would take my last name. It made me feel whole, complete, and it couldn't come fast enough.

Time was moving quickly—in less than a year Lottie would be leaving for Montana State University to pursue a career in the art world. She still hadn't decided exactly what avenue it would take her, but after a welding class last year, she was thinking about eventually looking into jewelry making or gemology. While the high school art club may have gotten her into some trouble, it also helped to shape her future and give her focus. To combat the rogue artists' desire to tag dicks all over town, I'd worked with the Chikalu Women's Club to provide a space for the art club members to freely design and create. The building for the Women's Club was on the end of a main road, and they'd agreed to let the club create a beautiful mural on the side of the building.

The concept took off, and year after year, several other businesses allowed the club to create a showpiece for their end-of-the-year project. It provided them an outlet, kept them busy, and kept smiling dicks with top hats out of my town. Still, the first mural would always be my favorite. Lottie added a special rainbow to it, and I couldn't help but smile every time I drove past.

Draining his beer, Colin stood. "I should get outa here, man. See you later for cards? Finn's hosting tonight."

"'Course," I answered and stood to shake his hand. Our monthly poker nights were going strong. It gave our ladies the chance to get together and do whatever it was they did, and I could catch up with my best friends in the world.

Linc was doing better than ever. Jo had talked him into counseling, and I couldn't remember a time when he'd had a bad episode. Their fishing guide business with Finn was flourishing, and with three kids at home, Lincoln was surrounded by the love he deserved.

Colin had recently turned down talks of a record deal. According to him, "That ship has sailed," and he didn't want anything taking him away from Honey and Chikalu. This town was baked into his DNA, and after leaving once, Colin realized he was a lifer. The bar and bakery had combined and was the most successful business in town. They'd even expanded to catering across four counties.

Everyone's lives were settling into place. Finn and his husband were talking about adopting and were in the middle of a home study to make that happen.

Once Colin and I said our goodbyes, I went in search of Maggie. This time of year I knew she'd likely be messing with the honeybees in the apiary. The honeybees went to work pollinating the acres of cut flowers and filler plants that Maggie grew on our property. Pride swelled in my chest when I saw her through the smoke by the beehives. Dressed head to toe in a beekeeper's suit, she was still the prettiest thing I'd ever laid my eyes on.

As I approached, I could hear her humming to the bees.

She thought it calmed them, and maybe it did. I kept my distance, and once she was finished, she flipped the drape of the hood over her head. Maggie removed the hat and peeled the top of the jumpsuit down, tying the sleeves around her waist. Her smile hit me right in the chest.

I loved that woman more than life itself.

Once I'd gotten my head out of my own ass, I knew I could never go back to pretending that Maggie didn't affect me in the best ways possible. I still loved to get under her skin, but over time, my thinly veiled, arrogant contempt had been quickly replaced with a deeply rooted love and respect. If I let myself think about it too much, I still beat myself up over all the time we'd lost, but it made me more determined than ever to show her every day how much her love meant to me.

"Hey, doll." I wrapped my arms around the baggy white suit, pulling her into me. "How're they doing?" I nodded toward the hives.

"Happy and healthy, best I can tell." She smiled toward the beehive boxes that I'd built for her last season. Having the bees on property nearly doubled flower production, and selling the honey in her shop was an added bonus.

"You running off?" she asked.

"Nope." I buried my nose against the soft skin of her neck and inhaled her sweet scent.

She squeezed my neck tighter, and her voice dropped an octave. "Good. Lottie is helping at the Women's Club this afternoon. I'll have you all to myself before you run off with the boys."

A groan rumbled from my chest as my arms dipped lower, grabbing her ass with both hands. "What did you have in mind?"

I pulled back to look at her. "Well, Officer." Maggie

unwound herself from me and walked away. She turned and winked over her shoulder and hurried toward the house. "I've got some ideas."

I couldn't help the slow grin that spread across my face as I chased after her. "Is that so?" I captured her, and a squealing laugh escaped her when I twirled her around.

When I settled her on her feet, she popped up on her toes and whispered in my ear. "Once we have the house to ourselves, you better get those handcuffs ready. I want to be thoroughly used when we're done."

"Baby, I love that dirty mouth." Anticipation raced through my veins as I ran through all the scenarios we might find ourselves in. Maggie was always a surprise—the way she yielded to me, took charge even when it seemed like I was in control. That woman held every piece of me in her hands, and I was more than willing to give her everything. All of me.

In the thousands of what-if scenarios we'd joked about over the years, none ever came close to the blissful reality of a life with Maggie Decker.

~

WANT a custom playlist for EACH book in the Chikalu Falls series? Subscribe to my mailing list and you'll get instant access to three playlists that inspired me while I wrote the series!

WHILE READING, did you get secretive, intriguing vibes from the little town of Tipp, Montana? The mysterious town is a new location for my next series, set at Redemption Ranch, coming in 2022. For a sneak peek, keep swiping!

. . .

As ALWAYS, reviews on Amazon and Goodreads help spread the word for your favorite indie authors. Please take a moment to review Protecting You, if you could!

ALL MY LOVE!
Lena

SNEAK PEEK AT REDEMPTION RANCH

COMING SPRING 2022

The Badge and the Bad Boy

Staring at how nicely Evan Walker fills out his Wranglers is an example of what I should NOT be doing. He's a criminal, a dangerous man with connections to the Chicago mafia.

But after a call that changed the lives of everyone involved, we're forced to hide in this small town that's eerily good at keeping secrets. As an up-and-coming female police officer, stepping onto the dusty pastures of a remote cattle ranch in Montana is a turn I did not see coming.

I'm only here until I can safely return to my job and prove I'm worthy of the promotion I've worked so hard for. But as we're forced to work together, I find that Evan is much more than I ever expected. He's strong, hard-working.

Did I mention the Wranglers?

We're drawn to each other in ways that are completely forbidden. If either of us gets caught sneaking around, we're kicked off the ranch, no exceptions—which would be a disaster for Evan since the protection here is the only thing keeping his little sister safe.

I know I shouldn't give in to his hot, smoldering looks or the way his lingering touch lights me up. It's reckless.

Addictive.

And the truth always has a way of coming out. In Tipp, Montana, secrets can save your life.

The only cost is your heart.

Find The Badge and the Bad Boy on Amazon

The Chikalu Falls Series

Finding You

Keeping You

Coming in 2022

Redemption Ranch Book 1

ACKNOWLEDGMENTS

Thank you for coming along on this amazing journey with me. I'm sad to think that our time in Chikalu Falls is over. I am so happy that Lincoln, Jo, Honey, Colin, Deck, and Maggie all got their HEAs.

There are so many more stories yet to tell. One day I hope to return and share Avery, Finn, or even grumpy old man Bailey's stories with the world.

I wouldn't have had the guts to even start typing had it not been for the unwavering support of my husband. He's always told me to go with my gut and write the stories I love to read. I love him more and more–even on the days when he gives me truly terrible plot ideas.

To my editor James, thank you for helping me put a beautiful polish on Deck and Maggie's story. Your perspective was so helpful during the process and it was an absolute joy working with you. I can't wait to see where our partnership takes us in the next series!

To Laetitia, maybe one day I will learn how to use a comma, but today is not that day! Thank you for your insights beyond proofreading and for always having patience and grace. I adore working with you.

Amy and Elsie, you are both my daily source of laughter and the only ones who truly "get it." Thanks for being in the trenches with me and always helping me see the forest through the trees. Writing can be a lonely business, but I never feel alone knowing you two are just a text away. Let's just work on getting in the same time zone for once!

Leanne, I don't know where to even begin. You hopped on this crazy train and never looked back. I am so thankful every day for your perspective, beautiful graphics design, organized spirit, and love of all things romance. Most importantly, you aren't afraid to ask me the hard questions or push me to be a better writer, marketer, and all-around author. I couldn't do it without you.

To the Vixens, thank you for your endless love and support. You have helped get the word out on the Chikalu Falls series and I can't thank you enough. I love that our group goes beyond books and true, valued friendships have formed. I can't wait to see where this journey takes us!

To each and every reader who took a chance on a new author and invested their time (and hearts!) to Chikalu Falls–I cannot thank you enough. There have always been love stories in my heart and I am so thrilled to share them with you. Thank you for loving broody men with gooey insides and strong female leads. I wouldn't want it any other way!

Made in the USA
Monee, IL
31 January 2022

90366076R00173